Henry's Stories:
Volume I

Henry's Stories: Volume 1

Henry Melton

Short fiction collected from the pages of the **Henry's Stories** online magazine

Wire Rim Books
Hutto, Texas

WRB

Printing History First Edition: March 2012

ISBN 978-1-935236-39-9

ePub ISBN 978-1-935236-40-5
Kindle ISBN 978-1-935236-41-2

Cover art includes works © 2011 by Candace Weigand

Printed in the United States of America

Wire Rim Books
www.wirerimbooks.com

Contents

A Word from Henry

Traditionally, a single-author anthology ought to have some glowing words about the writer on this page, and maybe on subsequent volumes, I'll find someone gloriously famous to write that for me. But lately, I've been running out of time and missing a few deadlines. You see, I'm what they call an Indie writer. That's the new term used to avoid the sting of being a self-published author. It now means an author constantly running out of time trying to be the whole publishing business by himself.

I just wanted you to know that in this volume, some of the stories were published by other people first. I've been in the business of writing short fiction since the 70's. Only since about 2007 have I taken my fate into my own hands and have begun publishing my own novels under my own imprint.

Starting in 2011, I branched out and created the on-line magazine, **Henry's Stories** http://henrysstories.blogspot.com where I could pull some of those old short stories out of retirement and also include some new works.

This anthology is a collection of some of the stories from that first year of the magazine, and I have every intention of keeping the on-line stories, and these anthologies coming. Some people read websites. Some people read books. I've got you covered no matter who you are.

So sit back and relax, and enjoy a few more words.

Henry Melton, February 20, 2012

Catacomb

First published in Dragon #97

This is my most popular short fiction with fan letters and emails arriving even today. Pardon the anachronisms. This was written back when both the Mac and the IBM PC were new and years before the web. This was before everyone knew to click a mouse or knew that underlined text was a hyperlink.

Lunae, assassin for the Witch Queen of the Hinterlands, paused in silence before the large stone door. <LISTEN, SMELL> There was no sound beyond the latched opening, but she had learned to distrust silence in this place. The walls were cubits thick. The door, though balanced to open with a light shove, was itself more than a foot thick and, when closed, was sealed nearly airtight. Sound never traveled far in this twisty, dusty place, but the smells that the men and the beasts left behind had proved especially trustworthy to her.

She moved her torch to her left hand and leaned closer to the edge of the door, where she might catch a whiff of the scents within. There was, as always, a faint man-scent and the musty tang of some beast that must frequent this set of corridors. She hoped never to meet that one ill the flesh. There was something ... compelling about that scent. She feared it. But now, there seemed to creep from behind the door a new scent, the smell of spice!

If there was any chance of a man behind the door, she had better be ready for a fight. The catacombs were more wild and dangerous than any other place she had been. There was gold here, and of course, there was greed. *Strike first!* had proved themselves sure words of wisdom in the seemingly endless time she had spent in the dark, dusty halls. Lunae took stock of herself. She had eaten hours ago, and she was in fighting trim. The tools of her trade were ready to her fingers. It was a momentary temptation to pass by this door, but she had no idea if this corridor would provide another exit soon enough to avoid the creature with the musty scent. There was no reason to delay. Her torch was more than half gone. Going back was out of the question.

<OPEN THE DOOR> The latch worked smoothly, but the hinges did not. The door moved unevenly with the popping grind of a stone pivot.

<LOOK> Glowstone lit the roomy chamber with its cool blue light. <PUT OUT TORCH> There were signs of travelers. A torn leather sack lay on a large, flat boulder next to a trickling spring. The rivulet barely parted the dust on the floor before vanishing into a fault-line crack. That dust was well stirred by prints of man and beast. The hoofprints amazed her. *Lead a pack animal down into the catacombs? The scents alone in this place would spook it.*

Two other stone doors faced her. This was a crossroads, if that term could be used in these underground passages. She quickly moved to check them. <LISTEN AT DOORWAYS> There was never too much caution in this place.

There were no sounds, and the smells of this oft-used waystop masked anything that might be beyond them. A set of conveniently placed boulders were at hand, so she blocked all three entrances.

"Thank you." It was a man's voice.

<PIVOT LOW. PLACE THROWING KNIFE IN LEFT HAND. LOOK>

She spun into a crouch, ready to throw her knife as soon as she spotted a target. Though it wasn't terribly bright, the glowstone light shone evenly enough to wash out shadows. A man could hide in two or three places among the jumble of boulders where the spring was sourced. Lunae was painfully aware that she was without the smallest boulder to protect her from any thrown weapon. She shifted her stance to give her better mobility. *Stupid! I've spent too much time getting this far into the catacombs to be killed by some clever thief.* There was nowhere to run. The doors were tightly wedged by the boulders she'd so carefully moved into place!

"Nervous one, aren't you? You could at least say 'hello'".

She had his hiding place located now. There was a crack between the stones through which he watched her. He was shielded from her knife, but if she could reach the brass vial of contact poison in her pack ...

<STAND UP SLOWLY. SAY: YOU STARTLED ME. I EXPECTED TO BE ATTACKED. TAKE A STEP TOWARDS MY PACK>

He had not attacked even though he had an obvious tactical advantage. Perhaps she could reach ...

He spoke. "I would appreciate it if you stayed right where you are!" She froze, her mind in high gear. He could have a nocked arrow aimed her way. If so, the aim would be hampered by the very rocks that protected him; no other weapon would have a better chance. He was either stupid or bluffing.

<DIVE INTO A ROLL. GRAB MY PACK. USE MY PACK AS A SHIELD . GET THE BOTTLE OF POISON> She felt the embossed bottle in her pack just as the stinging bite of a dart found her arm. Lunae fought for consciousness as a wave of buzzing darkness rushed over her.

YOU HAVE BEEN RENDERED UNCONSCIOUS ON A POISONED DART.

YOU ARE LOGGED OFF CATACOMB FOR 00:30 MINIMUM.

YOUR ACCOUNT BALANCE IS:

$ 0.78 FOR TODAY

$ 12.40 FOR THE GAME

$ 7.50 TREASURE BONUS {RESERVED}

...

Judith Cere stared morosely at her screen. Fat chance her treasure would be there when she checked back. Even money that Mr. Hide- and-Seek would kill her and she'd have to create another character. She bunched her right hand into a fist and hit the desktop. A stack of papers slithered off the desk and landed on the floor with a fluid plop.

"Judith?" her father's voice called from his office room down the hall. "Is anything wrong?"

Her finger stabbed the PAGE CLEAR key, and she called back, "No, Daddy. I just transposed a field. No problem." Her voice shook a little and her hand hurt. She didn't need to lose her temper. CATACOMB was proving to be a harder way to make money than she had hoped.

Her gaze rested guiltily on the scattered pile of handwritten invoices that she needed to key into a file as her task for the day. Best get to it. Father wasn't one to let the kids slide on their chores. Even if she was seventeen, he could make her feel like her brother Georgie caught with forbidden cookie crumbs all over his face. Maybe he wouldn't mind her CATACOMB adventures, but play before work was against the house rules.

She picked up the first paper and invoked the home database. *Get the file built, then check on Lunae again.*

···

YOU ARE UNCONSCIOUS FROM THE EFFECTS OF A POISONED DART.

LOGON TO CATACOMB IS NOT ALLOWED FOR 00:14 MINIMUM.

YOUR ACCOUNT BALANCE IS:

$ 0.78 FOR TODAY

$ 12.40 FOR THE GAME

$ 0.00 TREASURE BONUS

Thief! Well, at least he left her alive.

She cleared the screen and plopped down on her bed. Her flute case, half buried among books and cosmetics on her dressing table, was a black reminder of her problems. It was not going as she had planned. The ruby stolen from Lunae wasn't worth much in real money, but she'd counted on it to cover part of her time charges for playing the game until she could find more treasure. The three hundred dollars was due in two weeks. To be twelve dollars in the hole was not only depressing, it was embarrassing. She shouldn't have told Diana about her plan.

With a whoop, Barry skidded into her room and was followed by Jay, his friend from the house down the hill. A pair of suction-cup darts crossed in the air, one of them bouncing off the mirror of her dressing table.

"Barry, get out of my room this instant! You're messing up everything." She picked up the expended plastic dart and tossed it out the doorway.

"Hey! That's my dart!"

"Then go get it, brat!"

From down the hall, her father's voice silenced them both, "You kids be quiet. It's work time. Barry, do you want some file maintenance? Judith, are your invoices done?"

They both knew silence was the safest course. Barry gave her a silent sneer as his brotherly token of disrespect and waved Jay out with him. If there had been a silent way of murdering her brother ....

...

Lunae came to consciousness with the feel of her pack under her head as a pillow. Her thief had left her stretched out comfortably, concealed behind the rocks that had protected him. <TAKE INVENTORY> A quick survey of her pack and her person revealed only the ruby missing. Even her weapons were still in their places. She was puzzled. Most thieves would have left her dead and sold her provisions back to the Wizard of the Gate.

<SMELL. LISTEN> The smell of the thief was quite strong in the coffin-sized hidey-hole. He'd obviously spent considerable time waiting there for victims. She crawled from behind the rocks carefully. No one was in sight. A glance told her that the thief had cleared all three doorways and had obscured any footprints in the dust.

<STATE HOW I AM> The effects of the poison lingered in her system. She felt more tired than she ought, and quick motion was an invitation to dizziness. But it should wear off quickly. Her only question now was whether she should follow her thief in order to turn the tables on him and recover her ruby, or search out another treasure before her supplies ran out and she had to make for the Wizard's Gate.

Before she could shoulder her pack, the decision was taken away from her. A sudden wave of acid stench hit her. Out of nothingness stepped trouble. The dim light of glowstone was adequate, this time, to tell her quite enough: a Tor beast!

Adventurers into the catacombs perforce did business with the Wizard of the Gate to purchase their supplies, but more than gold pieces and bronze weapons were exchanged at the Wizard's market. Rumor and out right lies about the hazards and treasure in the catacombs were bought and sold as well. And nothing said about the teleporting half-man/half-beasts that searched the chambers was comforting. Some said Tor beasts were adventurers from another plane, given access by some other Wizard of the Gate, perhaps one of their own number. They were not animals. They walked upright and sometimes were known to use magic. They didn't use swords because they didn't need one.

<PLACE THROWING KNIFE IN THE LEFT HAND. PLACE SHORT SWORD IN THE RIGHT HAND> She didn't attack. Armored like a beetle, with hands like the paws of a tiger, the Tor beast topped her five-foot height by six inches and outweighed her by at least two hundred pounds. The pelt—if it was a pelt—formed a half-dozen rings about his torso, and a ridge of bluish-black shag from one claw, across the shoulders, to the other. The head was piggish, but the eyes betrayed an intelligent malevolence. Its growl as he spotted her was a deep bass that seemed to shake her insides. Nothing in the rumors she had heard told of how to kill one.

The Tor beast seemed to have no such worry. It turned and stalked towards her with the body-twisting gait of a bear. She threw her knife directly toward where a navel would have been, had the thing been born. The knife stuck, for an instant, before the beast shook it loose. The wound only made it more angry.

Lunae was moving up on the rocks before her knife had left her fingers. The beast was powerful, but she was much lighter on her feet. She picked up her pack by the straps and slung it at the thing's head.

Maybe the Tor beast walked slow, but there was nothing sluggish about the way it snatched the pack out of the air and ripped it wide open with its claws.

Her goods spilled out, and she felt sick as the beast, with all angry growl, ground her food supply and spare torches to mush and toothpicks.

Then the monster crouched and jumped ten feet in one motion, landing on the boulders just below where Lunae stood. She scrambled higher, using her sword to keep him at a distance. It didn't work. Its arm shot out, a blur. Then—pain; she barely held onto the sword as the beast batted it aside. With the stench of the creature wafting over her and the sick feeling that her sword was bent, she grabbed the hilt with both hands and forced all her strength into a sideways stroke. Her sword twisted and slid out of her grip as the warped blade slapped rather than cut the beast.

The thing roared. She could almost feel the bone-shattering slap she knew the monster could give her. But the slap never came. The moment of grace wasn't wasted. As well as she could with the ruined sword in her grasp, she rolled over the top of the mound, down into the coffin-sized pit where she had regained her consciousness.

The beast roared again. She knew the monster would be down on her the instant it navigated the rocks. The blade—not that she had a second to actually look at it—was in bad shape. Both bent and twisted, it would never take the force of an attack, even if the beast could be tricked into falling on it. It would bend like a hairpin. She gambled precious seconds in hopes of straightening the sword blade. She wedged the blade halfway into a crack in the rock and shoved all of her slight weight against it. When the blade was far short of perfection, but perhaps usable, she pulled the sword loose and held it ready.

For a hurried breath or two, she waited. There was silence in the chamber. Then the Tor beast growled, but it sounded ... weaker. Gambling again: <LOOK THROUGH THE CRACKS> The limited view gave a puzzling sight. The thing was staggering, struggling to keep its balance.

Enlightenment hit. The poison! She looked to the chamber floor, where the fragments of her belongings were scattered. Among the debris was a bit of metal that might have been the brass bottle smashed flat by a powerful foot.

What would the poison do to it? A human would be dead the instant a drop touched skin. Could the Tor beast shake off the effects? The creature was very powerful. Perhaps it had protective magic. If it recovered, she didn't want to be around.

But, there was always treasure. Magical beasts often collected treasure themselves. If her Tor beast died, she wanted anything of value it might have. She hefted the sword in her hand. Perhaps she could assist the poison a bit.

Shortly, the monster stumbled and fell. She was up and over her rocky barricade in an instant.

The beast was on its back, still struggling against the powerful convulsions the poison was creating in its muscles. Fighting against its own mutinous body, the Tor beast desperately grabbed at a black leather arm band that circled its left arm just above the elbow. The creature's life or death fueled its determination. If it could work the band's secrets, it might yet survive.

That's it! The Tor beast's magic is in that arm band! Lunae watched its struggles for an instant more, then danced in close for an opportunity to slash at the arm with her sword. It cut the monster's flesh, but not deeply. She did it again. And again. Finally, arm and body were separated. She kicked the still twitching member out of the beast's reach and waited for the monster to die. Blood, looking black in the blue light of the chamber, squirted forcefully from the severed arteries. Quickly, it stopped.

The trained assassin normally held no qualms examining a dead body, but something alien in it chilled her as she stepped near. The stench, now so much stronger in the spilled blood, made it difficult to breathe. The feel of the body was like an upholstered leather chair which remained warm from the life of the person who had sat there. It seemed surprisingly soft. Lunae expected hard, armor-like plate.

She searched the corpse for any natural or artificial pouches, pockets, or bags—anywhere the beast might have stored something of value. Within a minute, she admitted defeat. *Logical. Any being who can teleport won't keep too many possessions on his body, since he can go get them in an instant.*

As she felt the body, it grew softer by the moment. When she noticed this curious fact, she quit instantly and backed away.

Starting at the beast's chest, the body quivered slightly. Then it began to liquefy. In the light, her eyes could just make out thousands of sprouts, much like the fur on moldy bread. Tendrils of terribly rapid decay covered the body in half a minute. Slime from the rotting flesh dripped to the floor and formed a thickening flow to join the trickle of the spring.

In disgust, she turned from the sight to spot the beast's arm. It was whole. There seemed to be no sign of the decay that had already turned the body into an unrecognizable mound. Gingerly, she approached it. A cautious touch—first with the point of the sword, then with her hand gave the impression of teak wood covered with leather. There was no softness. Quickly, before the decay could start, she slipped the arm band off the dead limb.

The band was made of flexible leather with a ridge of worked metal along both edges. *It looks like silver, maybe. Almost the right size for a belt. It will sell. Magic always sells.* She eyed the claws. The arm, separated from the body, seemed to be spared the extremely fast decay. *That might sell too, but I want no part of it!*

The arm band slipped loosely over her shoulder like a coil of rope. As of the moment, it, her sword, and the pair of knives she had hidden in her clothes were her only possessions. What was not smashed was probably contaminated with the spilled poison. It would not be safe to touch for another day. With no supplies, no food, no torches for light, she might be dead by then.

The Wizard's Gate was too distant for her to travel without food, even if she could make the way in total darkness. There was really only one thing she could do: pursue her thief. Since he had spared her life, perhaps she could persuade him to give her provisions in exchange for some service. If not, perhaps she could steal from him what she needed to survive. Following him seemed to be worth the effort.

Yet the darkness still posed a problem. If only the glowstones could be used for lighting! But they were far too dim. Unless there existed a chamber lined entirely with glowstones like this one, the journey would have to be done in the dark.

She walked to each doorway and carefully sniffed the air. The stench of the beast covered everything, but her sensitive nose could still detect other scents.

"Judith! Supper!" Barry called from the base of the stairs up to her opened door.

Oh no! I must chase him before the scent gets cold.

"Just a minute! I've got to log off."

This was a horrible time to stop and search for a shelter. She grabbed a fist-sized piece of glowstone. Its light would be useless more than a few inches away, but it was the only light she had. With more desperation than confidence she glided as swiftly as she dared down the length of the corridor. With her sword sheathed, she let the fingertips of her left hand feel for openings in the wall. She believed she was passing a dozen perfect shelters on the right-hand wall. Only two things were clear in the darkness: her time was running out, and thief's scent was tantalizingly present.

If she had only gone back, retraced her path toward the Gate, she would have known exactly where to shelter. She imagined the crypt carved in the wall, where she had spent the night before her disastrous encounter with the thief. That would be ideal.

"Judith! It's getting cold." It was her father's voice this time.

"Coming!" *If I log off now, Lunae will seek shelter and attempt to fight off attackers like a dim-witted robot programmed and operated by the computer. Her only real chance for survival is for her to find shelter under her own power.*

At that instant her hand felt a carved doorsill in the rock. Not knowing nor caring what creature might be waiting within, she pushed aside the stone doorway. Groping about the room, Lunae found a foot-long stone slab that could be used as a deadbolt in order to seal the chamber from almost any terror that roamed the corridors. She dropped her glowstone and secured the door.

There was barely enough room to lie down in the closet-sized, cold rock crypt, but she didn't care.

. . .

Judith rapidly keyed the logoff and dashed out of her room, not waiting to view the message on the screen

```
YOUR ACCOUNT BALANCE IS:
$   1.58  FOR TODAY
$  13.20  FOR THE GAME
$  ??.??  TREASURE BONUS {RESERVED} {CONDITIONAL
= 53}
```

Supper was a table piled high with leaves. Even the meat loaf had green things in it. Mother was in that stage of gardening when she was spending fifteen hours a day just trying to keep up with the production.

A strong scent of spices and vinegar drifted in from the kitchen. Judith smiled at the thought that Lunae's sensitivities were infecting her own. She had seen other kids mimic the dress and habits of their on-line characters. But she wasn't going to start carrying a dagger up her sleeve!

Father had a distant, preoccupied look. Judith could sympathize with that condition better than her mother could. She and her father were the family members who spent the most hours on the terminals. The world on the other side of the glass tube absorbed one's attention.

Mother was giving a running commentary on her battles with the leaf miners and the fire ants. This was her year for trying totally organic gardening, and she constantly missed the use of her chemical weapons to fight against the ravening hordes.

Barry was unsympathetic. "Why don't you just use that white powder stuff you used last year? We won't tell on you."

"That's enough." Father had less interest in the war against the insects than Barry did, but there was such a thing as parental solidarity. "Barry, I won't need your help for a couple of days. It sounds like Mother could use a couple of spare hands with the garden. Starting in the morning."

"Aww! Come on, Dad! Jay and Toot and me we've got a COMMANDER game in the morning!" Barry visibly reined in his indignation and picked at the spinach leaves on his plate. To Judith's sisterly eye, it was an obviously staged acquiescence. Father would never stand for open disobedience.

"Just where were you going to have this game?" Father made the word sound indecent. "At home or at the arcade terminal?"

"Well," Barry spoke cautiously, "the graphics are better at Spacer's World than at home. And the faster baud rate there would give me an edge."

"Just how were you going to pay for the time?"

Barry glanced up at his father's impassive face and spotted the smirk on Judith's. He mumbled something no one could hear and took another bite of the salad.

Father continued, "If I recall correctly, you blew all of last week's allowance on COMMANDER. I heard you ask your mother for some money yesterday. Since allowance day is the day after tomorrow, I don't see where you could have gotten any money to pay for your game tomorrow. Since I don't suppose Spacer's World gives credit, you wouldn't be able to play there tomorrow anyway. And since your games-account suspension here at home doesn't run out for another two weeks, you couldn't play here either.

"So, it seems to me that you will have plenty of time to help your mother in the garden. Isn't that right?"

Judith felt a little sympathy for Barry. Not much, but a little. Father's logical traps were painful. There were ways to pay for game time that Barry could have lined up, but these were either forbidden or unacceptable methods. Who in the family could forget the time Barry's games account was suspended because he had charged several games to Father's business account?

"Judith," her mother asked, "could you help me clean up after supper? I need to run to the store."

Judith resigned herself to the delay and nodded. Now was not the time to plead that she had a game in progress. Barry shot her a sneer on general principles.

...

Barton Creek Mall had changed over the years. Judith didn't particularly like to shop there with her mother. It was a fun place if you went there with friends, but mothers were different. Most of the larger department stores had gone on-line and were gradually deserting the shopping malls. Sears and Penneys had left, leaving their areas subdivided into an Arabian maze of market stalls. The mall was the place to go to sample a dozen varieties of egg rolls, to buy hand-carved earrings, or to lose a few hours in a COMMANDER booth.

A trio of players, Just old enough to grow beards, were waiting for a booth outside the entrance to an arcade and watching the pair of them as they walked by. Mother didn't seem to notice, but Judith was glad she wasn't alone. Lunae could handle any trouble from the likes of them, but Judith wouldn't even know how to handle one of her sleeve daggers.

She shook her head to rid herself of the thoughts. Those boys weren't like her thief, out for trouble in a lawless world. Maybe the mall did have some permanent residents that were a bit smelly, but no one was going to accost her mother and her during prime time.

They shopped their way through a bottle shop, an herb market, and an office supply house. Then, at Judith's urging, they stopped for a slice of pizza.

"We're not too far from Reitz. Did you want to stop and get that practice book you asked for?" Mother asked.

"No. Not tonight." Diana worked at that shop. She didn't want to see her just yet.

Mother frowned and put down her pizza. "Now, Judith, you aren't going to give up on your music just because Brentwood Academy doesn't have a school band program, are you? They have a nice orchestra!"

"No! I'm not going to quit." Judith bit back. "I like my music. It's you and Father who are trying to take me away from all the good teachers and all my friends. "

"Now, Judith. You know we are only trying to get the best education for you and Barry. Brentwood isn't a big high school, but they have excellent teachers."

"And no music program."

"No band. They do have an orchestra. Are you sure you are interested in the music, not the football games?"

"Mother, that's not true!" And with a flushed face, Judith left the table and headed out the shop. Her mother, a little flushed herself, picked up the packages and followed.

Judith paid no attention to the other people in the mall as she made for the parking lot. *I'll show them. I'll get the money, go to the music camp, and make a slowing that'll force them to see where my talents lie.*

. . .

Lunae woke with only the light of a single glowstone to greet her. <TAKE INVENTORY. STATE HOW I AM> She was hungry. But there were no torches, no food, no water. The leather band was still looped over her shoulder.

If it weren't for that, she might have given up right there. Dying would cost her nothing, but reincarnating in another character would. And while still in possession of a rare, possibly magical, artifact, she just might survive and turn her find into a treasure bonus.

The chamber—from what she could tell by feel and from examination at a nose-bumping distance with glowstone in hand—looked exactly like the chamber in which she spent the previous night. She stuffed the glowstones under her tunic and unbolted the door.

<SMELL, LISTEN> The musty scent gagged her. If there were any scent of her thief, it was masked. She just stood there, engulfed by the odor. Something about it seemed to dull her reactions. To her right, from the direction she had come, she heard a scrapping, plopping, near-liquid sound, as if three tons of gelatin were moving down the corridor toward her.

<GET BACK INSIDE THE CHAMBER, LOCK THE DOOR> Her body started to move in response to her intent; however, it didn't follow through. Her arm reached for the door, but it stopped in mid-air. It was the numbing scent that had her in its spell.

<TURN LEFT> She half turned. The sound of the approaching creature was noticeably nearer.

<TURN LEFT> Now that she no longer faced her approaching doom, talk overheard at the Wizard's Gate came back to her. This was the CATACOMB's garbage collector. It was so huge that it entirely filled the width and height of the corridor; it digested anything organic in its path. Nothing she had heard, however, warned her of its stupefying scent.

<MOVE LEFT FOOT FORWARD> It worked! <MOVE RIGHT FOOT FORWARD> She moved. Okay Simple actions only.

<MOVE LEFT FOOT FORWARD. MOVE RIGHT FOOT FORWARD. MOVE LEFT FOOT FORWARD. MOVE RIGHT FOOT FORWARD. MOVE LEFT FOOT FORWARD. MOVE RIGHT FOOT FORWARD. MOVE LEFT FOOT FORWARD. MOVE RIGHT FOOT FORWARD. MOVE LEFT FOOT FORWARD. MOVE RIGHT FOOT FORWARD. MOVE LEFT FOOT FORWARD. MOVE RIGHT FOOT FORWARD. MOVE LEFT FOOT FORWARD. MOVE RIGHT FOOT FORWARD> She wasn't moving fast, but neither was her musty friend

<MOVE LEFT FOOT FORWARD. MOVE RIGHT FOOT FORWARD. MOVE LEFT FOOT FORWARD. MOVE RIGHT FOOT FORWARD. MOVE LEFT FOOT FORWARD. MOVE RIGHT FOOT FORWARD>

Fifty yards ahead of the gelatinous mound, the effects of the scent began to lessen, and she broke into a run. Still sightless, she tried to pace herself, so that striking a wall wouldn't hurt hew too badly.

Several times she scraped her arm against the left side of the corridor as she drifted too close to the wall. The surface wasn't exactly smooth, more like mason work than natural stone. This corridor resembled the one she had traveled prior to finding the glowstone chamber, so she was not surprised when her fingertips felt a large stone door. She stopped.

The blob of gelatin was far behind, but she had no doubt that it would get to her soon enough if she didn't find shelter. She tried the door. It opened with a popping, grinding sound.

To her light-starved eyes, the glowstone seemed to light the chamber brightly. The stench of Tor beast mixed with the old scents of spice, mule, and the faint odor of her thief. The same chamber? Was her sense of direction that far off?

But, first things first. She picked up a familiar boulder and barricaded the door separating her from old acid-and-quivery. Her warped sword slid quickly from its sheath, and she made a quick attack on the hidey-hole and skewered the empty air hiding there. Only then did she barricade the other two doors and take time for a survey.

The Tor beast was nothing more than a small mound of rich soil—as was the severed arm. The same decay had taken it as well. The beast had thoroughly destroyed her supplies, so nothing usable was left. Her thief was still her only hope. She found the source of the spring and drank, then she unblocked the doors and followed her nose.

It was puzzling. The air of this corridor did not include the musty scent, but was scented strongly with the smell of her thief. But it was the same one—wasn't it?—that she had looped around just hours before. She paced slowly and silently. The only sound was an occasional grumble from her stomach. When her finger tips failed to find the chamber again, she began to doubt her memory.

Okay, this is a different corridor. I missed a turn somewhere. But this is my thief's trail. She slowed her pace, trying to coax images from the darkness and to read messages into the scents.

The air was more moist here than in the glowstone chamber. There was the scent of her thief and other people, but his was the strongest. There was no trace of the pack animal or the spices, but torches aplenty had passed this way. There were a dozen fainter smells, some too elusive for her to place, but a mental picture of the place could be etched.

Her thief was just that: a thief. It wasn't a case of two paranoid adventurers having a casual shootout with the victor taking the spoils. Her thief regularly patrolled this set of corridors. He used the hidey-hole in the glowstone chamber—and undoubtedly secret places in other chambers—to waylay adventurers who passed by, collecting any treasures from his victims. No one who prowled this world could have any pretense of a moral position, but knowing what kind of person he was, it made it a little easier to do what she planned.

Finally, the corridor branched at a T-junction. The scent was freshest to the left, so she followed it. Not a hundred yards past the branch was a chamber door blocked open. There was no light within. He was in there. She knew it.

She made no sound, and she had no light. There was a very good chance that he was not expecting anyone. Even if he expected her to follow, he had left her with torches. Could she sneak inside and surprise him? Did she have a chance? She had no supplies. He was probably well stocked. At any moment, he could close and bar the door against the creatures of the catacomb for his nighttime snooze.

She shed the sword and hid the glowstone where it would not betray her position. One dagger she held with her teeth. Carefully, she slipped through the doorway and flattened out against the wall on the inside. She intended to stay motionless like that until he betrayed his location.

Pfft! There was the sound and the sudden sting of a dart in her left hand.

Oh, no! Not again!

<SLIP TOR ARM BAND HALFWAY DOWN ARM, TWIST ARM BAND INTO TOURNIQUET WITH THE DAGGER IN MY TEETH. PLUCK OUT DART, FALL DOWN, HIDE LEFT ARM UNDER MY BODY>

Her arm and hand began to throb uncomfortably under her, but the drug was contained, at least for the moment. With her good hand she fished out the other dagger. She played 'possum.

The sound of a rustle was masked by the rocks. The thief was lighting a torch.

"Very good, whoever you are. And if you are still awake."

The light flared, and she closed her eyes to slits.

"Oh, it's you! Little Miss Ruby with all the nasty stuff in her pack. You must be pretty hard up to track me down for just a little trinket like that. Or are you one of the feuding, vengeful types?"

She spotted him working carefully around the rocks The patter was just to lull her, if she were faking it. He was keeping shelter until he could get a real good look at her. Lunae added some protective coloration. Her mouth slowly opened, and a trickle of spittle drooled out. Consciously, she checked every muscle to make sure it was relaxed. She made no effort to watch what he was doing, relying on her ears to place him.

It worked. He came from behind his cover and stood beside where she lay. He wedged the toe of his boot beneath her to turn her over. He pushed.

As her body rolled, her bound arm snapped out and grabbed his ankle. She yanked. Standing on one foot and burdened with his blowpipe and sword, he toppled. Her dagger caught him in the arm. It wrenched from her grasp. Grasping for anything that could be a weapon, She caught his blowpipe. She clubbed him with it. The slender tube snapped in two, but he slumped out.

She stood. He was crumpled and bleeding from the knife wound, unconscious on the ground. His torch flickered erratically where it had fallen on the stone floor.

Lunae labored light-headedly for breath. A familiar buzzing sounded behind her ears. The tourniquet must have slipped a little in the battle. Another twist on the dagger's handle tightened the force on the arm band painfully. She would have to let it go soon or risk damage to the arm.

The torch flared yellow when she picked it up. There were two doors and she blocked them both. This chamber was slightly smaller than the other, but it too had a spring. Again, there was a small but comfortable-looking hiding place.

Sprawled on the ground, Lunae had the opportunity to see how large her thief really was; and he was big. She stared at the oozing wound for a moment before tearing a strip from his shirt and placing a pressure bandage over the wound. He was still alive and too dangerous to leave alone. She sought one of his darts from the broken blowpipe and stabbed him in the arm with it. Tying him up would be best, but ... it was getting ... very difficult to move. Waves roared in her ears.

She slumped down and prepared to sleep it off. The dagger slipped a turn or two, loosening the band. Her arm and hand were an unhealthy blue.

Horror struck as she saw his eyes open, watching her. She tried to tighten the band and to get to her feet, but her legs wouldn't move. Slowly, he pulled himself up on his hands and feet and crawled towards her. She forced one knee up. Her leg was a lead weight.

"Sorry." His words came slowly. He was weak. "Immune to my own venom."

She was trapped by her own weight. One arm was paralyzed; one held desperately to the tourniquet. She couldn't get up.

He came relentlessly on. "Should have killed me. I should ... have killed you." His hand reached hers and forced the tourniquet loose. "Both ... too civilized ... for this game."

YOU HAVE BEEN RENDERED UNCONSCIOUS BY A POISON DART.

YOU ARE LOGGED OFF CATACOMB FOR 01:30 MINIMUM.

YOUR ACCOUNT BALANCE IS:

$ 2.21 FOR TODAY

$ 13.83 FOR THE GAME

$??.?? TREASURE BONUS {RESERVED} {CONDITIONAL = 53}

...

Judith stared at the screen. It was almost midnight, and the house was silent and dark, except for those glowing green letters on her screen.

Defeated twice in one day! This was supposed to be entertainment? She was feeling depressed.

Another hour and a half. Could she manage to stay awake long enough to log back on then? It was her only chance to turn the tables. Tomorrow would be a busy day with no time for this.

The treasure bonus puzzled her. <RUN 53>

CATEGORY 53 TREASURES ARE GENERALLY MAGICAL IN NATURE AND ARE WORTHLESS UNLESS PROPERLY USED.

THEY CANNOT BE SOLD TO THE WIZARD OF THE GATE, SINCE HE WOULD TAKE THEM WITHOUT PAYING FOR THEM. THE VALUE SHOWN IS ONLY AN ESTIMATE OF THE TRADE VALUE OF THE ITEM.

Strange. There is no value shown. What does that mean? Is it the arm band? If so, I should have seen that message before.

Judith tapped a key that disconnected her terminal with the tieline. Then <RESPOOL, $.1800-2000> Back across the screen scrolled everything she'd seen or done on the screen between six and eight that evening.

There it is! I must have missed it trying to get down to supper. It has to be the arm band.

With that resolved, she put on her muffs, plugged them into the terminal, and keyed a wake-up.

...

Lunae woke to yellow light and the smell of bacon and fresh trail bread. As she tried to lift her head, her whole body shook from hunger, fatigue, and the residual effects of the drug.

"Ah, good. I was hoping you wouldn't be out very long. Here." Her thief handed her a trail sandwich. She had no heart to protest. It vanished quickly.

The thief was even bigger than she remembered, now that she was on the ground and he was standing.

"Not too bad looking," he commented, echoing her own thoughts, "even with some very sharp looking teeth." He sat down on a rock next to her and handed her a bottle. While she made its contents vanish as well, he rambled on, "Of course, in this world, all you see are beautiful specimens or characters who like to make themselves deliberately horrifying. But most opt for beauty and strength, when they have any choice in the matter."

Lunae handed him the bottle. <SAY: "THERE WAS SAND IN THE BOTTOM. BUT THANKS. I LOST MY SUPPLIES.">

"I noticed that." He took her bottle and put it back among his things, even turning his back on her. By reflex, she reached for her knives and found them properly sheathed. He turned back to her. "I knew you would be out for a while—what with two doses of the dart in one day—so I tried to find your supplies. The sword was close, but all bent up. I backtracked to the Blue Chamber and saw your stuff. Frankly, from what I saw, I am very surprised you are still here. What got after you?"

<SAY:"A TOR BEAST.", TRY TO SIT UP AGAIN.> She made it this time.

He saw her effort and offered her a hand to a more comfortable seat on a water-smoothed boulder. "Maybe it's a good thing I didn't kill you. It might be handy to know someone who can survive a Tor beast attack. How'd you do it?"

<SAY:"I KILLED IT.">

"That, I don't believe. But tell me the tale anyway. You wouldn't believe how lonely this job is."

And so she did. The whole thing. Maybe Lunae wouldn't have divulged everything without taking some advantage in trade, but it was late at night and Judith was a bit lonely herself. Her thief made an appreciative audience, commenting appropriately during the telling.

<SAY:"AND I WANT TO THANK YOU FOR NOT KILLING ME, TWICE.">

"You did the same for me. I didn't come to until you were halfway through with the bandaging. I appreciate it. Surviving another day here pays the grocery bill off-line."

<SAY:"YOU MEAN YOU REALLY MAKE A LIVING AT THIS?">

"This life of crime, you mean?"

<SAY:"WELL,YES.">

"You have it in a nutshell: I live on-line. What I make from CATA-COMB has to be enough to pay for my bread and access charges, or I go hungry. Thievery is just a matter of the odds. I tried searching for treasure in every cubbyhole, but it turned out that I made more by surviving attacks from other characters and pocketing their findings than I could make on my own. When I bought the blowpipe and turned thief professionally, it even had some moral advantages. My victims usually survived. I'm really quite good at it. Rumor back at the Gate has it that the Phantom Thief is a native of CATACOMB and can't ever be caught or killed."

<SAY:"I STILL DON'T KNOW WHETHER I COULD BE A THIEF, EVEN AS AN ON-LINE CHARACTER.">

"Didn't you say you were an assassin?"

<SAY: "YES, BUT">

"Yes, but what?"

<SAY:"I DON'T KNOW. YOU'VE GOT ME CONFUSED. LET'S GO BACK TO TALKING ABOUT YOUR SINS. WHY CAN'T YOU WORK FOR A LIVING OFF-LINE.">

For a moment there was no response. Then, "Don't laugh, but there is a very good reason. Denver's child wage laws keep employers from hiring people of my age. Next year I'll be nineteen, and I won't have that excuse. You'll have to wait until then to tell whether I'm a sociopath or just a bright kid beating the system."

<SAY:"FOR WHAT IT'S WORTH, I'M SEVENTEEN, AND I DON'T THINK AUSTIN HAS THAT KIND OF LAW. BUT WHY ARE YOU HAVING TO MAKE A LIVING. I'LL STILL BE IN SCHOOL AT YOUR AGE.">

"That, my sweet, is the fate of everyone who's unlucky enough to be missing a set of parents and too cantankerous to abide by the whims of the state juvenile system. As long as I'm not arrested for an off-line crime, the people here will let me make my own way. And to tell the truth, if I must be a thief, I'd much rather be one in a world like CATACOMB, where such behavior is expected.

"And now for your sins. What is a nice girl like you doing in a place like this?"

Judith told her whole plan. She spoke of her goals of making enough money to attend the music camp and to win a first-chair position. By taking her out of the public-school system and away from her friends and by putting her in the academy, she wanted to show her parents that they would be depriving her of her true vocation.

"Whew! Angel, you make me feel old. I'm not going to discourage you by telling you what I think of your chances, but I must say I have every respect for your ambitions. If I had a spare $300, I'd share it with you. But ... "

The dollar sign on the screen triggered a memory, and for a moment Lunae considered how to get the arm band back from her thief and how to learn its secrets. Then Judith spilled the beans. She filled him in on the unusual logoff message she'd received, even replaying it and the condition code description back from her terminal's local memory. Afterward, she explained her theory about the arm band.

"Angel, this is not how you're supposed to play this game. I'm supposed to kill you; you're supposed to kill me; and we're both supposed to steal each other's treasures."

<SAY:"AS GHOSTS, I SUPPOSE?">

"I wouldn't put it past us, in this world.

"In any case, you've hit me with a problem. If your theory about the Tor teleportation magic and the arm band is correct, then I am just the person to make the best use of it. I've used many of the magic spells of this world, and I know how they work. After all, that's how I spotted your last attack. Also, I've been all over the catacombs, and I know where there are several treasures only a teleporter could get at. So, I should cut your heart out, steal your artifact, and go to it. Instead I'll have to trade you for it. All I've got is a busted blowpipe and treasure worth about fifty dollars in real money."

Judith thought about it for a moment. The Lunae in her clamored for a better deal, a percentage of the take. But as it was past four in the morning, CATACOMB seemed far less real to her than a nice boy beating the system in Denver.

<SAY:"THROW IN A GOOD SAFE ROUTE BACK TO THE GATE AND IT'S A DEAL. I'VE BEEN LOST IN THIS MAZE FOR THREE DAYS NOW.">

...

The day was an ordeal because Judith never went to sleep, even after her thief shooed her off into a safety chamber and, thus, back into the off-line world. She could barely drag herself through her chores. And Barry was no help at all. Deprived of his COMMANDER game, his second-best sport was sister-baiting. She was grateful when Mother forced him out into the garden at spade point. Therefore, Judith didn't mind at all that she was stuck with the job of making sure that Georgie didn't get into anything but harmless trouble.

The day passed, but she never got logged back onto CATACOMB. Alone, finally, after the evening meal, she fell asleep.

Morning brought a tempest. Barry rushed out of the house with Jay, and a call to Jay's mother brought the information that the pair had gone off to the mall to play COMMANDER. The news of Barry's rebellion brought Father down from his office and put him into a black mood. He picked up the cane he always used for walking in public, drafted Judith to be his scout, and left for the mall with her.

Judith thought her father looked very impressive, especially so when he was angry. Though he limped and carried a cane in public, his image was of a man in control. Walking beside him through the crowd, her Lunae perspective made her wonder just how handy a club his cane would make. She headed for the arcade.

Barry was there, joking with some friends around a COMMANDER booth. The place was packed, mostly with boys Barry's age and older. Today, they seemed much less threatening to her. In an uncharacteristic burst of sympathy, she didn't report his location immediately to Father.

"Hello, Barry."

He was surprised to see her. "Hello, Sis."

"There's a man with a cane outside who has brought a message for you."

"Oh." His face paled a bit, but the light was low. "Jay, I've gotta go. See ya." And he was gone. His friends looked puzzled. Judith smiled sweetly and explained, "Business." Then she walked off.

Halfway to the door she overheard: "... played CATACOMB like never before. The *Alien Worlds* column said he made a mint."

There was an empty CATACOMB booth. She slid into the seat and fed the machine a pair of coins.

•••

Lunae awoke in a bed near the noisy babble of the throng at the Wizard's Gate. Her pillow was large, lumpy, and hard. Pinned to her sleeve was a note.

Dear Angel,

Sorry we didn't make this last connection. It worked. I've never had so much on-line fun since I started playing. Once I got to the right places, I found more gold in this world than I dreamed.

I've fulfilled my part of our bargain, though this Lunae of yours fights like a devil when you're not inside her. I had to drug her again to get her back to the Gate. The bed is only rented for a week, since I figure you'll connect up before then. This may be the last time we talk. I have a strong feeling they'll lock me out of this world when I go cash in my coins.

Kisses for my Angel, Your thief

Judith keyed the logoff.

```
YOU HAVE REACHED A SAFE PLACE.
YOU MAY NOW ADJUST YOUR ACCOUNT BALANCES.
YOUR ACCOUNT BALANCE IS:
$     0.05 FOR TODAY
```

```
$    18.34 FOR THE GAME
$   534.25 TREASURE BONUS
DO YOU WISH TO CASH IN YOUR TREASURE {Y/N}?
DO YOU WISH TO PAY YOUR GAME ACCOUNT {Y/N}?
```

...

Oh, Thief! We only bargained for fifty. I don't even know your name. And you don't know mine.

Judith closed out her character and the game. Her bank account swelled nicely. *There it is—all the money I needed, and more. How come I feel like I just lost the game?* On the screen, her bank balance timed out and erased itself.

She sat back for a moment in the booth. *They're waiting for me. I'd better go.* Her fingertips lightly tapped the keyboard. Then, on impulse, she typed: <$USANET$.ALIEN WORLDS//>

The screen began scrolling the article.

```
ALIEN WORLDS BY OSRET CHUNER{1}
CATACOMB{2} HAS BECOME THE WORLD OF THE MOMENT
SINCE YESTERDAY'S ANNOUNCEMENT {3} ABOUT A DEN-
VER PLAYER{4} WHO CASHED IN AT A REPORTED $50,000.
MANAGEMENT {5} OF CATACOMB, OF COURSE. MADE A BIG
SPLASH OF IT. HOPING TO ATTRACT MORE PLAYERS. AND
IT'S WORKING. IN SPITE OF MY WARNING
    <RUN 4>
DENVER PLAYER CASHES IN BIG IN CATACOMB.{1}
{DENVER POST}{2}
    EARLY THIS MORNING{3}, THE MANAGEMENT {4} OF
CATACOMB HELD A PRESS CONFERENCE. AWARDING A CHECK
FOR $50,355.75 AND A SPECIAL EMERITUS RANKING{5} TO
AN UNNAMED DENVER PLAYER{6} FOR HIS FEAT OF LIT-
ERALLY BURYING THE WIZARD'S GATE{7} UNDER SACKS OF
GOLD AND JEWELS.  IT WAS SAID BY PLAYERS
    <RUN 6>
INTERVIEW WITH DENVER PLAYER POST: I HEARD YOU
MENTION THAT YOU HAD HELP FROM AN ANGEL IN YOUR
AMAZING WIN.  DO YOU HAVE ANY SUGGESTIONS TO OTHER
CATACOMB PLAYERS FOR INVOKING ANGELS?
```

PLAYER: SORRY. BUT TO GET THAT CHECK. I HAD TO SIGN AN AGREEMENT THAT I WOULDN'T SAY ANYTHING TO ANYONE ABOUT CATACOMB.

POST: CAN YOU TELL US WHAT YOU INTEND TO DO WITH YOUR WINNINGS?

PLAYER: I THINK I'LL MOVE TO TEXAS. I HEAR AUSTIN IS A NICE TOWN.

...

At home, with Barry in the garden helping his mother, Judith again watched over Georgie. She played over in her mind all that her thief knew about her and all that she knew about him. Father, on the other hand, paced downstairs and never once went back up to his office.

Since he hovered around so long, Judith was finally prompted to say, "Daddy, don't worry so much about us kids. Barry wasn't being perverse. I noticed the expression on his face in the arcade when he realized his mistake. He was with his friends, and he just forgot about the gardening.

"As for me," she smiled, "I've been a pain about the new school. I'm sorry. I know it won't be as bad as I made it out to be. There will be plenty of new friends to make. And in fact, I can think of some advantages of being the only female flute player at Brentwood Academy."

Everybody Knows Bob

*Who hasn't wished for perfect freedom, to make their own rules
and to follow every whim. And to do that without battle or conflict
... even better!*

The security desk was an artwork in its own right, in dark tones. He ran
his fingertips over the dark burnished metal, admiring the gray-tinted glass.
Obscured, but watchful—some nameless architect had the soul of an artist.

He put his hand to the off-limits door and stepped quietly in among the
bewildering matrix of security monitoring screens. Three security guards
looked up as he entered, their expressions of alarm turning to recognition.
He put his finger to his lips and they nodded, turning back to their duties.

The arrival of the Monet, direct from the auction at Christie's had been
a featured article in the local papers. What better way for a rising star in the
software world to declare its solvency to potential customers than to pay an
extra couple of million for one of the world's most famous works of art, and
hang it in the lobby as a reminder?

Unfortunately, the painting was hung high and out of reach of the
crowd. Thus his search for a better view.

He settled into one of the black swivel chairs and randomly started
pushing buttons. The screen at his station flickered from camera to camera,
taking in the unseasonal crowd in the lobby, as well as views down the corridors and out into the parking areas.

On the display, a flash of elfin face with hazel eyes. His finger, moving too fast to stop, hit the key again and an unknown corridor appeared.

No. Wait. How do I get back? He fumbled with the unfamiliar controls and then gave up to look through the glass, trying to find the person belonging to the face.

A cluster of employees were arriving for the day, showing their badges and then passing down the corridors. All he could see of the group was their backs.

He nodded to the security guards and walked out. A wave at the badge-check guard earned him a smile and a nod. He moved briskly down the corridor, trying to catch up.

The taylor who made his favorite gray suit shared his love for subtle textures. He relished its feel—and today he needed it. The suit shouted *Upper Management* to workers as he passed the various offices. People waved, but didn't try to stop him. The suit gave him some needed distance.

This is silly. I haven't gone chasing a pretty girl in a long time. Still, he kept looking.

A glance in the next open office, done up in warm earth tones and trimmed with boxed ivy plants, showed it to be cube space for a hundred or more workers. The secretary, and everyone walking the aisles greeted him with a smile of recognition.

He gave them his standard smile, and a little wave, but kept walking. None of them wanted to bother him when he was busy.

On impulse, he turned down the third aisle, anonymous cubes on the outside except for the embossed Lucite name plates. He was perpetually grateful for those, as well as for name badges. Everyone knew him, but the reverse wasn't true.

"Hello Bob! Good to see you."

He glanced at the nameplate. "Kevin." He looked at the pictures on the inside walls, "How's your car?"

Kevin beamed. He pulled out the photos of his new Corvette, just like a proud papa with baby pictures.

He just smiled and nodded at the right times, pretending to listen to the automotive jargon.

Other co-workers started gathering, drawn by Kevin's enthusiasm, but as soon as they realized he was there, they all wanted to greet him too. He directed the conversation to Kevin's car, and slipped out as soon as he could.

He caught sight of her at the end of the aisle. Doing her best to tune out the socializing just a few feet away she stared intently at the diagram on her screen.

He paused, watching the back of Janet Gunn's neck, a pen between her fingers as she twirled one overworked lock of her short black hair.

Quickly, she sensed his presence and looked up. In that half-second before the smile, he read anger, frustration—fear.

But the mouth and those hazel eyes peeking out behind her long bangs—beauty made his heart beat faster. That single second on the security monitor hadn't played him false. Appreciation of the excellent was his call in life. He planned to bask in her presence much longer.

"Bob! Have a seat. Stay a bit." Whatever distressed her had vanished under the spell of his presence.

He took the second chair, and casually edged it to where passers-by wouldn't see him and stop. He could feel himself grinning. She was casting a spell over him, too.

"Janet, how are you doing today?"

Her smile sagged a little. "Oh, as usual." She waved her hand, taking in the whole building.

Something was troubling the girl.

"Tell me, Janet, who am I?"

She blinked. It was obvious who he was, and she hadn't really put it into words before.

"Well, you're my friend—a co-worker."

He nodded, "And you trust me, right?"

She looked at him with the left side of her mouth trying to break into a grin. "You have to ask?"

"Then tell me. What's wrong here? I have some power. I can make a difference for you."

She shook her head. "No, I wouldn't want any favoritism. That's part of the problem. It's..." She looked to the aisle, and shook her head.

He recognized the signs. "Let's go out for lunch, some place where we can talk. I can't have you unhappy like this."

She glanced at the clock. "No, it's way too early. Besides, I have to get this documentation ready for the meeting tomorrow. There's just no time."

He got to his feet, and held out his hand to her. "I can take care of that. Lead me to your boss."

She hesitated, but then her confidence in him wiped aside her worries. She put down her pen and led him through the maze. He fielded a half-dozen greetings from other denizens of the workplace, but his eyes were locked on her.

Janet was a perfectly cut crystal wrapped in a wrinkled paper sack. She wore drab clothes, pants and a shirt. Most of the men here dressed much better. She held her head down and her posture hinted at a hunched back and sagging shoulders in later life if she didn't shape up.

But when he was with her, something lit her up inside. Face to face with her smile, he was in love. Walking behind her like this, close enough to grab, his heartbeat rang like a fire alarm.

The boss had a real office, with a door that closed. He greeted them warmly. "Come in. Come in. Glad to see you." Greg Fielder said the name on the door.

"I need to borrow Janet for a few hours," he said in his best manager voice. Greg nodded.

Janet hesitantly said, "I told Bob I had the flow-charts to correct by tomorrow."

Greg shook his head. "That's okay, I can get Bartlett to do them. I'm sure whatever Bob needs is more important."

"Greg, you might want to note down that she's gone for training on your work sheet. We need to make sure training costs get allocated properly."

"Sure. No problem Bob." And then when his visitor's expectant silence dragged on, Janet's boss suddenly realized he was supposed to note it down immediately. He hurriedly pulled out the grid work sheet and filled in the hours. Greg beamed as he gave him a big smile and shook the man's hand. *He'd have forgotten to do it and she would've caught the flack.*

"Let me get my purse." Janet headed back to her cube.

I'll need a car. He meandered over to Kevin's cube.

"Hi, Kevin. Loan me your car?" He held out his hand for the keys.

Kevin shook, as if ice had gone down his spine. "Whoa. You know, Bob, if it were anyone else but you, I'd turn them down flat." He reached into his pocket and offered the keys.

Janet had gone back to her computer display, again with the pen in her hand.

"Janet. Your purse?"

She looked startled for a fraction of a second, but smiled and closed down the screen.

. . .

Kevin's Corvette was easy to find, and once Janet helped him remove the protective cover, he took a moment to admire the car's lines. Did the muscular shape trigger an instinctive reaction to the predatory beast, or was it sexual?

A moment later they pulled out of the parking garage and headed north.

Janet struggled with the wind in the convertible, but he told her to just push her hair back, and laugh into the wind. Soon enough, she did just that.

"I hope Greg won't get upset," she yelled at him over the wind noise, "by having my uncle pull strings."

"Oh, he won't. He trusts me. Don't give it another thought."

Driving the lakeside road in a red Corvette tempted his foot considerably, but he refrained from opening it up. He wouldn't get a ticket, but it might upset Janet.

A lush hotel appeared around the corner and on impulse, he pulled in. Tables among the palm trees promised a restaurant. The valet sprinted over. He glanced at the young man's name tag.

"Take good care of this one, Earl."

"You know it, Mr. Wilson." The attendant could barely keep his eyes off the car and took the keys gratefully. He was in the driver's seat and feeling the throttle in seconds.

Janet stood passively by as he came up to take her arm.

That's not right, he thought, affronted. *Earl didn't even see her.*

They entered the lobby, and he returned the volley of greetings from the staff. The restaurant entrance looked promisingly reserved, but he stopped first at the gift shop.

"Let's go in here first."

Janet followed his lead.

The sales lady was out from behind her cash register in an instant. "Yes, Sir James, what can I help you with?"

Janet was drawn to the array of clothes that graced the small, but firmly high-end store.

He pointed. "Janet needs something with a bit more color."

"No, Bob. I can't let you...."

"Now Janet. You know I can do this. It's a simple gift. Let this lady do her job."

The sales lady, who unfortunately did not wear a name tag, was sizing up his gray suit and estimating which class of clothes would fit his credit line. She smiled brightly. "Come along, young lady. I have just the thing."

"I'll be back in a moment."

"Certainly, Sir Robert. Take your time."

He walked back to the hotel's registration desk.

"Ah, Jason. Do you have a room with a good lakeside view?"

"Of course, Mr. Samson. How about suite 1201?"

"Fine. Charge it under the house account."

He received the key and scouted out the restaurant, then back to the shop before Janet could forget her intent to let him buy her the clothes.

...

She was dazzling. A brush through her hair, a simple dress just short of being too intense for lunch time, and a proud tilt to her head combined to make all of the attendants in the hotel take notice of her. He felt really good, being ignored for once.

They took a table on the veranda. He had a whispered conversation with the waiter and the menus were dispensed with in favor of the man's best judgement.

"You look lovely, Janet. I don't know much about color, but somehow your eyes are more expressive."

She dimpled. "I love the dress, but you shouldn't have."

He patted her hand for reassurance.

"Now. Tell me. What's your problem at work?"

She stared down at the bread plate. He reached over and tilted her chin back up.

"Now Janet, tell me who I am."

She brushed aside his hand. "Oh, you!" She recited, as if she had said it a million times, "You're my big brother and you have a right to take care of me."

"Right. So tell me what the problem is."

She sighed, playing with the butter knife. "You have to promise not to tell Mother."

"I promise."

"I know she means well, but if she thought I was in trouble, she'd be on a plane the same day. And I don't want that. I can take care of myself."

He waited, and then prompted, "Man problems?"

"Yes. No. Not really." Hazel eyes glanced up through her hair for a quick look at his face.

"It started with a man. No, maybe it started with my appointment."

"Appointment?"

"You know the 'Women in Engineering' thing. I've always wanted to work here. The projects are cutting edge. When an opening was announced, with a woman senior engineer as a mentor, and the promise of a full time job ... I jumped at it.

"But before I arrived, things had changed. My mentor had left for a new job, and while the company stood by its job offer, it wasn't the same. I was a kid no one wanted. It was nearly a month before I was assigned to any project. And even then, it was just minor things—spell checking other people's documentation, stuff like that."

"You said there was a man?" he prompted.

A flash of anger crossed her face. "Yes. The lead engineer on the project I was finally assigned to."

"Greg?"

"No. It wasn't him, and I won't tell you his name either. He didn't get into my bed. He just tried."

"Good girl. I take it there were repercussions."

"Oh, little things. He gave me a poor review, and every time there's any question about my work, he makes little jokes about 'Women in Engineering'. And the others laugh."

"Janet, now don't take this wrong, but can you do the job?"

"Ha! I don't recall it was you who got straight A's. It wasn't you who got all those scholarship offers!"

"Okay, calm down. You made your point."

She waved her hand. "Sorry. You touched a nerve. But yes, I can do the job. I've been doing it! I just don't get any recognition for the work that I do. I'm still just the part-time girl that gets handed the documentation jobs no one else wants to handle."

"So, what are you going to do about it, little one?"

She sagged. "I don't know if there is anything I can do."

He let out an exasperated sigh. He pushed back his chair and walked around behind her.

"Well, for one thing," he grabbed her shoulders and pulled them back, "your bad posture is going to be the death of you. Sit up straight, you have eyes that can kill, so use them."

He sat back down. She smiled at him tolerantly.

"And another thing," he said. "You are dressing to be invisible. That has to stop. Maybe you want to be just one of the guys, but that option isn't open to you. They already think of you as a woman, so make the most of it. If the jerk is slandering your engineering, he's probably casting doubt on your femininity, too."

With her head up, the anger in her eyes was all too clear.

He nodded. "Stand your ground. You're a talented engineer. With a little work, you should be able to play the people skills game much better than you have been."

She nodded, "I'll try. I don't know why I have to wait for your visits to see the obvious." She consciously straightened her shoulders.

The waiter and his attendants approached, carrying the trays for the next course.

. . .

Luncheon was done in a couple of hours, and they strolled down to the fountains, arm in arm, to settle their meal.

"I'd better get back to work," she said finally.

"Okay, but mindful of my advice to dress better, I do think you ought to return to work in the same clothes you left."

She suppressed a laugh, "Yes, I think you're right there. But where are they?"

"I had them sent up to the room." They headed for the elevator.

The door to the suite opened to a glorious view of the lake, framed in green from the hotel's elaborate landscaping.

He gave it a long look. It had taken him years to realize his place in life. There was beauty in the world. His duty was to admire it.

"Could you get this hook, please."

He turned. She'd removed the dress and was struggling with the bra fasteners. He pulled in a long, slow breath before he moved to help her.

He moved behind her, and released the hook. As short as she was, her hair was close enough to bury his face in.

"Janet," he whispered, "who am I?"

"Oh, you and that question! Did you forget your vows again, husband of mine?"

His eyes were closed, and he breathed in the sweet scent of her.

"Do you trust me?" His voice wavered a bit.

"Why? Do you have a suggestion?" she asked slyly. She turned in the circle of his arms. "Why don't you take off that coat?"

She helped him out of it, and started on his vest.

"Wait." He shook his head. "Come here." He drew her to the bed.

He held her tightly, reclined against the mound of decorative pillows. She reached for a button, but he shook his head.

"No. Let me tell you a story."

She laid her head on his arm.

"Once upon a time, a man fell in love with a girl. She thought she was in love with him, but she was wrong."

Janet stroked fabric of his vest, an admiring smile on her face. "This is for one of your television shows isn't it? I love it when you tell me your stories."

He continued, "She thought he was someone else."

She nodded, "He had another girlfriend, or a secret life as a criminal."

He shook his head, "No. It was a true delusion. She thought he was someone she had known all her life, but he had just met her. He could tell her the truth, but it would do no good."

She frowned, "How can he know, until he tries?"

"Because it's happened before, many times before. Everyone believes they know him. Strangers offer him money in seconds, women offer him love, and yet if he turns his back and walks away, all memory of his existence is gone as quickly as it had come.

"The girl believes she's in love with this stranger, but it will vanish like a soap bubble."

Janet puzzled through the complications. "But you say he loves her?"

"Yes." He gently pushed aside a stray wisp of hair that obscured her face.

"Then, how serious is the girl?"

"She cheerfully crawls into his bed."

"And then what? Does he get her pregnant? Ooh! She gets pregnant, but when she forgets, she thinks she's a virgin, but the doctor says no. A horror story!"

He kissed her on the forehead.

"No. Like I said, this time he loves the girl."

"Real love?"

He shrugged. "When the moment comes that he holds her in his arms, in spite of the hammering of his heart, he knows her happiness means more than his own."

"And she'll forget him, when he walks away?"

He nods, and whispers, "Yes."

"Bummer. So what does he do?"

He tried to make the moment last forever. He held her close. He tried to soak up her scent, and her unconditional love.

"I don't know what he does."

He kissed her, and then pulled himself out of her embrace.

"But for one thing, he tries to do her as little harm as possible. He takes only a kiss.

"He'll put her safely back into her real life, and then walk away and never see her again."

"Never?"

"If he stays, he'll harm her. Best to let her find happiness like everyone else. Happiness she can remember."

He reached for his coat. She lay there, a thing of beauty that would crack the heart in a statue of granite.

"Get dressed," he whispered.

She nodded, "I was just thinking about your guy. Sad story."

He nodded, unable to speak as a wave of longing struggled to destroy his façade. He cleared his throat. "Do you need help with your hooks?"

...

Janet was back in her work clothes when they turned into the parking lot—smiling and erect, she even made drab look good.

He noticed a pair of police cars at the main entrance and pulled up to the side entrance. "Go on in. I'll meet you there in a bit." She kissed him and hopped out. He watched her go in, feeling her evaporate from his cheek.

By the time he looked up, Kevin and the police were walking towards him. He pulled abreast and stopped the convertible. One by one, their faces sparked with recognition.

"Mr. Jefferson. Good to see you in town." The older policeman greeted him with a nod.

"Hello. I'm just in for a short spell. Is there anything I can do for you?"

The policeman was plainly uncomfortable. "Well, we had a stolen car report."

"Kevin? You didn't report it stolen did you? It's Tuesday."

Kevin actually slapped himself on the forehead. "Tuesday! Of course!" He turned to the police. "I'm so sorry. I totally forgot what day it is."

He gave the policemen a nod that it was okay, and tossed Kevin his keys. "It is really a nice car. Sorry gentlemen, if I've caused you trouble."

They left with little more than a grumble at Kevin. Kevin offered to loan him the car for another day, but he turned it down. He was done with it.

. . .

"Greg, close the door. I need to talk to you." Janet's manager looked up, startled for a second. Then he smiled.

"Yes, sir. I didn't know you were in town, or I'd have invited you to lunch."

"No time for that. I just got wind of a potential problem." He waited for Greg to close the door.

He lowered his voice. "There may be a sexual harassment claim if we don't take action immediately. I need to look at your personnel records."

It didn't take long. The official records were all on-line and Greg had the passwords.

Five minutes of reading pinpointed the engineer who had tried to take advantage of Janet. He found the bad review, and just a two-word edit changed it from damning to respectable. He edited the jerk's action plans to include mandatory sexual harassment awareness training, and added it to the recommended list for everyone else in the group.

As he worked, he explained what he did to Greg, and got his help making the system work. He knew Greg would forget, but he favored his own delusion that some hint of his actions would remain in the people he met.

At least, the computer changes were permanent.

Greg shook his hand and thanked him profusely as he left.

Janet's cube was several aisles over. He found a decorative planter in the corner and stood next to it where he could see over the tops of the maze of cubes.

Closing time. Janet stood up, but he could only see the top of her head. A minute later she stepped into the aisle. *Is she standing straighter?* He couldn't tell.

Her gaze swept his side of the room. There was no sign of recognition. At that distance, she was outside his influence.

She was gone.

He walked over to her cube, sat down in her chair, and opened the box that contained her new dress.

Rummaging a pen, he wrote a note:

"Stand straight, and use those killer eyes.

—Your Secret Admirer"

He dropped the pen back into the drawer, and noticed a graduation photo. A year or two younger, but her shoulders were back, and her face proclaimed her ready to take on the world. He slipped it into his coat pocket and walked away.

Litterbug

Nothing ever really goes away. A discarded wrapper doesn't vanish when you drop it.

"Dad!" Jerry yelled as his father tossed the banana peel out the open window of the pickup truck.

He turned toward his 17-year-old son, mildly surprised. "What?"

Jerry Foley sighed, "Dad, don't litter like that!"

"Why? It was just a banana peel." As always on this subject, he was unrepentant.

"Because," he declared, "littering is against the law."

The elder Foley shook his head, "Son, you'll have to do better than that. Illegal isn't the same thing as immoral. These days, there are so many laws that you can't get through a day without breaking some of them. I refuse to live my life by the rules a high paid debating team comes up with."

"There is a big fine. Several hundred dollars."

Mr. Foley slowly, and pointedly, looked up and down the little country road they were traveling. There was no other traffic, and the farmhouses were far apart. "You gonna turn me in?" He grinned.

Jerry crossed his arms. "That's not the point. Littering is wrong. You shouldn't do it."

His father was enjoying himself. "We have a couple of minutes yet before we reach town. Go for it. Convince me you are right, and I am wrong."

Jerry hated it when his father opened himself up for argument. Greg Foley never lost his temper, nor lost his grin. And he almost never lost the argument either.

But he knew his father played fair too.

He quickly ran his reasons through his mind. The littering laws and being a good public citizen were already crushed. He would have to think of something else.

Luckily there was one reason immediately obvious.

"It takes tax dollars or other people's efforts to clean up the mess you leave." He pointed down at the plastic trash bags he was going to be using in a few minutes as part of the Hutto clean up campaign.

"Good point for an abandoned refrigerator, or even an old newspaper. But that was a banana peel. In a day, it will be black, dried up and invisible among the weeds. Before another month or so, the county will have a crew through here to cut the roadside weeds. Litter or no litter, they will be here to turn Johnson grass, baby trees, and old banana peels into mulch. No additional cost to anyone, as far as I can see."

Jerry pointed, "You gave a bad example." His father had harped on just that point in another argument earlier in the week. Not that he would have smoked the cigarettes anyway. He just wanted them to test his gadget.

His father pursed his lips and nodded, "In other circumstances, I might agree. But, who was here to see this? Only my environmentally brainwashed son who would never litter so much as a used blob of chewing gum if his life depended on it."

"You were also giving me an example of ignoring a public law if it didn't suit your private preferences! What if I see you doing this, and I use the same logic to stay out past curfew or slide through the stop sign at Jake's Hill road."

"Would you?"

Jerry put a pause on his tongue. There were hazards no matter what he said to his parent. He decided to go with honesty.

"I don't know."

His father nodded. "Good enough. Obeying the law is a good solid default behavior, and you should never break one just on impulse. But following every little subsection of the traffic code when a tornado is bearing down on you is suicidal. I have purposely ignored stop signs with as little excuse as being very low on gas. If you get caught, then pay the fine with a smile, because it was your decision. Just don't be brainless, and break a law on a whim."

Jerry smiled, "So, what was your reason for tossing the banana peel, other than your whim?"

Greg Foley curled his upper lip. "Fruit flies. I hate 'em. Leave a dead banana in this pickup for any time at all and they appear as if by spontaneous generation. You ever snort in one of those critters by accident? Murder! I tell ya."

. . .

Jerry shook his head in capitulation, grateful that they were pulling to a stop at the Highway 79, Ranch Road 685 intersection. He got out with his bags and looked along the stretch of railroad tracks that were his personal cleanup duty.

"Call me when you are done."

Jerry tapped the pocket where he had his cell phone and nodded. After the pickup drove off, the first thing he picked up was the note trapped under a large flat rock. His part of the cleanup was the rails and southern side of Highway 79 from the intersection to a marker he would find closer to town.

He opened his first bag, stuffed the note in and got to work.

. . .

The cleanup was inspired by the Presidential whistle-stop campaign now working its way through this part of the state. The President's special Amtrak train was due to arrive in Hutto tomorrow morning, before heading east. Stopping only at small farming communities, it was the President's latest attempt to repair the PR damage he had taken over last year's Omnibus Farm Bill.

Hutto farmers who shared morning coffee at the little diner room at Wag-A-Bag next to the Co-op hadn't said a kind word for the President there all year. Yet the community had pulled out all the stops to sweep the streets and polish the stop signs on the half-dozen streets that faced the Union Pacific rail siding. There was still glitter in the Presidency, no matter how hard the actual politicians tried to tarnish it.

It also helped that the locals were being given the prime seats. The press were relegated to a special parking area over amid the metal silos at the cotton gin. By doing his part in this cleanup, Jerry had locked up one of the limited seats on the bleachers hastily erected next to the tracks.

...

Beer cans, stained paper plates, shiny candy wrappers, and plastic drink cups emblazoned with the sun-faded logo of a fast food place eight miles away in Round Rock, Texas—there was plenty of trash to fill his first bag. It was taking a lot longer than he had thought. His stretch of roadway was much less than a mile, but there was a lot of stooping and picking.

Jerry wished he had one of those remote grippers or even a spike on the end of a stick. He could already feel it in the muscles of his back.

Still, this was a good selection of stuff for his gadget. Household trash wasn't the same as road litter.

When he saw his end-point memo next to the switch where the siding left the main line, he was ready to quit. He picked it up and added it to the little bit of stuff he had in his second bag, and then called his father.

As he waited, he looked at the switch. Even though he had lived in the Hutto area all his life and on most days trains barreled through town about every fifteen minutes, he had never really gotten this close to the tracks. The local police were pretty quick to chase off kids who played on the rails.

He patted his pocket where he had stashed a rusted railroad spike, an unexpected treasure. There were lots of them in the rocks next to the tracks but he had not realized they were there.

The switch was interesting as well. In the back of his mind, he had wondered what would happen if someone switched the tracks as a joke. Now he realized it would never happen. The switch was simple. It was clear how to make it work—step on the release and flip that heavy bar over to the other side. But the most massive padlock he had ever seen latched the bar down. It made the padlock on his school locker look like a toy.

Plus, there was some kind of wiring hooked to the switch and he suspected there was some huge central office that could read the position of every track on the line.

...

His father drove up after a while, and rolled his eyes as Jerry put the full and partial trash bag into the back of the truck.

"We're taking that stuff home?" he asked.

Jerry grinned. "I want to test my gadget."

"I've raised my son to be a trash man." He shook his head.

At home, the first order of business was getting a canned coke out of the refrigerator, and then he hauled the bags out to the barn.

...

His gadget stood over twelve feet tall. A roller coaster for trash is what his father called it. He called it a Refuse Separator.

All three switches on – *click click click*, and the barn was alive with the hum and rattle of the fans and the conveyer belt. Unceremoniously, he dumped the first bag into the hopper, and then fished out the railroad spike and placed it on the top of the pile like a cherry on a sundae.

Already, the bottom of the pile was being dragged off, up the conveyer belt and dropped from the top. The fans separated the paper, while a huge electromagnet attempted to bend the fall of the iron and steel into a separate catcher bin. Glass and aluminum and other inert stuff landed in the center bin, which was shaking in an attempt to sort light from heavy.

Jerry still wasn't happy with it. The gadget started as a science fair project last year, and although he got a second place, he couldn't stop playing with the design.

"Having fun?" His father came out, sipping a drink of his own.

"I'll know in a minute." He pointed at the railroad spike. "I want to see that drop into the iron bin."

His father nodded, finishing his drink, and then tossing the aluminum can into the trash.

"Dad!" Jerry fished it out and dropped it into the aluminum recycle bin. "I told you. Aluminum is prime recyclable. Old cans are valuable."

"As valuable as my time?"

Jerry spoke slowly, as if his father was too stupid to understand. "Separating the recycle streams at the very beginning is the most cost efficient method!"

"Ah ha! Cost efficient for whom? It's not cost effective for me. I could care less whether I make a penny by tossing the can into the pretty colored bin. It's only cost effective for the people like you who are trying to manage the environment. And the way I look at it, I'm doing you a favor."

"What?"

His father gestured at the separator. "Your gadget will be most valuable, not for managing new trash, but for mining out the valuable metals that are already stashed in the existing landfills. So I am doing you a favor by making sure that the mine has good quality ore."

Jerry just shook his head. He would never make his father understand.

But just then, the spike started to climb up the conveyer belt, and Jerry moved closer to watch it drop.

Ker-chunk! Success!

His father patted him on the back. "Good job son."

. . .

After his father left, he reached for the little bag and dumped its load into the hopper. Even with the limited range of things the separator could handle, it still made his job of sorting the recyclables easier. His father ribbed him about the electricity he spent on the job, but at least he was willing to chalk that up as an educational expense.

The smaller load went fast, but just before it was done, he caught sight of something shiny shooting out of the drop stream. He walked around to the backside of the gadget and retrieved the silvery candy wrapper.

"'Brokies'—I never heard of that one." He tossed it back into the input hopper and a few seconds later, just as before, it shot out of the drop path in an unexpected direction.

"What is going on?"

A third time, he sent it on its way. He kept an eye on it the whole way.

It was the magnetic separator. The wrapper was being pushed out the back by the electromagnet.

"Why is it being *pushed?*"

He grabbed up the flimsy wrapper and looked it over. It looked just like all the other aluminized plastic wrappers so popular with candy makers. He went over to the paper bin and fished out a peanuts wrapper that looked identical in material and put the both of them into the hopper.

They flickered through the separator one after the other. The Brokies hit the magnet and was ejected, but the peanut wrapper dropped past it without a wobble and hit the airflow that pushed it over into the paper bin.

"Dad!"

. . .

"I think I have heard of this," his father said as he looked over the shiny wrapper. He looked at Jerry, "Do you still have that assortment of magnets you ordered? Go get it."

One by one they tested different magnets. Each pushed the wrapper. When they found the little samarium magnet, Mr. Foley spread the wrapper flat on the bench and the little rare-earth magnet floated in the air above it—suspended by the magnetic field.

"No doubt about it, Meisner effect," he pronounced. "You have a superconductor here." He frowned. "A room temperature superconductor."

Jerry shook his head. "I don't believe it. I've read up on superconductors. You need super cold conditions to make superconductors."

His father shrugged, and tapped the little magnet. It wobbled, oscillating with nothing to dampen out the motion but miniscule air friction. "Do you believe what you read, or what you see?"

Jerry took a deep breath. "I don't understand what I see."

"Good. Neither do I. I could maybe see someone inventing a superconductor and then keeping it secret. But a candy wrapper?"

Mr. Foley tapped the magnet aside and picked up the wrapper again. He read the text, and then examined the inside, and even the edges for some clue.

"Jerry, there is something different about this. Here, take a look."

At first glance, the Brokies wrapper was just like all the other wrappers he had seen. There was a bold text banner across the top proclaiming the name, with an enticing image of the treat itself–some kind of caramel glazed chewy treat. It was when he looked the back side that it struck him just how strange the wrapper was. There was no fine print. Both sides of the package were the same.

He grinned up at his father, "There is no recycle logo."

"Ha! Trust you to notice that one."

"Also, no ingredients list. I thought all food things had to have a list of ingredients."

"And no trademark symbol next to the product name, nor a use-by date, nor a copyright on the text. If it didn't say 'Made in San Antonio' there plain as day, I would have suspected it was from some other country, one where the product laws were different."

They were both silent for a moment.

Jerry asked, "Okay, maybe it's an experimental lot. Somebody in San Antonio is getting ready to release a new candy and has given out samples for people to test."

"Hmm. Maybe. What is that dot?"

On the upper left of the package was a large gray dot, nearly a half-inch in diameter. Jerry looked closely.

"Wait a minute." He dashed over to his workbench and rummaged in a drawer. He pulled out a large magnifying glass and examined the dot.

"Come look." He repositioned the lamp to shine a brighter light on the wrapper.

His father adjusted the glass. "I can't see as well as you do. I think I see a pattern."

Jerry nodded. "There is a pattern. That dot is a dense maze of digital information. And it seems to be laid out in some kind of spiral pattern."

The elder Foley nodded. "Now it makes sense."

"What makes sense?"

He set down the magnifier. "Somebody has invented a way to put all the junk information into this dot, like a super IPC product bar code. I'd bet that all the trademarks, ingredients, and product history is all encoded into that dot."

"No way. That doesn't make sense at all. You still have the laws, and nobody is set up to read the dot. Even if the big stores and warehouses have dot readers, it's the end-user, the consumer that needs to be able to read recycle markers, ingredient lists, and the date the food goes bad. The dot is useless."

"Unless everyone has a dot reader."

Jerry shook his head. "Everyone doesn't."

His father waved his hand. "Hear me out. Digital watches are so cheap right now that they give them away. How much more so when the electronics get generations more powerful and smaller. I could see a day, fifty years from now, a hundred, when stores have a giveaway pile of things smaller than a dime that could read the dots. Marketing would love to get rid of anything on the package that isn't advertising. Not too far in the future, everybody will be able to read the dots, with a dirt cheap free reader."

"Maybe in the future, but not now."

His father just stared at the wrapper, frowning.

Jerry asked, "You aren't serious?"

"If there were cheap ways to make room temperature superconductors, just think how nice it would be to use it as a candy wrapper. Your whole production line could just move the things around on magnetic fields." He pointed at the rubber and metal conveyer belt that was part of Jerry's gadget. "Wouldn't it be cheaper to use and maintain than that?"

"Well yes, but the future? You can't mean time travel."

"Because it's impossible? Well there is more than one kind of impossible. What's scientifically impossible changes every day, but what's economically impossible has a little more staying power. That's based on human nature. Your idea of an experimental product is possible, but no one could be stupid enough to hide a breakthrough like room temperature superconductors so they could make candy wrappers.

"Son. I don't think you should go to that whistlestop thing tomorrow."

"Why?"

"Because I can't think of any reason for a time traveler to come visit Hutto unless something bad is going to happen."

. . .

They argued most of the evening over it. Jerry was adamant that he had paid his dues and had done the cleanup chore and he deserved to be there to see the President.

It was going to be a once in a lifetime event, and the only argument against it was that *maybe* time travel was possible, and that *maybe* there was something bad that would bring visitor to Hutto.

Jerry fought with tenacity. He could never tell for sure when these arguments were bogus. His father would argue over anything, and often didn't really believe his own position. Still when they headed for town in the morning, his father wasn't done.

"Safety should come first. After all, the whole event will likely be on the television."

"Dad, give it up. You are repeating yourself. I am going."

"Disrespectful youngsters. I promised myself I would avoid this exercise in political self-gratification at all costs. And now look at what you are doing to me. I have to stay there all day to watch out for you."

"You could have gotten a good seat if you had helped with the cleanup."

"I'm not that hypocritical. The farther I can get from the event the better."

Jerry wondered again whom his father voted for. For as long as he could remember, the polling place was an early morning visit on election day. But he would never find out which way Dad voted. He would debate against any politician under the sun, but there was never a kind word for any of them.

"If I am right," Mr. Foley said as they pulled up next to the Co-op's silos where cars were being parked, "it will at least prove one good thing."

"What is that?"

"That in spite of all the ecological brainwashing, there will still be litterbugs in the future."

...

Even though the train wouldn't arrive for another couple of hours, the makeshift parking area was nearly full, and the bleachers were mostly populated. Jerry brought his binoculars and camera, and had to wait in line as the Sheriff glanced over his items before he would be let in through the barricade. It would have been annoying if it weren't for the news crews. Second class citizens, they had to wait by their remote broadcast vans until all the locals were seated.

Jerry went for the top row. He settled in next to the football coach and the school board president.

"Good morning, Jerry. Did I see your father here?"

"Yes coach. He decided to come to keep me out of trouble."

They laughed, and the men went back to their discussion. Jerry pulled out the binoculars and scanned the area.

It was a long wait. In spite of the fact that he had heard the band practicing 'Hail to the Chief' all day long at school this week, it was a relief to be able to watch them from his perch.

The long wait also gave him time to worry about his father's time traveler theory. Suppose someone was here from the future. Why here? Why now?

Why would I want to travel back in time?

He would like to watch a lost treasure being buried, so that he could find it in the present day. He would like to go back and see Jesus do a miracle. He would like to watch the JFK assassination and see if there was really someone on the grassy knoll.

That last worried him the most. This President was really hated by the farmers. Suppose one of them tried to do something about it.

He looked over the area again with his binoculars.

It was amazing how many people in uniform there were. All of the local police and DPS officers were in attendance, as well as a large number of men in black suits with little earplugs snaking up out of their collars.

He was startled when one of them turned and stared directly at him. He waved, but there was no response. How many of these events did a Secret Service agent attend before he grew tired of all the same people?

Besides, Jerry thought, he should be looking for the time traveler. What would a time traveler look like?

Not somebody he knew. Probably not any of the police or Secret Service, because they would recognize a stranger in their own ranks. His best bet would be to find someone ordinary who had something strange about him—because if the time traveler had a perfect disguise, then he would never spot him anyway.

Of course, there were a huge number of ordinary strangers in Hutto today.

He settled down to scan the crowd systematically. He was bored stiff, and anything was better than watching the grass grow.

. . .

He knew the train was coming five minutes before he could actually see it. The black suits started moving at a quicker pace, and the police started using their hand held radios. He stood up to stretch and ease the soreness on his backside before the main event. The SS agent watched him again. Jerry was pleased. He had never thought of himself as a suspicious character before. He waved at the man again.

The rest of the crowd started standing as the little silver train approached. The band struck up its piece as the three-car Amtrak special pulled into town.

From his perch, he watched as a railroad worker, accompanied by a black suit, worked the switch and directed the Presidential special over onto the north siding. The rumble of the engine almost drowned out the music, but the Hutto Hippo band played gamely on.

There wasn't a long wait. The door swung open and the President of the United States of America came to Hutto Texas.

Jerry, and everyone else, took a picture. It was amusing how many flashes went off in broad daylight.

Barely had the speeches started, when he had a worrisome thought. *Why did the time traveler litter yesterday?*

Maybe Dad's whole theory was wrong and it was unrelated to today's event?

But that didn't make sense either.

He shifted in his seat, and heard the faint rattle of the wrapper in his pocket. Why had he brought it along?

He pulled it out, and while the President spoke about his future plans to help the farmers, Jerry stared again at the shiny plastic.

It was frustrating. The packaging did look futuristic, in many subtle ways. For example, the seams were really merged, not just hot crimped like normal. Even the font that advertising text was written in was like nothing he had seen before, yet clean and crisp and very readable. And that info-dot—how far into the future before everybody easily used things like that?

But if it was from the future, it had to be related in some way to this event. If the traveler dropped the wrapper yesterday, he had to be scouting out the area before today's festivities. Why?

He looked over the scene again. It was a mob, packed with people all around the stands and nearly up to the train. Even Highway 79 was blocked off. All traffic, road and railroad, had to stop while the President gave his speech.

Jerry glanced along the rails.

He stood up and grabbed his binoculars. Far to the west, there was something on the tracks. The heat shimmer made it hard to see, but it looked like another train was coming.

Vividly, he remembered picking up the Brokies wrapper, wedged against the rails—right next to the switch. It was almost the last bit of litter he had picked up.

The switch!

From his position on the top row, he could make out the yellow-tipped handle that controlled which position the rail was in. It was just like they had left it when they directed the special onto the siding.

But surely the oncoming train would stop. They had traffic signals and there was a red light on the tower. He could see it plainly.

He turned his binoculars again on the oncoming train. It was coming closer. But something looked wrong. There was no engine.

A runaway!

His father had told him something like this had happened before. Eight miles away in Round Rock, several cars had been parked on a siding. They were all connected to an air-hose that controlled the brakes. A loss of air stopped the car. The rules were to bleed the air out of the hose when parking train cars, but someone had taken the short cut and left them pressurized.

The land between Round Rock and Hutto looked flat, but there was indeed a grade, enough to keep Brushy Creek flowing swiftly, and enough to accelerate the cars to dangerous speeds.

Those are tanker cars. Chemicals.

For the first time, he felt afraid.

He looked over at the town. *Of course.*

The tanker cars would come barreling into town and smash into the Presidential special on the siding. The tanks would rupture and splash flaming death over the President, the news crews, and all the people of Hutto.

And me too.

There! The man in the black suit was watching him again. He waved his arms wide and shouted, "Train! A train is coming!" He pointed.

The people from Hutto frowned at him. Trains coming through town were nothing new.

But the Secret Service man was talking into his radio, and instantly, there was motion all over the stage. Men stopped the President in mid-sentence and were hustling him off the stage. The locals were starting to panic.

Jerry looked around for his father.

Back at the edge of the crowd, almost to Main Street, his father was resting against the two-story brick general store. Back there, they hadn't noticed anything wrong.

And at the corner of the building, a man was avidly scanning the scene with a camcorder. There was nothing odd about that, except for the strange color plaid baseball cap he wore. Maybe there were plaid baseball caps somewhere, but he had never seen one before.

There was shouting below. The compact wedge of Secret Service men protecting and moving the President shoved their way through the crowd at the base of the stand. They were making for the parking area, where other agents were trying to get a car free of the jammed space.

They aren't going to make it.

Jerry looked back along the track. The runaway was much closer.

The yellow end of the switch handle was barely visible. That was the pivot point. That was the difference the time traveler had examined yesterday.

The President wouldn't make it to safety in time. The news crews and all their videotape would be destroyed in the inferno. Other than a fragment of live broadcast, there would be little to document what happened to cause this great catastrophe. Future researchers would die to know what exactly transpired.

It was all clear in his head, but there was no way he could reach the switch in time to avert the onrush of history.

Below, in the mob, the shouts were getting more strident. His SS agent was one of them. Yelling at his radio.

Jerry jumped over the edge of the stands, and landed painfully in the mass of Secret Service men. A pistol was shoved immediately in his face.

Jerry yelled, "Somebody get the switch changed back to the main line! The runaway is heading for the siding!"

His agent put a hand on the pistol and pushed it down out of his cheek. With the other hand, he was already on his radio, yelling for the railroad workers.

But the agents didn't stop for him. They were getting the President to safety no matter what.

Jerry pulled himself up off the ground and started shoving through the mob on his own. He had to reach his father.

Up ahead, trying to buck the stream of panicked people, there he was, looking for him.

And filming the whole thing, the man in the plaid ball cap was standing in the doorway of the large brick building, maybe the safest spot in the whole town. *A time traveler would know which places came through unscathed, wouldn't he?*

Jerry gritted his teeth. *Let us all die, but get your video!* He turned and stalked straight for the time traveler. The man glanced up from his viewfinder.

Jerry pulled the wrapper from his pocket. He waved it and yelled. "I know about you! It's not going to happen!"

The man with the camera looked at him. Jerry could see his eyes focus on the wrapper, and comprehension come over his face, like the face of horror.

There was a sudden wrench, and Jerry stumbled, and almost fell.

I can't panic now. This will be the safest place in town, I just know it!

There was the growing rumble of a train coming, and as he rounded the corner of the building, the string of a dozen tanker cars blazed through town on the main line.

They made it! The surge of relief was cut short by the flash of an explosion as the cars finally jumped the track just past the old baseball field at the far edge of town.

But I'm alive. I'm alive.

. . .

"I understand we have a real live hero!" The President came into the room and the Secret Service men who had been questioning him backed out of his way.

Jerry shook his head, "Hardly a hero, sir."

The President held out his hand and Jerry shook it.

"I am quite sure I owe you my life, and maybe two thousand other people could say the same thing. I think that qualifies you as a hero. That's what I've been telling the press, and you know they believe everything I say."

Jerry was uncomfortably aware of the blaze of camera lights that had accompanied the President. He could only smile timidly.

But the President wasn't done with the moment. "How did you know that the train switch was in the wrong position?"

Jerry shook his head. "Just instinct, I guess. I had been on the cleanup crew yesterday–picking up litter along the tracks–and I had looked at how the switch worked. From where I was in the stands, I could just tell that it was wrong."

"You have good instincts. And a good heart working for you town like you did. You ought to go into politics when you get a little older."

Jerry tried to hide the thought of what his father would say about that.

One of the other men in suits came up. "The boy's father has arrived."

Greg Foley entered, a little shy of the lights. He ignored the President and came straight to his son.

"Dad, you made it." They embraced. Camera lights were concentrated and hot.

"I was in the pickup before the sound of the explosion reached the house. But they almost didn't let me into town."

The President moved into the lights with them.

"I am sorry about that. But let me thank you, too for your son's efforts."

"You are the President, aren't you? What did he do?"

"He tackled a squad of Secret Service agents and made them switch the train tracks back to the main line. He saved the day. He saved the town too."

. . .

It was several hours later before they made their way back to the house.

"You know," said his father, "I almost think I'm a little psychic."

"What do you mean?"

"A moment before the explosion, just a few seconds really, I was hit by the sudden feeling that I really should be in town. It was so clear. I was already out the door when the flash happened. I've never had a feeling like that before in my life."

"I know what you mean. When I saw the train coming, I just knew where I had to run to try to escape the explosion. Instinct I guess."

His father nodded, absently, and finished off his canned coke. He crumpled it like always, and then hesitated for an instant, before tossing it into the aluminum recycle bin.

"Dad?" Jerry was shocked.

His father grinned. "Okay! So maybe I'll stop being a litterbug. After all, I have a famous son I shouldn't embarrass. Logically, I know I was right. But..."

"But what?"

He shook his head. "I can't shake this feeling. Logic isn't everything. Nobody can predict all the effects of his actions. I'd hate to litter and have it come back to haunt me." He shrugged.

Jerry smiled. "I'm proud of you Dad."

Patterns

It can be frustrating to be able to see the way the world works when everyone around you is blind to it. But maybe if you were born that way, you could tweak those patterns.

MONDAY

Ted took the sheet and his number 2 pencil. He flipped open the test questions and quickly went down the list, tapping the answer sheet with his pencil in the correct spots. He'd fill them in later. As usual, he finished the first stage quickly. Setting aside the questions, he stared at the standardized test form. Yes, he should go through the list and fill in the ovals where the dots representing the correct answers were marked. But that was boring.

The pencil marks made a pattern, a bit random, but suggestive. He rolled the pencil in his fingers. If he filled in this set...and then moved that set a few millimeters that way... and added this one..and that one... and left the rest alone, then it was clearly a house beside a stream. A bit minimalist, but enough for him. Of course, that would drop his score down to a low C, but that was still enough to avoid trouble. He smiled, added a little density by filling in some of the ovals darker than the others, and erased the stray marks, and he was done.

He wrote TED LAMBERT on the sheet and turned it in to Ms. Calvin.

...

Hillside High School was not the first item on his favorite places list, but it was better than home, and there were girls to watch. Soon enough, he would like to progress to the level of actually talking to girls, but watching was interesting enough for now. There were social rules to be observed, and he was only a freshman. He was content to spend his time trying to make sense of all the social patterns.

"Hey Ted," Bill Monty walked past in the hallway and slapped him on the shoulder in passing. He didn't wait for a response, because Ted never gave one, but it was a friendly enough gesture. Most people gave him a few seconds to respond to their greetings, and when he didn't, they flagged him as slow, or autistic, and never tried again. That was okay by him. The hardest thing in the world was to hold a conversation with someone. He was smart, but he wasn't glib tongued, and that's what it took to hold a conversation.

He had a few minutes for lunch, and since making decisions in the lunch line was too uncomfortable, he always brought his own. A square of wooden flooring, just behind the flag at the side of the stage was his favorite spot. He leaned against the wall and unwrapped his sandwich, while watching the other students.

Different clusters of people gathered in predictable groups. There were the football players, and there were the younger cheerleaders. The older cheerleaders seemed to attach themselves to dominant males, and so migrate from one cluster to the next as status changes occurred.

Betty was always the center of an art focussed group, and they were always working on some project. Leanna was the anchor of a fashion oriented group. Samuel was surrounded by a tight group of males, that were always turning to look at various girls. From their expressions, the discussions were salacious.

Fully a third of the students were in flux, sitting with one group one day, and changing to another the next. Fifteen percent appeared to be loners, sometimes watching the groups with envy. Ted classed himself with them, although a 'group' of loners wasn't a reasonable description.

Isis Kelly had caught his attention. He spent fifteen minutes watching her every move before pulling out his pad of blue colored sticky notes.

With careful block letters he penned:

Bob's favorite color is yellow. At 4:52 daily, he exits the boy's gym after seeing nothing but guys for two hours. There is a comfortable place to stand there, next to the trophy display case.

Folding the note in half, trapping a short piece of string, he wrote **ISIS** on the outside. He put his trash in the barrel and left the caffetorium and walked quickly to locker 742 and slipped the note into the grill on the door. The other end of the string, bound into a small wad of poster putty, caught in the grill, just out of sight. He was gone in two seconds.

. . .

Ms. Nelson, of Economics class had been the source of his greatest stress. It appeared to be her personal goal to make everyone participate in her class discussions. He had been given detention for causing disruption twice, although he had not intended to cause trouble. In fact, his goal was to cause as few ripples among the faculty as possible.

"Mr. Lambert, do you think Angela is correct?"

Progress. The only safe question to ask him was close ended, with a yes or no answer. The only problem was to choose one which would elicit fewer follow-up questions. Angela was obviously incorrect, art was a marketing expense, not a charitable one, but if Ms Nelson asked why he disagreed, that could be difficult, and might lead to another detention. The case could be made that a company could fund an art project as charity, but wasn't that public relations, which was branding, which was marketing? Unless the company had charity functions as part of its charter, but that might just be so that their stock could be sold at a premium to people who valued charity. Of course, the whole argument was false if it was a privately held company, not answerable to stockholders.

"Yes."

It was obviously not the answer Ms Nelson wanted, but the long delay before his answer served its purpose. Eventually, she would either stop asking him questions, or else only give him very easy yes/no questions.

She went on to ask another student their opinion, and if history was accurate, he would be safe for the rest of the day.

. . .

On the bus ride home, he sat three rows behind Isis, who had not attempted the 4:52 rendezvous since that their bus, number 7, departed at 4:15. Besides, she was wearing a brown and white outfit today. But he did see her pull out the blue colored note and read it again. She looked around the bus, but her eyes did not lock onto his. To most of the students he was invisible.

He was the only one at his stop. His house was on twenty acres, with nothing visible beyond the tree line. His father would be home in a few hours, and he would be pretending to do homework by that time. He went in through the front pasture, following an imaginary labyrinthian path. He stared at the dirt underfoot, kicking at pebbles and scuffing the topsoil. There was a pattern here, even if he was the only one who could see it.

TUESDAY

Ms Calvin handed out a math study sheet and told everyone to work quietly. Ted took his and waited until she had passed by before looking at the second sheet, stapled to his worksheet only. It was the test page. Up at the top was the computer printed 72 score, but it had a red line marked through it and a hand lettered 100. Red ink covering his pattern. In very fine lines, red ink marks had circled all the ovals where he'd erased his initial correct marks and left betraying buff marks on the paper. She had also seen his pattern and outlined its major strokes showing the house and stream.

He showed no reaction, but it was a wake up call. He wasn't as invisible as he'd thought. The initial correct marks had been a mistake. He should just have memorized and visualized the initial pattern, rather than rely on the marks as a crutch. It shouldn't be difficult. He'd memorized everyone's locker numbers, hadn't he?

But what should he do with the worksheet? Whatever he wrote would be examined. Leaving it empty would be a sign of defiance and possibly lead to more attention.

The real question was, was Ms Calvin trustworthy? She was likely watching him. However, she had not written any personal questions on the test sheet. It was a chess match. His move.

He read down through the problems on the worksheet and then in tiny letters, wrote all the correct answers in the bottom margin. He turned the worksheet over and closed his eyes.

In the darkness, he listened to the sounds of the school—the classmates scratching away at their worksheets, the air-conditioner whistling faintly though the grill that had accumulated dust and lint on its white painted louvers. Footsteps in the hallway marked their owners by their pace and the texture of the steps. Slow and massive was a male instructor. Likely Coach Haskins, given this time of day and the corridor. Fast and light, with the swish of a skirt had to be a late student. He went through his mental checklist and guessed it was Louise Watson. She was frequently late. That was a puzzle to follow in a few days.

At the back of the room, he could identify Ms. Calvin's steady breathing. Slight variations in the sound told him she was looking around at the class, not fixated on him. That was good.

In fact, she appeared to be more concerned about someone to his left. Indeed, someone was breathing hard, showing signs of distress, sniffing and sighing. He turned and looked. It was Martha Lister. She was on his project list, part of the loner group, and had been displaying signs of depression for a month or so. He raised her priority.

Ms. Calvin turned her eyes on him. He didn't look away, glancing back at Martha before turning back to face forward. Hopefully she would turn her instructor sympathies towards someone who needed them more than he did.

"Sign your worksheets and pass them towards the front of the class." He marked his and added it to the stack moving up the row. The bell rang and he made his escape.

. . .

Isis wore a bright yellow dress, and it suited her. When he was ready, he'd like a pretty girlfriend. That was no time soon, however. For now, he was content to watch. Bob Denton, sitting with the other football players glanced her way a couple of times, which he hadn't before.

Today's person of interest was Martha. If dark eye makeup could conceal facial bruises and long black sleeved dresses could hide other marks, wouldn't that be an ideal costume to wear if bruises were an unresolved problem? It was only conjecture, however. She'd been wearing dark clothing since the Christmas break. It was notable at the time, but he couldn't recall her dressing that way before. Had something changed in her home life at that time?

After ten minutes of careful observation, he was convinced. She was favoring her right arm, and possibly a bruised rib. She moved carefully, but the very care showed patterns.

Unfortunately, while she could report abuse herself, she had elected to hide it.

He pulled out a blue pad and lettered:

Your bruises have been noticed. Teachers are concerned. If you do not want help, discard this note in the trashcan to the left of your locker.

He marked it with **M.** and left it inside her locker.

...

Every available minute between classes, Martha lingered near her locker, watching people, checking to see if anyone looked into the trash can. Ted, as first mover, had the advantage, watching the watcher from various vantage points. She did not discard the note, not in that trash can. She had torn it to tiny bits and scattered them on the lawn. She was terrified that her problem would be discovered, and yet was loathe to cut off an offer of help.

...

Isis did not take the 4:15 bus home.

He paused at the fence line, and ignored his path through the front pasture. He went directly into the house and logged onto the computer under an established alias.

Martha Lister's mother Sue was a checker at a Freshmart grocery store, with 8 years work history. The store's HR records were well secured, but her union's computers were not. He filed the data and started researching her house and medical records. One list of data had leads to others. Soon a pattern developed.

Martha's father Edgar had vanished from the record five years ago. However, six months ago, the archived images of her house on Google's mapping system showed a red pickup that was not listed in Sue Lister's financial records. A lucky angle by the street view system gave him a license plate. The number, from two states over, led to a stolen vehicle report, from six months ago.

A number of possibilities existed. Was the driver of the red pickup Edgar, or a new friend of Sue Lister? What were the family dynamics that were in play? Was the mother aware of Martha's abuse?

Ted's father came home before he could complete his research. He wiped the traces of his research from the computer. His memory was good enough to retain the data.

He opened his school books to his fake homework assignments and started at the pages without reading.

An anonymous tip about the stolen vehicle could remove the driver from the household. There were any number of ways that the abuse could be 'accidentally' discovered. And there was no guarantee that other teachers hadn't picked up on the situation. How had Martha avoided gym class disclosures of her bruises? Had she been reporting sickness to get out of gym, and if so, was her mother complicit to give her excuses? He needed to get more information, and he needed more information from Martha herself.

Making changes in her life 'for her own good' might just make things worse. Sometimes a defective home life was better than none at all. He had offered to help, not to make her life fit his patterns. He had to watch that impulse. It was too easy to pull strings.

WEDNESDAY

From his early morning lookout from the second-story window in the library, he watched a red pickup pull into the circle and drop Martha. The driver's face was hard to make out, but he looked roughly the same hair and skin color as Martha. It could be Edgar, but it wasn't a positive ID.

Isis was also dropped off by parents. She was in another yellow outfit and Bob walked up to greet her before she was half-way to the steps. They chatted animatedly as they dropped out of his view.

"Hello, Ted."

He didn't look back. "Hello, Ms Calvin."

"I had heard that you spent the morning before first period up here in the library. It's pretty quiet this time of day."

"Yes." He normally would have ignored her. Silence put up many effective barriers, but with the Martha issue, he had to be careful to keep his options open.

"I just wanted you to know that I'm holding the advance placement tests in a couple of weeks. It would be possible for someone with your abilities to get college credit without having to take the normal classes. Even a freshman could jump ahead to more challenging material. Would you be interested in something like that?"

This was all old news. He'd researched it all years ago. He turned to watch her face.

"Sometimes," he said, "other things take priority."

She nodded, puzzled and then frowned. "Are you talking about your things, or someone else's?"

"Ignore me for a month."

She hesitated. "If you're sure, I can do that."

He nodded. Giving her a fixed time span gave her conscience a way out. And in a month, he'd have to have a plan to deal with her.

She turned and left. He looked back out the window. There were still several people on his list he needed to see.

. . .

The phrase he dreaded flickered past in the hallway. Two girls were whispering, heads together near their lockers. "...blue post notes..." He kept walking, but emptied his pocket of string and poster putty before he reached the next class. He knew he'd left a pattern others could detect, if they compared notes. The blue note pad joined a collection of others on a teacher's desk.

It would have been useful to use the blue notes to converse with Martha, but he wasn't ready to be identified. His little notes had affected the lives of half a dozen girls and a couple of guys. It was bad enough that two of them were comparing stories. If it got around, and he had to deal with more people watching for someone leaving notes at lockers, the side effects were unknowable. Let the blue note mystery stay contained, and not connected to him.

. . .

Computer class was a minefield, where teachers expected students to get off the lesson plan and hack the system. That's why the computers were all on a special firewalled network, where 99 percent of the Internet was off limits. But he had made sure that the rules had exceptions. The classroom computers had addresses ending in .2 through .63, all given out by a server. Since teachers also had to use the network, they were assigned addresses ending in .64 through .127, with the firewall restricting the lower numbers but not the upper range. One early morning, a few months back, he'd gotten on the librarian's computer and accessed the server that handed out the student computer's addresses and added an exception that allowed a computer to reassign its address to the higher range if it made multiple requests in short order. By clicking the Renew DHCP Lease button at a certain pace, the address would flip up into the unrestricted range. This gave him full access to the Internet, but it also made the school administration computers visible.

His requests were quick and to the point. Martha's requests to skip gym class were signed by her mother, but no one had followed up on the phone. It was possible the names were forgeries. The requests were for a week each, and had occurred three times, the most recent being yesterday. Just time to heal, but not enough to cause raise too many flags.

There was also a parent/teacher conference note that listed Edgar and Sue Lister in attendance from five months ago. It was Edgar. While the abusive parent could be the mother, the statistics and the stolen red pickup pointed at Edgar.

Using the student chat system, he queued up a message for Martha:

M.

Login to Goodreads.com as ANNAJ with password HoneyBee9$ and leave honest reviews on the last three books you checked out at the school library. I have to know what you think.

. . .

Using a Gmail account he had established months back, he left an email to Sarah Miller:

Hi Sarah,

It's me again. I just had an idea. Wouldn't it be great to look around you and discover someone dark, vulnerable, and in need of simple friendship. You could invite them for a sleepover, and just give them an evening of safety and welcome openness.

Z

Sarah was a nice person. It was her defining personality trait—wanting to help people. Z was a fictitious, like-minded person that she'd only met online. As a result, since he couldn't reach out and be warm and fuzzy when his projects demanded that, Sarah had become his proxy. He had to be careful that he didn't drain the goodness out of her, since there was always the risk that a hand of friendship would be slapped away. Long term, he wanted to hook her up with someone like Bill Monty. Good people should find each other. Unfortunately, Bill was two grades older than she was, and he suspected that would be a problem.

...

He had a cell phone, supposedly for the sole purpose of calling his father if there was an emergency, but it had a limited web browser. It was just enough to allow him to check for new reviews by AnnaJ. Anna was also fictitious, the name deliberately chosen to avoid any accidental association with another student at school. He had checked the library records, and Martha had three books checked out recently. For privacy reasons, the titles weren't logged, but the dates were, and check-in dates of books were also recorded to keep track of which were popular and might need replacing. A couple of loose matches gave him titles. A quick look at the shelves showed stories of girls in stressful home situations.

It was a perfect opportunity for Martha to speak out, wearing AnnaJ's mask, if she took it.

...

Gym class was between sport seasons, and so Coach Gleason was random about his activities. Organized days were better for Ted. He could do exactly what was expected of a weakling freshman with no sports skills and get by. Random games outdoors just get some fresh air were more dangerous.

"Hey Ted!" It was Hank Waer, from the Junior class. He was twice his size, and he knew it. Ted ignored him. Play autistic. It worked more often than not.

"Come on. Let's see you run."

Coach was off on the other side of the field, talking to his more promising athletes. Maybe he'd come to the rescue, but that wasn't the way to bet. Hank and his buddies circled around Ted, now that he'd been cut out of the herd. He avoided eye contact and stared at a spot on the ground about ten feet ahead of him.

"Ted? You hear me?" They were in street clothes. Coach hadn't thought anyone would likely get sweaty today. Hank snagged his collar and lifted him off his feet.

"Hey, you don't weigh a thing do you?" There were laughs from others in the class. It was all good natured fun. He grabbed him by the ankle and dangled him upside down. "Nothing to say?" He didn't.

"Psst. Hank." There was a warning that Coach was looking their way. Hank lowered him enough so he could put out his hands and cushion the drop, but not before loose change and his cell phone fell out of his pockets.

Crunch. "Oops." Hank had put his mass to use before walking away. As Ted ignored him still, concentrating on picking up everything that had fallen out of his pockets. The cell phone had a smashed screen and the buttons were misaligned. It was useless.

There was nothing to be done about it. Fighting would be counter-productive. He had no reputation to defend and passive prey were no fun. Complaints to a Coach weren't likely to be well received either. Tugging at a few invisible threads and making Hank suffer might feel good, but what was the point? He had played his autistic card, and it worked with no permanent damage.

Unfortunately, the phone was dead, and getting computer access to check on Martha would be difficult.

...

There were no after effects of the Hank incident. No one commented on it, nor tried to followup on it. It was like it had never happened. They were in different classes and had no interaction other than mixed grade gym classes like that one.

Lunch showed Martha and Sarah sitting together. Sarah always talked with her hands gesturing wildly, which made it easier to decode the conversation from across the room. Sarah was inviting her, and making her case about how much fun it would be. Martha kept her eyes on her food and shrugged a lot. She said little, but there was no outright rejection. He would just have to see how it played out. At least Sarah had made overtures of friendship, and that could be useful in the future.

In the hallway, he passed Bob and Isis chatting with his friends.

"...she was just standing there like a golden trophy herself. I'd be an idiot not to ..."

So it had worked out like he'd planned. The clock was ticking. He'd given Isis her heart's desire, but what she did with him was going to be up to her. He would monitor it from a distance. People were too complex for him to make more than a few little adjustments. Real changes came from within, as a result of trauma or self-realization. Staging something like that was beyond his capabilities. Which is why punishing people like Hank would be a futile exercise.

...

Ted walked off the school campus as soon as he could. Home was an hour and a half walk, but he needed a new phone.

Across the highway from the Best Buy was a gas station and convenience store. He walked in and looked around, checking out the people as well as the racks behind the cash register. After a few minutes he walked up to a man who was standing on the curb, scratching off the numbers on his lottery ticket.

"Pardon me, sir. But if you could buy one of those tickets, I'll share the winnings with you." He held out two dollars. He was clearly under age to make the purchase on his own.

He frowned down at the little kid, but he had little to lose. "Get the bingo ticket and let me scratch off the numbers."

A minute later the man was back. Ted stared at the numbers, just to make sure it was the same one he had examined a few moments before. Using the frequency of the exposed numbers on the 'bingo' cards, he chose the concealed numbers to scratch off, and the card proved to be a $20 dollar winner.

"You're a lucky little guy."

"Not luck. I can do it again."

"For real?"

He nodded.

They went in together and bought five more cards. Ted looked them over. "This one is trash. But this one..." He revealed it to be another $20 dollar winner. As were two more. With two duds and three winners, the man pocketed his $30 cut and was ready to try another round.

"The clerk is looking at us funny. Let's go across to the Shell station." The man knew a hot streak when he was on it, and was happy to let the little kid call the shots, as long as they were still winning.

After his adult purchaser was trained to watch for Ted's signal—choosing only winning tickets, letting other people get in line ahead of them when a dud was showing in the display, they quickly made more progress. When Ted had enough, he took his share of the winnings and said, "Thank you. I have to meet my dad now."

"We're done?"

Ted nodded.

The man counted his gains. "Come by any time. We can do business again. I'm here every day."

. . .

With the cash, Ted played on the Best Buy lady's sympathies, pleading that it was a present for his mother, and let her use her own driver's license number to fill in the form. "Your mom will have to buy top-up cards on her own, you understand?" He nodded. The starter card he'd purchased ought to last him a couple of months of careful use.

Now, for the first time, he had an untraceable cell phone with a thousand texts available to use. He hid it carefully in his backpack and started on the hike home.

. . .

Martha's book reviews, as AnnaJ, were revealing. She was scathing in her review of the characters in the first book, kinder in her assessment of the second, and ridiculed the last. Making the translation, it was plain that she was on the road to hating her father, but her mother was emotionally dependent on him and if he left her again, her mother would have a hard time recovering. Probably the mother was unaware of the beatings. Considering the way AnnaJ talked about one of the book characters, Martha's abuse was likely bruises only, and not sexual.

Well, then, it was up to Sarah.

. . .

When Ted's father walked in the door and saw the smashed phone by the door where he set his keys every day, he was lectured about how expensive phones were. His defense that another student had stepped on it made little difference.

"I just can't afford a replacement right now. Now go do your homework."

. . .

Sarah had emailed Z about her attempt to invite "this cute little goth girl who can't smile to save her life" to her house. She was optimistic about her chances.

Z emailed back her encouragement.

A little research while his father went out to the grocery store produced a cell phone number for Martha Lister. Confirming his own cell number was suitably anonymous, he sent her a text:

M. Accept the overnight. It will be good for you.

There was an immediate response.

Who are U?

He considered possible responses. Finally settling for:

I'm here if you need help.

She didn't reply to that.

THURSDAY

Taking the pre-dawn bus as usual, he was at his second story perch as the students began to arrive. When the red pickup appeared, he took special note of the blue tote bag Martha was carrying in addition to her school books. It was likely her clothes for an overnight.

Now, he had to decide. While Martha was out of harm's way, he could feed an anonymous tip about seeing a stolen red pickup to the police. If he were going to act, this way would be best. If Sue Lister was emotionally vulnerable, then having her husband arrested might be less damaging than being abandoned again.

In any case, he didn't know Edgar's daytime schedule. Sue would be working today at the Freshmart. What did he do during the daytime?

He would have to make sure Sue wasn't arrested, leaving Martha with no parent.

After starting at the horizon for a while, the class bell rang. He would make the decision later. This thread was a little more substantial than the others. The potential side effects could be worse than the problem to be cured. Any police arrest could turn violent.

· · ·

Louise Watson was late to first period. He saw her dashing down the hallway.

By the time computer class rolled around, he still hadn't decided to pull the plug on Edgar. He set up some alerts so that any mention on the internet of the red pickup's license tag, Edgar's name, Martha's home address or several other key items, would trigger an email that would vibrate his cell phone. He would wait for more information or an explicit request for help from Martha.

Louise was an interesting case, and looked to be much less serious than Martha. School records were incomplete. Sometimes Ms. Fletcher flagged her tardiness, and sometimes she didn't. But all the incidents fit a Tuesday/Thursday pattern. It wasn't the school's pattern, that art class started the same time every day of the week. It had to be Louise's ride.

On a hunch, he checked school records for 'Watson' and discovered her brother, Jason, who had graduated two years ago. Soon enough, he had the reason. Jason attended the local city college and had a French class that started thirty minutes later than the high school class. He must have been drafted as Louise's transportation, and did not care to get to his class early so she wouldn't be late.

So how to solve the problem? Force the brother to be more considerate? He suspected Louise was already working that issue, either by an appeal to the brother or to her parents. It wasn't working.

Make the brother want to be at school early? Was there a suitable girl he could get interested in that shared his class? Since he didn't have any way to observe the people, it would be unlikely he could find the threads to pull there. He should stick to what he could affect, rather than speculate about things he couldn't reach at this time.

Alter Louise's patterns? She could take a bus like he did, couldn't she? He checked her home address and identified the bus. Number 12. He would check who got off of it tomorrow morning. He listed her classmates—people who she knew well. If one of them took the same bus, that might give her incentive to ride it as well. More research was needed.

...

Lunchtime observations showed Sarah and Martha chatting more comfortably. They actually talked and looked at each other. Ted could understand Martha's remaining hesitation. Bruises would still be visible from the last known incident, but she was used to hiding them. She could probably manage.

He noted everyone Louise associated with. He memorized that list, along with the larger list of her classmates.

One table consisted of three girls in intense conversation. It was the two girls he'd overheard before and Isis. She pulled out a blue note and passed it around. A second note came out, and they began comparing handwriting. It was good that he had used a stylized block printing method for those notes different from how he wrote his class papers. Until this blew over, he'd have to avoid that style entirely. The cell phone texting would be useful, but he'd probably have to investigate other ways to leave anonymous messages. Perhaps more email aliases, like Z. He should start building them now, rather than wait until he needed them.

He spent Economics class creating life histories for imaginary Kent, Saul, and Jasmine. Kent and Jasmine dated. Saul lived in London. He'd have to do a little research on British English speech patterns for him.

As he watched Sarah and Martha head off with Sarah's mother, he was reasonably satisfied with his descision to chicken out and fail to call the police on Edgar Lister. He had the thread and could pull it at any time, but it was Martha's life. She had his number if she needed the help. Maybe new friends would be sufficient.

...

As he walked the pasture, his head filled with the details of the lives of his imaginary friends, he wondered what he would have to do when Ms. Calvin insisted that he join the standard culture of school grades and academic plans. If she had spent the time to become a school teacher, she would not be open to a child his age choosing an alternative career path. He had seen the patterns of American life. There was the public school life he was faking, private school versions of the same and home schooling which required more effort from a parent than his father could give.

Until his growth spurt hit and he appeared more like an adult, he was constrained to this life, or to gamble on a runaway's life that appeared considerably more dangerous than gym class.

He let his hands pass through the tall grass that grew in this unoccupied pasture. If he'd grown up in another time, maybe he would have found something appealing about the patterns of land and cattle and crops. But that wasn't his fate. The world of computers and finance had lots of potential in a few years, when he could sign his name to a contract without committing fraud.

Until then, Hillside High School was his playground, and the students there his to care for.

FRIDAY

Bus 12 unloaded, and he quickly identified each student that unloaded, carrying bags and books.

Oh, ho. Hank Waer stepped down and looked around. He hefted his load and walked toward the back of the athletic building where guys in letter jackets tended to collect in the early morning hours.

Hank Waer had been in Louise's class for years.

He stepped over to the shelf of class annuals. A quick check confirmed that she and Hank had been a couple just last year. Louise was avoiding the bus, risking regular tardies, just to avoid Hank. No wonder her brother was lacking in sympathy. A break-up had happened. When? And what caused it?

. . .

Martha and Sarah exited out of the Suburban and chatted, arm in arm. Martha was even wearing a sweater Sarah had worn a few days ago. The overnight must have gone well. Still, Martha was wearing her bruise obscuring long sleeved clothes and eye makeup. He would need to be right on top of any email addressed to Z. Somehow, in spite of the new friendship, he doubted Martha had opened up about her problems.

In Ms. Calvin's class, Martha showed signs of being on top of her class work. Perhaps he could just put her project on the wait list for now. If she could just get past the bruises and avoid getting new ones, expanding her social range would probably solve the depression problems.

In computer class, he narrowed down the Hank/Louise breakup to the past month. That was when the tardies started. There were no related reports, no public fights or anything like that. A cross check against social events showed nothing suspicious. A date gone bad?

There were times when he wished he were more connected to the school grapevine. This is a situation where gossip would be invaluable. Unfortunately, his public persona, the near-autistic little kid, was a poor match for that kind of thing. Gossips wanted to look you in the eye, and gain social points for knowing something you didn't.

That was a possibility. What about an underground social network, just for the Hillside, where people could text their latest tidbits and earn social standing for being the most plugged-in person on campus?

I actually have two personas now. Ted the wallflower, and Blue Note.

Perhaps Blue Note should make an appearance. But that would require some preparation to set up an anonymous website. In addition, gossip was frequently mean-spirited, and Blue Note only gave good advice. That would have to be resolved.

. . .

Ted located Hank's cell number.

He tracked him until Hank was alone on the bleachers, waiting for buddies.

Hank, whether it was your fault or not, you need to apologize.

He pulled out his phone and frowned. He tapped on the keys.

Who are you? And what are you talking about?

Ted was probing the waters. He had to step carefully.

She's pestering Jason, remember him, just so she doesn't have to ride the bus with you. You don't want Jason on your case.

Hank looked around, but didn't notice him. Jason, Louise's brother had a school record in the hammer throw. He must have been strong, and around when Hank was younger.

It was an accident. I didn't know she'd be upset. And now she won't talk to me.

Jackpot.

I'm not saying you'll ever get back together. I'm not saying it's your fault. But YOU HAVE TO APOLOGIZE. This is girl logic, here, and they gossip. Apologize and they all know you're a stand-up guy.

Who are you?

Just a guy trying to get Jason's little sister off his back.

A group of guys walked up the bleachers and called to Hank. He waved back, but left them there as he stalked back into the school building.

. . .

Ted watched Martha get back into the red pickup when her father picked her up. Was she moving with a quicker step? Time would tell.

He had watched ten seconds of an intense conversation between Hank and Louise as he walked through the hallway. At least they were talking. That was progress.

But it was Friday, and he had a weekend to deal with. It was enough to dampen the glow of seeing progress on his other projects. He packed his bags and climbed into Bus 7, waiting for the other students to join him. The door closed without Isis. Perhaps she had a date with Bob. He would have to find out on Monday. The bus began to pull out of the parking lot.

His phone vibrated. He fished it out and cupped his hand around the screen.

Are you there? It was a text from Martha.

What is the problem?

My dad! Police are after him. He dropped me off in the middle of nowhere and police cars are chasing him. I can still hear the sirens.

Ted's mind raced through the possibilities. Either an old alert about the stolen car, someone else's 911, or else a new crime had alerted the police. In any case, they would catch him.

But Martha was stranded and alone.

Where are you, exactly?

St. Johns and Highway 1245.

In four minutes, school bus 7 will come along the highway. Walk into the lane and flag the driver. David has a soft spot for stranded girls. Call him by "Mr. Ellis". Your father's car was stranded and you need a ride. Sit with Ted Lambert. He is a little flakey but safe.

But I need to call my Mom.

There was an alert showing up on his email system. Edgar was arrested.

Right. But that can wait until you are safe. Exit with Ted and he will keep you safe until she can get free. Once you are safe, you can call your mother.

I'm waiting for the bus. What will I tell Mom?

Tell her your father put your safety ahead of his escape, and that he has been arrested and she needs to go be with him.

The bus began to slow. From where he sat, he couldn't see, but the driver pulled to a stop and opened the doors with a metallic squeak. They spoke and many of the students strained to hear what she said. David nodded and she stepped back to his row.

"You are Ted, aren't you? Can I sit here?" He nodded and scooted over to make room for her.

He didn't make eye contact, and had his cell phone hidden in his pocket with even the vibrate turned off.

She smiled a bare minimum. Tears had caused her eye makeup to begin to run. He was tempted to offer her a tissue, but it would have been out of character. Everyone knew Ted was terrified of girls.

She pulled out her phone and typed. He could read her screen, just barely.

What do I do now?

Ted pressed a key in his pocket to send the message he had already composed.

Stay with Ted. He will exit in just a minute. Call your mother when you get off the bus. Your father was arrested. No shots were fired.

When his exit showed up, he pulled the cord as usual and stood up. She got off with him, attracting considerable attention.

The bus pulled away on its route.

Ted stood motionless, watching her.

"Could I wait at your house until my mother comes for me?"

He nodded.

"Do you mind if I make a call?"

He shook his head.

She called the Freshmart number and asked for her mother. There was a wait until she could get free to make it to the phone.

"Mom?" She turned away from Ted. "The police arrested Daddy. No. I'm safe at a school friend's house." She told the story in a halting fashion, interrupted by her mother's questions. "Just go to the jail. I'm okay for now. Tell him I'm safe. I'm sure he is worried."

She put away her phone. Her eyes were a mess. He hesitated, then handed her his little pocket packet of tissues.

"Thank you."

He took a couple of steps toward the gate, then turned to see if she was following. She did and he led the way. When they got to the pasture, he pointed at the rut in the dirt that his daily route had cut. "Follow this."

She nodded, puzzled. After a couple of minutes of walking the convoluted, twisty pathway, she giggled. "What is this?"

He just pointed ahead and kept on going. As they went through the next gate and entered the front lawn, he led her to the porch and pointed back to the pasture where they had trod.

She looked, "Oh!" She saw the image that the pattern of trails made in the grass. "Who is she?"

"Mother." He unlocked the front door and went inside. He set down his bags and waved her to a seat while he went into the kitchen and brought her a coke from the refrigerator.

After a couple of minutes, he pressed the send button on his hidden phone again and the message he'd keyed while in the kitchen appeared.

I assume you are safe at Ted's house. If you need anything else, send a message, but otherwise just wait for your mother's call.

Martha looked at her phone and keyed, **Yes, I'm safe.**

She sipped and looked around. "This is a nice place." She got up and walked to the mantelpiece, where there were a few pictures and an urn. "I'm sorry about your mother." The inscription told the basics—the date was nearly the same date as Ted's birthdate. One of the pictures was the model for the pattern in the field.

She pointed. "Could we sit on the porch?"

He nodded and they went back outside where the sun was slowly setting over the waving grasses.

. . .

Several hours later, after Sue Lister arrived to collect her daughter and thanked a puzzled Mr. Lambert for his assistance. Ted's phone flickered with a message:

Thank you for everything.

No problem. I assume you are home safe?

Yes. But, I was wondering. I don't know who you are, but you help people. I met Mr. Lambert, Ted's father, and he's nearly as closed off as his boy. It's sad. Do you think you could do something for that family?

Possibly. I'll look into it.

The One

Everyone's dreams are private, or so we think.

The girl was dramatic, he'd say that much for her. Sam Delany took in her ankle-length black dress, black shoes, very black hair, and dark eye makeup. Why she was staring at him, he had no clue.

"Who is that?" he asked.

Jason looked over his shoulder. "Teri Perry. And she hates her real name. Goes by Agatha when she can get away with it. Full on goth, I guess."

"What's the deal?"

"My sister claimed she tried a seance at a party once. Really into spirits and demons and stuff."

Sam rubbed the back of his neck. "She's creeping me out. She's been staring this way for an hour or more."

Jason shrugged. "You're the new guy. Someone who isn't on to her tricks yet."

He gave up on watching the baseball game and went back inside to get his books out of his locker. Switching to a new school midway through his senior year was not his idea of a great time. At least his cousins were here. That was something, right?

He was half-way to the parking lot, his mind tallying up which books he'd need to take home, when he turned a corner and there she was, head to toe black and barely as tall as his chin.

"Ah. Hello?"

She seemed to be looking past him, but she said, "You're new here, right?"

"Yes. From Wilmington."

"I've been waiting for you for three years."

"Huh?"

She blinked, looking a little vague. "Not what I was expecting."

"What is going on? I saw you watching me."

"Your aura was surprising. I wasn't sure until I got close up. But you're the one, all right."

"The one what?"

"My mate."

He took a step sideways. "Okay. I was told about your tricks. Just lets not get crazy."

She smiled tolerantly. "You can fight it, but you'll come around. It's destiny."

He nodded, humoring her. "Okay. Destiny. Right. Later then." He waved and headed out as fast as he could without actually running.

She didn't follow. He was grateful for small favors.

He waved at Jason in the stands on his way out, but he wasn't really in the mood to share the latest revelation.

He got in his Jeep and headed home.

. . .

The next morning at school, there was a page on pink paper, ripped out of a small spiral notepad, folded in half and taped to his locker:

Teri Jo Perry A.K.A. "Agatha"
5'2" - 102 lbs. Birthday 1/12

It went on for two paragraphs, detailing her phone number, her favorite colors, her favorite foods, etc. She had an IQ of 132, she had her appendix removed when she was 14, and she was on the birth control pill. There was a list of favorite musicians and favorite authors. She didn't go to movies and was an only child.

It was more information that he knew about anyone, let alone a girl. It was *much* more information than he wanted to know.

And it struck him that it was hazardous for it to be out there for someone to discover. Didn't she know about identity theft? He folded the paper carefully and stuck it in his wallet. He wouldn't want random people knowing all his medical history and favorite foods and stuff. He was surprised she didn't just go ahead and include all her accounts and passwords while she was at it. Really!

Did this dingbat really believe her auras and destiny and stuff?

He chuckled. *Am I being stalked?* Flattering, but he could do without. He needed to find Steph.

· · ·

When lunchtime rolled around he searched for his other cousin and finally found her.

"Hey, Steph, can I borrow you for a minute."

She introduced him around to her girl friends at the table. There were a few speculative eyes watching him as he pulled her off to talk in private.

"What do you know about this Agatha person?"

She chuckled. "Sam, don't tell me you're interested in her?"

"No. It's not that. I think she's following me around."

"Seriously?"

"Maybe. I don't know. I only talked to her once, in the hallway. She said something about auras."

She waved her hand. "Don't mind that. She got on that aura thing, oh—years back. She does a fortune telling schtick when we're at parties."

He frowned. "Is she...could she be dangerous?"

Steph shook her head. "Naw. It's all an act. Other than the goth stuff, she's pretty ordinary. She'll even wipe the eyeliner off when it's time for the two-act play contest. She played a cute little Betsy Jones last year. Nobody could believe it was her."

He nodded. *A trickster and and actress. Good to know.* "Okay, just ignore me, and don't spread any rumors. I'm just trying to find out who is who around here."

She looked a little puzzled. She nodded back towards her table. "I can probably fix you up with a date for this weekend, if you just say the word."

"Maybe next week. I've still got stuff to do at home."

· · ·

There was another pink note taped to his locker. He snatched it off with a growl.

Julie Smith has an erratic spike in her aura. Danger. Don't get her pregnant.

Agatha

What in the world? Who is Julie Smith.

And he was seriously angry that she would think he would get anyone pregnant. Who did she think he was?

He went looking for his dark nemesis. He stalked through the hallway and out to the parking lot. He was halfway across the athletic fields when he saw a figure in a black dress. He changed course.

She saw him coming, her face serene.

He clutched the paper. "Don't leave notes on my locker!"

She blinked, then nodded. "Ah. Okay. How do I get messages to you?"

He was almost speechless. "Why do you need to? We don't know each other. We're not friends. And don't say a word about auras and destiny!"

She nodded again. "I understand your concern. How about you give me your number. I can send texts. Would that be private enough?"

He shook his head. "Why don't you just leave me alone?"

She spread her hands. "But I can't leave you in danger! That doesn't make sense. You'll trust me eventually, but until then, why not texts?" It was again as if she wasn't looking directly at him. He was tempted to brush his hair or something.

She was so frustratingly dense. Off in another world.

"Okay. Texts only. No locker messages, no meetings in the hallway. Got that?"

"Understood."

He gave her the number and she immediately entered it in her cell.

"Good. We're making progress." She smiled.

He didn't know whether he'd made a big mistake or not. But he couldn't have her leaving possibly scandalous messages on his locker for anyone to intercept. Without another word he stalked off.

...

This late in the year, it was impossible to join any of the sports teams or start to learn an instrument or anything like that. There was chess club, and he was good at that, but it was reluctant to open that can of worms again.

He was spending far too much time with his cousins, as much as he liked them.

And it was too easy to spot his stalker wherever he went. Like sitting in the entrance to the library eating an apple and pretending to read a book. Her eyes tracked his every move.

"Jason! There you are."

"Sam. What's up?" He had his hands full with one end of a large banner. The other end was being tacked up on the wall. "Beat the Wildcats!" it said. Jason was one of the beefy guys who got to throw the cheerleaders into the air at games.

"Not much. I thought I'd have trouble getting up to speed in my classes, but I was wrong there. I'm at loose ends."

He nodded. "I wish I could help, but I'm booked solid. Go talk to Steph. She was pestering me about some project. Let her pester you."

. . .

Steph practically rubbed her hands with glee. "Yes, I can use you. Come with me."

She led him into the stage area, where three girls were hammering away at some boxes. "I brought help", she called out. They all set down their tools and came to meet him.

"This is Sam, my cousin. Girls. He's all yours."

She wandered away.

"What's up?"

The large dark-haired one took his hand. "We're building stage sets for the play."

The little one, a bit chubby, but cute, said, "We've got the plans, but they're not going together very well."

The one with the light brown hair said nothing, but smiled.

He took a look at the plans.

"Do we have a budget for the materials?"

"Not much. We're supposed to re-work the stuff from last year."

He nodded. "Show me."

. . .

With Candi's help, since she was the biggest, they hauled a few of the set pieces out of storage. It was plain bits and pieces of the flats had been reused for years. He could see lettering in French in places on the back, hidden side of some of them. A previous crew had just turned their hand-me-downs over and painted fresh buildings on the back side.

"I wonder how many layers down it goes," he said, chipping at the paint with his fingernails.

Suzy, the little one, and Clare, the quiet one, began arranging the set flats according to the diagram.

"No," he shook his head. "We need to reverse the blacksmith shop. Candi, would you help?"

Soon they had the old sets laid out in roughly the same order as the diagram. It was like a jigsaw puzzle, only with nails and wing nuts.

"Now all we have to do is put facing on that one, and paint them."

The girls all clustered around the diagram and they agreed.

Candi got them to show up after school to help with the painting. Sam agreed to help.

"That's great. We don't usually get any of the cute guys to help," Suzy confided.

"Why not?"

"Sports and stuff. They're all taken, and the geeks like to play with the lighting and the sound system. Plus," she whispered, "we can sometimes get a little rough."

"Oh?" He grinned. The idea that Suzy could get rough with anyone was a little humorous.

She nodded. "Man eaters, all of us. Except maybe Clare. She just licks them to death."

Clare was blushing like mad and bashed Suzy on the head with a three ring binder.

"Hey, cut that out."

But they all behaved themselves when the bells rang and they spread out the drop cloths to catch paint splatters. Candi eyed him up and down when he picked up a bucket. "Do you have any grubs to change into. You don't want paint all over you."

"I'll be careful."

"It's not you who will cause the spills."

He nodded, but started covering wide areas with sky blue. The girls retired around the corner and came back with their hair bundled up in scarves, and wearing old, splattered coveralls. He sighed. He didn't have any old grubs. But maybe what he was wearing would soon be assigned to that job.

. . .

They had the flats soon covered in broad areas, but it'd take another day to get the detail lines in place.

When Suzy asked if Clare could take her home, he offered. "I've got a Jeep. I'll drop you off."

"Great."

Candi raised her hand. "I could use a ride as well."

"No problem."

Clare pouted.

Suzy shook her head, "It's your own fault for having a car."

They laughed.

Suzy pointed to a bench. "Stay right there while we change, unless you want to come help?"

He smiled. "Oh, I'm okay."

She unzipped her coverall down, showing a hint of lace and sauntered out, hips swaying.

Candi shook her head. "Don't mind her. She loves to tease."

Clare patted him on the shoulder and shook her head sadly at the doom that awaited him. She picked up her books and left.

. . .

Suzy rode next to him, with her hand on his leg as far as her house. She winked. "You're welcome to stay longer."

"I'm still here," reminded Candi from right behind her.

"Spoilsport."

Candi moved up to the front seat. He said, "You should have asked for the front seat. It's tight quarters back there."

"Suzy wouldn't have put up with it. She needed to get her hands on you."

"So she's the man eater she claims to be?"

She shrugged. "I think it's all an act, but one of these days, she'll get some guy to take her up on her offer."

He nodded. "I've heard some girls are just ready to get pregnant."

She chuckled. "Don't discount a girl's hormones.

"But look here." She plucked at his sleeve. "I told you. Paint splatters all over this."

He looked down. "I hadn't noticed. They're tiny."

"But they need to be treated quickly. Here, this is my house. Come on in. I've got something to deal with this."

He followed her in. She dropped her books on the table. "Take that off and I'll run it though a quick wash cycle. The paint is water based. We might get it out."

Looking around cautiously, he didn't see signs of anyone else about, but taking off clothes in a girls house sounded risky. He waited, with his fingers on his buttons.

She shook her head. "Don't be a baby." She began unbuttoning them herself. Soon he watched her stalk off towards the washing machine.

The house looked normal enough. He didn't feel like sitting down.

She came back, bright eyed and carrying a coke. "Here. I hand-scrubbed it a bit and I think the paint will come out. Have a seat." She sat down on the couch and patted the space beside her.

"I probably should head on home."

"But without your shirt? It won't take too long." She reached out and took his hand and he sat.

She leaned toward him. "So, you're Steph's cousin? What made you change towns?"

He sipped the coke she handed him. "Um. Parents. Dad took a new job and so we moved. Couldn't have happened at a worse time, either."

"Oh, why?"

"I was varsity. Baseball, football, track, all that. It was a small school, so I was in demand, you know? In this place, it's so big, I'm lost in the whirl of too many people with better seniority than I'll have time to get."

"Lost in the maze, huh? I get it." She took his hand. "I've been pretty lost in this school too."

As he looked in her eyes. He couldn't help notice that in all the shuffling to get his shirt in the washing machine, somehow, she'd managed to lose her bra. Her breasts were swaying under her blouse, and he could see the nipples making their indentations.

He nodded, and leaned back. "Yes. I guess it's easy for anyone to get lost at a big school." He looked over at the stack of books on the table.

"What kind of classes are you taking?" He snatched up a textbook. "Calculus, huh?"

"Just the usual old boring stuff." She squeezed his free hand.

He saw her name on the cover. Julie was scratched out and Candi was written in in bold letters with a heart over the 'i'.

"You change your name or something?"

"Yes! I was so tired of being a 'Julie'. Everybody knew me, knew what to expect out of me. It was the start of a new year, and I wanted to be a new me. Other girls were changing their names. Why not me?"

"Like Agatha."

"Yes. Like her. And 'Angela'. I was surprised she didn't buy herself a pair of wings. She had angel stickers all over everywhere."

He looked at her. "Why Candi?"

Her eyes glittered and she licked her lips. "Because I could be very sweet—to the right guy."

He nodded. "You probably would be."

Pretending to be oblivious to what she was doing, he picked up another book. "Oh! History. That reminds me. I have an essay due. I was having so much fun with the painting and all, I forgot about it. I really need to go take care of that."

He dropped her hand and stood up. "I guess I'd better take the shirt now, even wet as it is, and go deal with it. Sorry. I shouldn't have taken your time with it."

She protested, but he was firm. "It's my fault for not being prepared for the painting like you guys were."

With a downright sullen look, she stopped the wash cycle and extracted his shirt. He wrung it out over the sink and put it on.

"Really sorry, but I've got to go."

He almost ran back to the Jeep.

. . .

"Doing laundry?"

"Hi, Dad. Just a shirt. I got some paint splatters on it at school."

He chuckled, setting down his laptop case. "I thought that went out with grade school."

Sam sighed. "I was just helping some girls paint stage flats for their drama class."

"Oh, girls, eh? Any of them pretty?"

He nodded. "Sure. All of them. In their own way."

His father was a little overweight from sitting at a desk day in and day out. He sighed. "I remember when I could go play with the pretty girls."

"Dad!"

"Don't tell your mother I said that."

. . .

Charlie Whittacker set down his books next to the girl in the long black dress during the pep rally. "That's the one you're thinking about?" he asked, staring across the basketball court, watching Sam escort three girls to sit on the second row to the left. Charlie and Agatha talked in low voices and never made eye contact with each other. People could tell, just by the way he was dressed, that his mind was already in some ivy league school, and he looked a little out of place sitting next to a goth girl.

"Yes, if he doesn't get himself in trouble."

"Why do you think it's him?"

"His aura, I told you."

"Anything else? Something a real person could understand."

"It's the right year. He's new, and there's no one else in school that's a candidate. Besides, he's the guy in my vision."

"The one where you die."

"Right."

"Then I should think you'd want to keep your distance from him."

"It's fate. There's nothing I can do about it."

"Maybe I should talk to him."

"Don't. He's resistant enough. Anything you say would just push him farther away."

"Have it your way." He grabbed his books and moved on down the row.

. . .

Sam saw Agatha across the way at the pep rally. He always saw her. At first he thought she was following him around, stalking him, but now he wasn't so sure. She was just extremely visible, dressed the way she was.

Suzy yelled in his ear, "Did you play baseball at your old school?"

"Yes. All the sports."

Candi added, "He was a regular sports hero."

It had been a week since the shirt incident, and although he finished the painting job with the girls and even hung around as the play started rehearsals, he was careful to flirt with them all openly and evenly. Candi had lost interest in that game.

Still, having someone to hang around with was better than being alone.

He tapped Suzy on the shoulder. "Who's that guy?" He pointed at the tall red-haired guy moving down the aisle.

"Charlie Whittacker. Math geek. He was in Drama class last year, but he's all tied up with science fairs and junk now. On the scholarship track."

He nodded. One by one, he was learning his way around the school's social circle. In his old school, the senior class numbered less than fifty. Here it was more like 500. But as always, there were the leaders, the club presidents, the ones in the race for class standing. There was no way he was likely to get in that league, not with his late start, but it was good to know who they were. And if they knew who he was, he could make some connections. More than those his cousins passed his way.

Not that he didn't enjoy all the fuss and frantic busy-ness of the Drama group, but it wasn't really his play, and he'd never been an actor. Mr. Dyson had asked if he were interested in reading for one of the lesser parts, just as a standby, but he declined. There were people who needed that opportunity, and he didn't.

The cheerleaders came out and the band blasted into the fight song. All pretense of speaking were gone. It was 'yell loud or no one could hear you'. He glanced to his left and saw Clare yelling too. He tried to listen, but he couldn't hear her contribution. She even yelled quietly.

He'd learned not to discount Clare's intentions. Suzy had been dead on, right from the beginning. Clare was interested in snagging a man as well. The one time he'd spent more than ten minutes alone with her, she'd talked in a low sultry voice that could easily get a guy thinking bedroom thoughts.

"Did Candi getcha outta yer clothes?"

He'd been surprised that her intentions had been that plain to the others.

"Just the shirt, for about two minutes. I had to leave."

"I'd've tripped you and held you down 'til you quit strugglin'. I al'ays knew she's too timid. But, still, she'll be after that cousin or yer's, Jason, next. Bet money she'll have a man the old way by June."

He'd chuckled. "Probably."

Clare had given him a good long stare. "Why're you still be'in a loner? Ya been here two week, what?"

It was a reasonable question.

"I won't throw you outta my bed if ya get lonely. No chains an no babies. I'm ona Pill."

Between cheers, Clare looked his way. She had looked like a quiet polite girl the first time he'd seen her. She gave him a smile and a twitch of her eyebrow that had a whole world of different meaning now.

But the question she'd asked that day still stood.

With all these girls throwing themselves at him, why was he playing the eligible bachelor?

Across the way, Agatha was still watching him.

. . .

You said Julie. Her name is Candi.

He watched as Agatha looked around for her cell and finally dug it out of her tote bag.

She looked across the noisy gulf at him and tapped.

Sorry. She's been Julie for all my life. Don't tell me she trapped you?

He chuckled.

Nope. But she did offer some 'special services'.

That ought to give her something to think about. Washing clothes is a service, right?

Agatha stared intently across the way.

I can see from here she's still on the prowl. Be careful.

He looked over at Candi, and she was watching the crowd intently.

She noticed his attention and yelled, "Why don't you introduce me to that cousin of yours?" Jason was out on the court, a big letter on his chest, holding two cheerleaders as part of their cheer.

He yelled back. "I'll let him know you're interested."

Suzy rolled her eyes.

. . .

He caught up with Jason later.

"Hey."

"Sam. What's up?"

"One of my lady friends, Candi Smith, is interested in meeting you."

"One of... How many do you have?"

"I lose track."

"Right. Who is this one?"

"You may know her as Julie."

He frowned, thinking. "Maybe. She doesn't want you anymore?"

Sam looked cautious. "I have been told that she's looking to snag a mate the old fashioned way."

Jason smiled, and then frowned. "Ah. Does that mean...?"

"Don't get her pregnant, unless you're ready to settle down, like right now."

"Okay. I understand."

"Still, she's a good looking girl. If you're in the neighborhood of the play rehearsals, just ask around. I think she's one of your sister's friends too, come to think of it."

"I'll think about it."

. . .

Home in his room, with books spread around as if he were doing homework, he got onto his computer. He pulled down his buddy list. A familiar name was online.

Billy boy, how are things back in Wilmington?

   Is that you, Sam? I thought you'd dried up an blowed away.
Yeah, new school, but it same ol, same ol.

       Uh, oh. Girl trouble?
More or less. Too many of the wrong kind.

     Too many hotties or too many dogs?
You'd never believe me.

  Sam, have I ever not believed you. Even with the dream girl thing.
        You can tell me.
Well, I've got three medium hot 'buddies', one of which is looking to snag a daddy.

      Steer clear, son. Steer clear.
I am. Just smiling and keeping my shirt buttoned, at least after the first time.

         Tell. Tell.
"Oh let me wash that paint stain. Now sit beside me on the couch."

          And?

I got the message when her superstructure was missing a harness and bailed.

Whew. That's the one looking to get a big belly?

Yep.

The others?

Flirty buddies. I can handle them.

Anyone else.

Yeah. Spooky goth. Sees auras. Claims we're destined mates.

Uh, oh. But I guess she's no worse that that girl you see in your dreams.

Totally different. But there's something about this one. She's everywhere I look.

Looker?

I dunno. I can't get past the black goth stuff.

I've seen some pretty sexy goths.

I'll take another look. I just wish I could find the right girl.

She won't be the right one without "red hair, pixie cut and deep brown eyes"

Give my dream girl a rest.

Why? You compare every girl to her. Look around. Maybe she's out there looking for you.

...

Dinner was lasagna. Not the TV dinner kind.

"Sam, how is school?"

"Okay, Mom."

"And your grades?"

"They're coming up. I took a hit, making this move, but I should be okay soon enough."

His father's eyes were tracking the ball on the screen in the other room, but he was doing his duty and eating at the table with them. "Going for valedictorian?"

"Dad! You know that's not possible. Be happy with B's."

"I'll be happy when you put more effort into it. I know you can do better. You're just coasting along. You'll never get scholarships this way."

"I'll manage."

He sighed. It was an old argument.

. . .

Chess club meets Wednesday 4pm. 1222 Blackburn Hall. I told them you would come.

Sam was horrified as he read the text. What gave her the right? And how did she even know about Chess club. Was it on his records somehow?

He tapped away angrily.

None of your business what clubs I join. Stay out of my hair.

There was a quick reply.

School spirit. Cross town games coming up. You know you'll win.

He turned off his phone before he was seen. No sense in getting a teacher down on him as well.

But how did she know about chess?

Steph! Steph knows her. I bet that's it.

. . .

He plopped down at Steph's table at lunch.

"Howdy ladies." Candi and Clare were there as well. Steph was one of the main actresses in the play. His trio were extras on the stage—townspeople with no real lines. But their play was coming up and that's all they talked about.

"Sam! How are you? You just missed Jason. He and Candi are planning a double-date to the movies on Friday with David and me. You could come too."

He shook his head. "Still trying to catch up on the homework. Dad wants straight A's this time. Never gonna happen. By the way, did you talk to Agatha recently?"

She looked puzzled. "No. Since she dropped out of Drama last year, we don't do much."

"So, you didn't say anything about chess?"

"Oh, do you play chess? That looks too hard for me."

"Yeah, I played some back at Wilmington. Just trying to track down some things."

. . .

Okay. How did you know about chess?

He sat in a corner of the library, fuming. Her reply came a couple of minutes later.

Are you going to the meeting?

No. Answer my question.

I'll tell you everything, after the meeting. Just attend. You don't have to play.

He grumbled. It was almost time. He had sworn off chess. At least Chess club. He didn't want to go back.

But he had to figure out what Agatha was up to. And he had to know how she knew about his chess skills.

He walked over to Blackburn Hall and located the room.

"Hello, are you interested in chess?"

There were three guys there.

"I've played a little. I'm new to the school."

"Great, we need another player. Have a seat."

There were two boards—a standard sized board with plastic pieces, and a fold-up pocket board with tiny pieces that plugged into holes in the board. He hadn't seen one of those in a while—what with the digital players so common.

He couldn't help himself. He took black on the little pocket board. The opponent, Greg, was a decent player and no one talked much. There was a little discussion of their rankings, but Sam disclaimed any knowledge of his own ranking number.

"Check." He said absently as the game progressed. He slapped the little clock that tracked how many minutes he spent versus his opponent.

Greg grumbled. "That's probably mate."

It wasn't. Sam reluctantly pointed his finger at a rook.

"Oh. Sorry." Greg made the move, but a minute later it was over.

"You're good."

"Lucky."

"Did you want to join the tournaments?"

He shook his head. "I'm too new here. I'd better wait a bit."

"Are you that guy Agatha mentioned?"

"Oh, what did she say?"

He shrugged. "Just that she'd seen you play and were pretty good."

"Really? I haven't played since I moved here."

"Don't worry about it. Agatha is always getting information from her 'visions'. Maybe that's where she saw you play."

They all chuckled at that. Apparently, she was a known source of odd stories.

. . .

When they broke up, Sam wandered down the hallway. His phone vibrated.

Library

She was waiting at a table, her painted eyes watching for him.

He pulled up a chair.

"Okay. I went to the meeting."

She nodded. "You won." It wasn't a question.

"Well, yes, but that's not the point. How did you know I played chess?"

She sighed, and looked down at the table. "I suppose you don't believe in clairvoyance?"

"I don't believe high school girls in black clothes that talk of auras are statistically likely to have useful clairvoyant skills."

She chuckled and smiled up at him. "You sound just like...someone else I know."

You look so much better with a smile. Her brown eyes glistened. Billy had been right. He should take another look at her.

"Okay, I've had this discussion many times. Forget the word 'clairvoyance'. I am intuitive. I come up with testable information without obvious research."

He nodded. At least she knew words he could understand. 'Testable' meant she'd predict things that could actually be checked—proved true or false. Not just claim knowledge about past lives or secret thoughts that no one could test.

"Okay. So you just guessed I knew chess."

"Exactly. I knew that you played chess. I know you are good. Some number in the two thousands keeps popping up in my head but I can't make sense of it. Is that a ranking?"

"And you didn't go online and look up my Elo chess rankings?"

She nodded. "I wouldn't know how to do that. I can understand how you might not believe me, but that's what's happening."

"You told Greg, at the chess club that you'd seen me play."

She smiled. "I've seen you doing many things. Some in the past, some in the future."

"Like what?"

She looked off to the side, and blinked, as if recalling something.

"I saw you without a shirt, talking to Julie. I saw you playing chess with a large group of people—lots of games going on at the same time. I saw you crying in a Jeep, on the side of a mountain. I saw....other things. Lots of other things."

Sam was quiet. *The rumor mill could have relayed the shirt incident. She could have made up the chess tournament. But nobody knew I went up on Baldy that night. Nobody.*

"Why me?"

She shrugged, and it occurred to him that there were tears in her eyes. *Why?*

"We are linked. I said so from the first. We are mates." She straightened in her chair, and cleared her throat. "I'm more likely to pick up emotional events. Although, personally, I hardly think playing chess is all that emotional—but that's just me."

"You said future events?"

She nodded. "I've seen you and me. Together."

He didn't ask for details. She could be lying, or projecting, but it was so close to his own recurring dream that his thoughts veered away from thinking about that too closely.

"Three years. You said something about three years ago."

She nodded. "I've had dreams all my life. Little things mainly. I'd even seen you. But they were all vague."

She looked behind him again. "It was the auras that changed. I put a few pieces together and realized you would be coming." She looked down at the table again. "It's hard to explain. Especially when we don't share the same concepts."

He nodded. "Like auras. You mean like the Kirilian photographs?"

"No. I know about those, but those are just some kind of electrostatic things. The auras I see are different."

He was frustrated. He'd read about auras. But none of the descriptions made any kind of physical sense. If you couldn't photograph auras, then they weren't light. And if they weren't light, how could people *see* them.

She was smiling at him, now.

"Okay, do you have the magic piece of information that would help me understand it?"

"Nope. I just see them. I can make testable predictions based on what I see. And I can't make anyone else see them, or understand what I'm seeing." She shrugged. "I don't try to make people believe me. But I can't just lie and hide what I'm experiencing either. I'm content with people thinking I'm crazy. What does it matter in the long run anyway?"

She reached to her side and picked up her bag. "I've got to go."

"No. Wait. I have more questions."

"My ride is here. I have to go. We'll talk more later."

He got up with her and walked with her to the entrance. He wanted to get another close look at her eyes, but she just kept on going, walking out the entrance sidewalk right as a car drove up to meet her. He watched as she got in the front seat with her mother, black haired like her. As they drove off, he thought he saw her lean her head against the woman.

. . .

She'd been depressed as she walked out. Was that just part of the goth thing? There was so much he didn't understand about Agatha, and for some reason, he really wanted to know her.

But there was much about life in general that he didn't understand.

He'd tried not to think about the people he'd left behind in Wilmington. Susan Casey hadn't taken his move well. He'd thought he'd gotten past his dream girl and began dating a real live blonde that liked what he did, or at least liked him well enough to put up with his enthusiasms. They'd been going together for a month or so. That night, when she told him plainly that if he moved, that was the end for them—it had been the worst night of his life. He had thought she'd work with him—make plans for trips back and forth, to plan a college they could both attend.

But that wasn't how it worked out. She was hurt, and blamed him, somehow, for his father's new job. He'd waited until she slammed the door on him, and then he'd driven nearly a hundred miles in the night, and up to the top of the mountain.

Had he really thought, that night, that the universe would acknowledge the depth of his suffering and change everything? Well, after watching the moon cross the sky, he finally gave up and managed to get back home before dawn. His parents hadn't even realized he was gone.

...

A bright face with dark brown eyes, crowned with bright red hair so short it was almost a skull cap turned to see the dawn glow brighter. He loved her so sharply he could barely breathe. He could feel the danger coming, but her smile was joyous. "It's nearly time." She locked eyes with his, and he could feel her love for him. "It's how the world is supposed to be."

Sam woke with a shock, still feeling the warmth of her body in his arms. *No!* He didn't want it to vanish again. As it always had.

He fumbled for a pen and opened the closest notebook to an empty page. He sketched rapidly, as the image of her face began to lose focus. He got the shape of her head, the eyes, her nose—but his strokes began to fumble. He wasn't an artist.

He tried to make her stay, staring at the crude image.

Carefully, he tore it out of the notebook, folded it, and put it in his wallet. He pulled out the other sheet, in pink. Paying a lot more attention this time, he re-read the details about the new girl.

Could my dream girl be Agatha?

There were significant differences, but were they distortions of the dream, or a disguise she wore?

Long after the details of his dream girl's image faded, he could still feel the echoes of their love. That was alway what lingered.

The dreams had been coming for a long time, years. Nearly always the same one. *Were there others?* Memories of dreams were always tricky things. He'd thought he had several, but could some of those memories have just been dreams about dreams?

He'd constructed a bigger memory. The two of them, lovers, waiting for a dawn that could destroy the both of them. But how much of that was conjecture? How much was really in the dream?

Hadn't she said, "This is how the world is supposed to be." Something like that. What if she was Agatha? What if she had the same dream? She'd know that that moment was pre-ordained, that they were destined to meet it together. It sounded like something Agatha would say.

But he could be making stuff up again.

He put both pieces of paper back in his wallet.

. . .

"How did your date with Candi go?" Sam clapped Jason on the back as they met in the hallway Monday.

He looked around, with a tense grin on his face. "She's got another puppy on the leash."

"Already?"

He nodded. "She bailed on the double-date. I hear she's gotten real intense with Abe Harris over the weekend. No details, but poor Abe's gotta funny smile on his face this morning."

"Should someone warn him?"

"I don't think he's listening right now."

. . .

On the walkway between the cafeteria and Foster Hall, Agatha briefly matched pace with Charlie.

"Progress?" he asked.

"I don't know. We're talking. But it's not at all like I imagined it."

"He didn't immediately fall to his knees and propose?"

"That's not it. We just talk a different language. He's a lot like you, all logic and science."

"We get along okay," he protested.

"We've had years to discover each other. It wasn't easy, if you recall."

"Don't I! Well, later."

They took different routes. Charlie walked into the entrance and turned to the left.

Sam was waiting for him.

"We need to talk."

Charlie looked surprised. "Do I know you?"

"Probably. I need to ask you about your sister."

He paused. "I don't have a sister. Only child."

Sam shook his head. "Agatha, Teri Perry. Whatever her name is. I see you two talk from time to time." He looked carefully at the read-haired guy. "The features are too close. You have to be related."

Charlie shook his head. "No, I'm afraid you've got it all wrong. Different last names and everything. I know Agatha. I don't deny that. But I only met her a few years ago here at school."

Sam was still skeptical. "I know what I see."

"Here." Charlie fished out his driver's license. "See. Charles Whittacker. I live over on Terrace Avenue. I think she lives on Boulder."

Sam handed it back. "Same birthday, I see. Fraternal twins?"

Charlie winced, and then glanced down the hallway. Classes were nearly starting, and no one was in hearing range. "This is our secret. No one has guessed, not in all these years. Not our parents, no one. I'll talk, but later, in private."

Sam nodded. "Fine. I'm not trying to cause trouble."

Then he scribbled a number on a scrap of paper. "Text me when you can talk."

Charlie waited in the hallway as Sam made his way to class.

Agatha appeared around the corner, silent as a ghost. "Believe me now?"

"Yes. How could he have known?"

"He's probably seeing our auras, even if he's not conscious of it. Believe me, I don't look anything like you."

He sighed. "The time really is approaching, isn't it?"

Her smile faded. "Yes. But I'm at peace with it. It's how the world is supposed to be."

"I'm not so sure."

. . .

Sam was on autopilot through all his classes. He checked his cell for missed messages several times an hour. He pulled the papers out of his wallet when he could and stared at their messages. He had to make sense of Charlie.

That Agatha had a brother was no real shock. Lots of people had brothers. That she had a red-haired brother knocked big holes in his doubts about her and his red-haired dream girl.

It was the last puzzle-piece. Agatha was a real life, breathing confirmation that his dreams all these years could be more than just a reflection of teen guy hormones. It made the love he'd been feeling tangible, something more than nighttime sex dreams. If she were real, that love was real too.

Inexplicable, with their current history, but a real anchor, there in the future, for him to grab and hold.

Every time he talked with her, she felt more familiar, more like an old love, met again.

Charlie had been a rude intrusion. Fantasy romance dreams had little place for 'the other guy'. He'd seen their meetings. Elusive encounters, a few words passed as stranger's paths crossed in the hallways. They never looked at each other. They were hiding something.

The sour thought that they were secret lovers, and that Agatha's performance was a role to make him dance for her amusement had come and gone. It was a logical enough speculation. High school entanglements could be Machiavellian in their depth, but other than his brief observations, their relationship had just been a guess.

Only seeing them walking together, fresh after staring at his sketch, made pieces fall into place. But even now, with a semi-confession out of Charlie, Sam needed more information, more evidence.

His phone vibrated.

Meet after classes. Star cafe.

He didn't know the place. He hit the search engine. It was twenty miles away, in the next town. A brief suspicion that he was being led to some kind of a trap flickered and vanished. So what. He needed to know what he was missing.

. . .

The cafe was a casual internet and coffee place, with lots of little tables and cozy nooks. Sam saw Charlie in a dark corner. There were three chairs.

He nodded. "She's on her way. She had to go home and borrow her parents car."

Sam sat and tried to read the guy's character from his face. There were secrets there, and sadness.

"What can you tell me about your sister?"

He laughed. "That's a wide-open question, isn't it?" He shrugged. "Besides, I'm under orders not to scare you off. She won't be long."

"Then tell me about you. Rumor has it that you're a math geek. Scholarships and fancy schools circling around, waiting for you to pick one."

He chuckled. "That's partly true. I am good at math."

Sam had a pen in his hand. It went tap, tap, tap against the tables edge. "How good?"

Charlie frowned. "What do you mean?"

Sam hesitated. "I have ... skills myself. Skills I've taken to hiding."

Charlie nodded. "I understand." He looked at the paintings on the walls, debating things in his head. "I'm very good. There are 6,776 square inches of artwork in this room, not counting framing and matting. You weigh about 231 pounds, given your dimensions and apparent muscle development. I never solve sudoku puzzles, because there's nothing to solve. The answers are immediately obvious. I've got notebooks hidden away, filled with math proofs, including a few I'll make public some time in the future when it makes tactical sense to build a reputation."

He shrugged. "Like I say, I'm good. What about you?"

Sam glanced around to make sure, again, that no one was listening. "I've memorized the chess play books. I know all the openings, the middle games, the endings. If I turned myself loose at tournaments, I could be internationally ranked in short order. I'm not brilliant, but I'm formidable. I read my textbooks once at the beginning of the year, and after that, I use them as props, pretending to do homework. Anything I've ever read, I still retain."

He sighed. "The only things I struggle to remember are my dreams."

"Dreams? Like visions?"

The question was unanswered, as both turned in their chairs at the same moment to watch a car drive up in the parking lot.

"She's here."

And a moment later, a figure in black came in carrying a tote bag. She saw them, but gave no sign other than by walking straight to their table.

She smiled at them, timidly. "Both my guys. I guess you've been talking, so it's my turn to ask questions. Sam, how did you guess Charlie was my brother?"

He pulled out a sheet of paper and unfolded it. "I sketched this upon waking from a dream. A dream I've been having for years."

He tapped features with his pen. "The eyes are yours. You two have the same nose. And the girl in my dreams has bright red hair—the same shade as his. When you walk together, you move with some of the same mannerisms. Finding out that you had the same birthday was just icing on the cake."

Charlie muttered, "So much for your theory that he was seeing my aura."

"Don't be so sure." She picked up the sketch. "That's very short hair."

Sam nodded. "Yeah. But that's how she...you, looked." He swallowed. "The dream event is very short, the same way every time. I don't know any details of what's happening. But we're in the country, and it's dawn."

She nodded. "We're in each other's arms. I know. I've seen it. I just never looked at my own hair."

She set it down and dug into her bag. She pulled out a mirror and began wiping her face clear of dark eye makeup.

· · ·

"I knew there was a guy out there in the world, waiting for me. I've known since I was ten. But the details were always fuzzy." She talked around the mirror.

Sam was fascinated as she struggled to change her image right in front of him.

She looked at her brother, "When I saw Charlie for the first time, I thought it was him. I mean, he had the right aura. We clicked right off."

Charlie grumbled, "Lucky we were only what, thirteen, at the time? No chance for any sticky romantic issues before we discovered the truth."

She smiled at him, "Well, romance at thirteen is a very different thing than at eighteen. I thought you were quite romantic."

Charlie turned to Sam. "The birthday thing was a big red flag. I have always known that I was adopted. My folks told me at an early age that my birth mother died in childbirth. I was placed straight out of the hospital."

She added, "But I didn't know that. And I was resistant to the idea."

"But since it wasn't a secret to me, I could track back to the hospital records easily and a little sleuthing showed that I was one of a pair."

She was sweeping her hair back in a tight ponytail. "I asked a few leading questions, and finally got the truth. My folks were afraid I'd start one of those quests to find my 'real' parents, but I already knew the truth. A single mother who died in childbirth doesn't lead to many happy reunions. And I'd already found my brother."

Charlie opened a notebook. "I cashed in a couple of bonds from my college fund and had both our DNA tested, once we noticed just how odd we both were."

She chuckled. "He was thinking we were aliens or something, with a mysterious father somewhere."

He spread out the sheets on the table. "But it turns out there's nothing unusual with either of us. Siblings, of course. Mainly Irish, with a little Cherokee from a couple of generations back."

She picked up Sam's hand. "We thought that our talents—his math and my intuition—were just a hand me down from our parents. And now, there's you."

...

He nodded, intensely conscious of the warmth of her fingers, and the softness of her skin. With her face cleared of the dark makeup, she looked so much the image of his dream girl. He tingled all over, like echoes of the love in his dream.

He cleared his throat. "My family was from Kent, with German and Danish influences, according to Dad's family tree software. And photos of him when he was my age look practically identical to me, so I have no doubts there."

"But you have ... talents?"

"Yes, I was talking about that with Charlie before you showed. Excellent memory, analytical skills. A good IQ, for whatever that's worth. And I've had dreams."

She nodded, taking another look at the sketch on the table. "Prophetic dreams. And I contend you are probably seeing auras, but not recognizing them as such. When did you first notice Charlie, and why?"

He thought back. "At a pep rally. Why do you ask?"

"Why did you notice him in particular?"

"Ah, he sat beside you, then went away."

"What about the guy who sat on the other side of me?"

He tried to remember. "No clue."

She nodded. "For no obvious reason, you picked Charlie out of a crowd. For no obvious reason, you were particularly aware of him, even when we just passed in the halls. And for trivial reasons, you accosted a guy you'd never met and demanded to know about a sister that you had no logical reason for knowing about."

"Well, it so happens that..."

She raised her hand to silence his objection. "Why did you start to pay attention to me?"

"Well, you were staring at me all the time."

"All the time? I doubt that."

"I thought you were stalking me. Every where I turned, you were there, a black figure in the distance, watching me."

She nodded. "So, you were looking for me in every crowd, hunting for a glimpse of me."

"Well, you in your black outfit, you were hard to miss!"

"What about the six or seven other goth girls at school, who also wear black? Did you notice them?"

Sam frowned, trying to visualize. "I don't remember."

"You have excellent memory, but you didn't *see* them. You just saw me. It's what I've been trying to tell Charlie all this time. You do sense auras. You just don't realize it. It's like a subconscious neon sign hovering around him and me, pointing us out in a crowd of thousands of people.

"And we sense the same thing about you."

Charlie grumbled again. "She sees it. I know what she's talking about, but I don't *see* them either."

Sam asked, "So your talent? I assume you're seeing more stuff in auras than what we're experiencing?"

She smiled. "Oh so much more! I see auras on everyone, not just you guys. I even see auras around buildings. I could tell when the school billboard was due to blow down, remember Charlie?"

"A month before it happened. I'm not willing to call that a prediction. You just saw that it was weak."

"Well, interpretation is the thing. I've made my share of bad calls. Some things are clear as can be. Others are just indications."

She leaned towards Sam. "We are meant to be together. And that's as clear as it comes."

He nodded. "I'd say the same." And he meant it. Doubts were vanishing by the minute.

Charlie cleared his throat. "Romance is all very well, but it gets us no closer to solving our main mystery. Why are we different? What made us this way? And is there a purpose to all this?"

She laughed like a crystal bell, "That's Charlie grumbling about my world view. How is Sandra doing these days?"

"Sandy is doing just fine. Not an aura or vision in sight. She's an 'A' student due to her own hard work."

She smiled fondly at her brother. "Are you treating her well?"

"Dinner last Saturday night cost me $120. And she likes me for my sense of humor more than for my math skills, thank you very much."

She turned to Sam. "And yes, I did check out her aura before I gave my blessing. She's a good soul that worries about my goth phase." She looked down at her outfit.

"Pardon me guys. I'll be back in a minute."

...

Sam looked at the guy across the table. Whether her claim of destiny was true or not, the idea that she was his mate felt wonderful now. But that made him... "I guess you'll be a *de facto* brother-in-law. *De jure* as soon as I can swing it."

Charlie was still gloomy. "Propose to her, not to me. She can check out my girlfriends, but I have no say of what she does, or who she likes."

Sam nodded. "Do you have any ideas about the 'main mystery'? Sounds like you've been thinking about it for a long time."

"Aliens. I don't know who or why. And if they're responsible for my birth mother's death, they have a lot of explaining to do."

"Not a fan of spirits or angels?"

"No."

Sam tapped the table again. "And I'm not a fan of random happenstance. There's something driving this pattern of events."

She came back out of the ladies' bathroom changed.

The black dress was poking out of the top of her tote bag. She was wearing a pink light-weight garment that was probably an underwear slip or something, but with a belt and an attitude it was as decent as other clothes Sam had seen girls wearing at the mall.

She dropped a big bundle of severed black hair on the table and shook her radically shorter remaining tresses. "I've been dying these black so long, it's going to be strange to go back to red. But I'll have to visit a hair salon to get it cut closer."

She grinned and her eyes sparkled at the effect she was having. "Agatha's days are over." She took Sam's hands.

"Charlie probably told you about his math puzzle things—how he doesn't solve them, the answers are just *there*. Well, that's how I see life. I don't question your prophetic dream—our prophetic dreams. They just are. That's just how the world is supposed to be.

"So in the morning, at school, I want us to be a couple. It's time. We don't need elaborate cover stories for our friends. Are you okay with that?"

"Yes I am."

"And it's Teri, from now on."

He nodded. He wished he'd remembered a ring in his dreams, but there hadn't been one. He had no more doubts. She was the girl he'd loved for years. "From now on. You and me."

She smiled, suddenly timid. Then she abruptly dropped his hands and grabbed her bag. "But I have to go now! The transformation has to be complete before all the shops close."

He snagged her free hand and pulled her to a kiss.

She brushed at her head, where there would have been hair. Another timid smile, and she was off.

Sam stood up. He picked up her discarded hair and began stuffing it into his bag. "I guess I'll go too."

Charlie reached out and gripped his wrist like a vise. "Sit back down. There's some things you need to know."

. . .

He had trouble looking Sam in the eye. His mouth was a grim line. He was testing lines, ways of saying what had to be said.

"If I weren't such a wimp, I'd knock you over the head and sink your Jeep in the lake."

"What?" Sam couldn't understand the abrupt change in attitude.

Charlie leaned across the table.

"My sister has visions. And they're nearly always right. I've been around long enough to believe what she says."

Sam nodded.

"Well, a while back, maybe two or three years ago, her visions of you started to get clearer. She could see the two of you, together, and it was a bit more intimate than just holding hands."

Sam didn't have to acknowledge that. In his dream, they'd been wrapped together so tightly there'd been no doubt.

"So, she knows you're destined to be lovers, and she could sense her love for you and yours for her. Every girl's dream, right?"

"Now here's part two. The two of you are swept up in some danger. There's a brilliant flash of light, and then...nothing. She believes, and I have to think she's right, that she finds her love, has a night of passion, and then dies."

His fist hit the table, still not able to look at Sam. "I really, really hate this Romeo and Juliet tragedy stuff. And I should just get rid of you. Make the vision not come true."

Sam was struck silent. His mind raced back over all the times he'd lived that dream. Yes, there was the dawn. She realized it was time. He felt the danger, and she tried to comfort him with her fatalistic belief. *This is how the world is supposed to be.*

Charlie was watching him. "Your dream, how does it go? And skip the icky parts."

He told him. "But mine ends before any flash of light—before the danger hits. Why does she think she dies?"

"Because there are no more dreams past that point in her life. She's had prophetic dreams all her life, and they've come true. Things she's experienced alone, and some that I've been in. They always come true!

"And then, the flash of light, and that's the end of them."

Charlie put his face into his hands and stared into nothing in particular. "She'd been thinking about it a lot. That one last dream was pretty much the climax of her life. And she accepted that there was nothing for her past that point."

He looked him in the eye. "She went kinda off-balance for a little while. She changed her name. 'Agatha', because she thought it meant 'death'. She started dressing in black, and died her hair to match her mother's. Some of the goth stuff was just theatrics, but it became her life, something to hold onto. She became death as an armor against her own."

He brushed some of the black hairs from the table.

"But you're here now, for real, and she's decided it is time for the final act. You saw her—she just killed 'Agatha' without a hint of regret because your sketch showed her in red hair and no eye makeup. She'll dive right into her romantic vision and smile into the face of death as it comes for her."

Charlie sighed. "I'd fight her over it, but you see—I'm not in that dream, just you two. She'd just kick me aside and go on with her destiny anyway.

"You see why I'm tempted to get rid of you—to spoil the vision."

Sam nodded. "She doesn't die in my dream. I won't let that happen."

. . .

He pulled the Jeep into the driveway, went inside and turned off the TV.

"Hey, I was watching...," his father complained.

"In the kitchen. Family meeting."

He found his mother cooking. He turned off the stove.

"Everything can wait."

His parents settled around the kitchen table. "This had better be good."

Sam remained standing. "Dad, I need to see my birth certificate."

He frowned. "Well, I'm not sure. I haven't seen it around in a long time."

Sam shook his head. "I don't buy it. Half the house is filled with filing cabinets. It was a joke when we moved. You know right where it is. I need to see it."

His mother asked, "Why?"

He took a deep breath. "Because I have reason to suspect that my birth mother may have died." His parents exchanged glances.

"Well that's ridiculous. I'm your mother."

He put his hand on her shoulder. "It's okay, Mom. It's really okay. I just have a critical need to know. A look at the birth certificate would put my worries to rest, now wouldn't it?"

She looked at her husband. The wordless moment grew long.

He sighed, "Okay, I'll get it."

The document spelled it out. Three months before Teri was born, Ginger Delany gave birth to Samuel, but it was only signed by the father. The mother's signature line had been labeled DIED IN CHILDBIRTH.

Sam's Mom's name was Elizabeth.

He pulled up a chair and sat down between them. His eyes welled up and he felt crushed, over a woman he hadn't known existed.

"I'm sorry, Sam. I didn't mean to hide it from you. I just thought, when you were older, it would be better."

"It's okay, Dad. Mom. I'm not angry. I'm confused, but I'll get over it. Can you...can you tell me what happened, medically?"

He shook his head. "I was in the room. It was as normal as it could get. She started having contractions and we went to the hospital. We had a bag packed and everything. It was all clockwork, until her water broke. Suddenly, she was in terrible distress. They rushed her into the delivery room for an emergency C-section. You came out fine, but her heart had just stopped. The doctors didn't know anything.

"Your grandmother Doris came in from Denver to help me out, and Lizzie here, her neighbor, came with her. She was in pre med, and was practically your mother from the first week on. I was a wreck, and she pulled me out of it, too. We were married before you were six months old."

What happened to me is the same thing that happened to Charlie and Teri. Something killed our mothers.

He straightened up. Everybody's eyes were wet. It was a family tragedy, and he'd brought it out into the open.

"I'm sorry I was so...abrupt. Sometimes I know things, dreams and intuition. Some things happened today and I just had to know for sure."

"It's okay, son."

"Mom, did I ruin supper?"

She tossed down a wash towel she'd been twisting in her hands. "No, but I'm a wreck. Bud, call for a pizza."

...

Teri Perry was the sensation of the day at school. The hair dresser had trimmed her hair down to nearly the scalp before they'd gotten rid of all the black. With a bright, light, and short dress and makeup that made the most of a cheery smile, everyone wanted to come see the creature formerly known as Agatha.

Sam was there every instant he could shake free of classes, making known his claim. Charlie joined them for lunch.

"How did your mother take your transformation?" he'd asked her.

Teri smiled. "I think she was relieved. When I went goth, she'd expected it to last only a month or so. And she knew I've been worried about something lately."

Sam asked, "Are you ready to tell her about me?"

She shook her head. "Too many questions to deal with right now. And I don't want to waste the time we have."

Charlie exchanged a look with Sam.

He changed the subject. "Guys, I have news. It seems my mother died in childbirth."

"When was this?" Charlie asked.

"Three months before you guys were born, and in Kansas City."

Teri squeezed his hand. "So you didn't know."

"Nope. I had no clue. Mom and I have some re-bonding to do. I have to convince her I feel the same as before."

Charlie asked, "Do you?"

"Pretty much. It's that strange woman who had plans for my future that she never saw that I'm conflicted over. Who was Ginger Delany?"

He quit rambling when he realized his thoughts were drifting too close to his own future worries for comfort. What was Teri thinking? How do you live your life when you don't really believe you'll have a future?

...

They were sitting on the hood of his Jeep the parking lot after the last bell.

She watched the other students walk by. Some waved, many looked, and some weren't sure who she was.

"Sam. How short is my hair, compared to your dream?"

He took a careful look, running the tips of his fingers through the fine stubble. "It's pretty close."

She leaned closer, her eyes shut, as he touched her. "Sam, if I asked, would you run away with me."

"Yes." He didn't think before he said it. "Why?"

Her brown eyes opened close to his. Every breath included her perfume. "Because I don't think we have much time."

He nodded. "Charlie told me your worries. I don't share them."

"He's tried to convince me the world is nothing but sunshine and roses, too. I tend to believe the world I see."

"So you think the world is going to end today?"

"My world, and at dawn." Her voice had a slight waver.

"And if it's not?"

She smiled sadly. "The hair length was just confirmation. I've been feeling it coming for months. It's like the auras. When you see the dawn getting brighter, you know the sun is coming, whether you're ready for it or not."

Henry's Stories: Volume 1

She gripped his arm. "Sam, I can feel the minutes slipping away. We only have hours left to us. We will be in that field at dawn. And you will be loving me."

He couldn't deny her. "I have one requirement."

"What is that?"

"We stop by the county clerk's office on the way out of town."

. . .

She had planned ahead. Her mother thought she was going to study with friends. She had no luggage, no books. "I won't need them."

Beautifully timid at the clerks office as they applied for their marriage license, she kissed him for the gesture. Sam grumbled mightily at the 72 hour waiting period. "I don't believe I'll ever get to see this filled out," she held the paper in her hand, "but I love it."

A stop at a Walmart for a night's snacks and a sleeping bag, and they hit the road.

"Do you know where we're going?"

She shook her head and giggled, "And I don't care! Wherever we stop will be the right place."

Her euphoria was contagious. "The last time I drove blindly across the countryside, it was a much different situation."

"The other girl." She nodded.

"What do you know about that?"

"The night you cried on the mountain." She struck a dramatic pose, like one of the silent actresses with her head back and the tips of her fingers to her forehead. "She...Sue?"

"Susan."

"She abandoned you. Broke your heart."

He nodded. "But it's better now."

She giggled and wrapped her arms around him as he drove.

"Hey! I don't want to have an accident."

"We won't. We don't die until dawn, remember."

He let his breath out through his teeth in exasperation.

"I won't let you die."

She gave a long sigh. "I love you."

"And I love you."

110

"So find a place to stop already."

He nodded and took the next turn and he started taking alternate rights and lefts as they meandered far from the highway.

"Turn off my cell phone. Yours too." He suggested.

"GPS tracking?"

"Right. I think we want to be unfindable."

She dug into his pocket and took longer to find it than was actually necessary. But she brought it out and found the way to turn it all the way off. She did the same with hers.

"Oh, Sam! Look!"

There was a little rural campground complete with a bathroom, and in the distance was a low ridge. He recognized it instantly from his dreams. This was the place.

. . .

They had the grounds to themselves, and he had a campfire going before the stars came out. He toasted marshmallows, and soon she was licking sticky blackened sugar off her fingers.

He leaned up against a rock and stared at the stars.

"Whatcha thinking about?"

He smiled. "I've got a buddy. Bill, back in Wilmington. I've grown up with him, practically. I've even asked his advice when I met you. I was wondering what he would think about me now."

"What advice did he give?"

"'Give the goth girl a closer look.'"

She chuckled. "Well, let him know...." She winced and shook her head.

"What?"

"I've got to stop thinking about the future. It's a bad habit."

"Come here." He patted the rock next to him.

She sat down on his lap instead.

He put protective arms around her. He could feel all the tension leak out of her body. He planted a kiss on her head.

"I'm a horrible person."

He kissed her again. "I differ."

"Whatever is coming in the morning. It could kill you, too. I should never have begged you to be here."

"Silly. It was in the dream. Both our dreams. If these things are as immutable as you say, then there was nothing you could have done to keep me away."

"But I should have tried!"

"Table all regrets until tomorrow. Tomorrow at noon. I'll listen then."

She was quiet for a bit. "Sam?"

"Yes."

"If you were going to die tomorrow, what would you do tonight?"

"Just hypothetically?"

"Yes."

"I think I'd want to spend it proving to my wife how much I love her."

"Oh, you have a wife somewhere?"

"I've got a piece of paper somewhere—now where did I put that?"

"Not signed yet."

"Details, details. If God wants proof, I'll blame it on bureaucracy. I didn't *have* the stupid 72 hours from the moment I knew about your *dead*-line."

She slapped him playfully.

"Cut that out—Wife."

She sighed and her body tried to melt into his.

She mumbled too faintly for him to hear.

"What was that?"

"Oh, I was just trying it out. 'Teri Delany.' 'Teri Jo Delany.' It's got a nice rhythm. Not so choppy like 'Teri Perry'."

"I like the sound of it."

She shivered slightly.

"Getting cold."

"Well, the fire is turning to coals."

"We do have a sleeping bag."

"Yes, we do."

. . .

He found a spot near where he'd parked the Jeep where tents had been set up in the past. It was flat and had been cleared free of stones. And it had a clear view of the ridge they'd be seeing in the morning.

She hesitated, suddenly bashful, with a hand on her buttons.

He cleared his throat. "There were a couple of things I learned from my vision."

"Oh?"

"One was just how much I loved you. And the other was just how much I enjoyed the sight of your body in the morning."

"You got a good look, did you?"

"Not good enough."

She corrected the oversight.

He joined her in the sleeping bag. They clung to each other, desperate for an anchor of stability in a moment poised to fall over the edge into infinity. If he could have, he would have taken the high road, and waited out a chaste 72 hours. He did not have that option. The other choice was to give his wife so much joy and love that she wouldn't be able to fear the dawn.

Squeals of delight and other sounds echoed off the row of trees next to the campground while the stars above gave their silent approval.

. . .

Sam sniffed the dew on the sleeping bag. He pulled his head back in where a warm bundle of love had her legs twined with his.

"Still dark," he whispered.

She squirmed, mostly asleep.

I can't lose her. The idea that some danger could come out of the sky and blot out the most precious thing in his existence was impossible to grasp. But other impossibles had become real. He had to face it. The threat was too close. It was breathing down his neck.

He peered out. There was a hint of light to the east. And then, a streak of light crossed the sky in a fraction of a second. He flinched.

"Sam?"

"Nothing. Just a meteor."

There were meteor showers all year round, but his infallible memory didn't have a listing for this calendar slot. Still, sporadics could happen at any time. *It's okay. It's normal.*

Teri tugged at the padded fabric. "It's getting light."

"Not yet."

She put her hand on his chest. "Come back in here, just for a bit."

There was no time for more than kisses and caresses. Still in the tight warmth, they were soon slick with sweat.

She opened the zipper and folded the sleeping bag top half back to let in air.

He marveled at her bright face and felt like he could get lost again in those dark brown eyes. There was enough light to highlight her bright red hair, so short it was almost a skull cap.

Sam loved her so sharply he could barely breathe.

But this was so familiar, and the danger was *right out there* coming for her.

She smiled at him, joyous in the light of the dawn. "It's nearly time."

No. It can't be.

She locked her deep eyes on his and he could feel her love for him, trying to wash away his fears. "It's how the world is supposed to be."

I will not let you die.

He gripped her tighter. Her eyes widened, and all around them it got brighter and brighter. Behind his head, she was watching something coming at them.

There was an incredible flash, and a shock that shook his jaw with the force of his teeth clashing together.

For an instant, it seemed he was spread wide across time and space.

He collapsed, half draped across her.

. . .

He pulled in a great gasp, desperate for air. *It knocked me out.*

"Teri?"

Her body was warm, but she wasn't breathing.

"No!"

Memories of CPR diagrams flashed through his head. He opened the sleeping bag wide and heedless of the cool air on his skin. The cell phones were in the Jeep. Step one was always to call 9-1-1, but he couldn't think clearly enough to deal with that.

He tilted her head back and lifted her chin. Still no breathing. He breathed into her mouth twice, quickly.

With his hand in the center of her chest, he pushed down a couple of inches, counting.

After a thirty count, he breathed into her again a couple of times.

He was halfway through the second compression count when she slapped weakly at his hands.

"Teri?"

"Big heavy man. Back off."

He collapsed beside her.

She leaned her head his way. "Am I dead?"

"Not anymore."

She nodded. "Good."

They rested, side by side for a minute or two. He draped the cover back over them. When the silence dragged on, he checked her breathing again. She responded to his touch, but didn't wake up.

"Teri?"

She shifted position again, but kept her eyes closed.

He got to his feet and snagged his jeans out of the Jeep. He located his phone and called Charlie.

"Where are you?" a worried voice demanded. "Are you okay?"

"The thing happened. Nearly got the both of us, but I recovered and gave her CPR. She spoke, but I think she's still in shock. I need help."

"Okay. She's alive?"

"Yes. Alive and she griped at me for the CPR."

"Position?"

"Deliberately lost. Can you locate my cell?"

"Not quickly. Not without hacking the system."

"Okay. Pull up a map."

He talked Charlie to the exit he'd taken and the general direction he'd followed.

"Okay, I see your campsite on the map. It's marked."

"Good. Sandra there with you?"

"Yes, how did you know? Never mind. What do you want?"

"Tell her to bring some extra clothes for Teri. Something comfortable. She left with just the thing she had on in school."

He dressed the rest of the way and went back to sit with her.

. . .

It took over an hour, but Charlie pulled up in a SUV. He and Sandra got out.

Sam led them to where she slept. "It was like a massive electrical shock. I think she's okay, but she's having to adapt to what it did to her. See if you can wake her. Gently."

Charlie knelt down beside her. "Teri? It's Charlie. It's time to wake up now." She reacted. "Come on Teri. Don't be lazy. You're already late for school."

"Go 'way. Naked."

He chuckled, and stood up. "Sandy. Maybe you should try."

He walked a few paces away with Sam.

"What happened?"

"You were right all along. Aliens."

"What?"

Sam struggled for words.

"It was a space probe. They dumped it off in the cometary belt a long, long, long time ago. It eventually entered the inner Solar System and came in as a meteor. Only, one that was designed to download information into the first life form with a brain it could find. That was Teri and me."

"So they loaded you with info?"

Sam nodded. "Sort of. Only they were working blind. Their sensors knew there we had developed brains, but brains would still need to be modified to handle the download."

Charlie nodded slowly, taking it in.

Sam continued. "So the zap sent a ripple back through time to the moment when our brains were most adaptable and it made the alterations then, so that when the info dump arrived, the brain would be compatible.

"The zap was designed for just one brain, but since we were practically glued together, it got the both of us."

Charlie was gazing at the horizon, unfocused. "And so when Teri's zap got all the way back to the womb, where we were in close contact, it altered me as well."

Sam added cautiously, "But there was a flaw. Or maybe just a design limitation. When the zap attempted to jump to the host..."

"It killed our mothers."

"Right."

They looked back at the girls and then turned back. Sandy was helping Teri get dressed.

...

"I told you I wouldn't let you die."

The four of them sat in a cozy booth at a rural pancake house.

Teri was still a bit groggy. "I couldn't let myself believe. The visions. They stopped at this point." She leaned against him again.

"The prophetic visions weren't part of your skills. They were just a side effect of the zap moving back in time. It dragged memories, emotionally significant memories, back to an earlier part of your life. It did the same for me. Your other talents, like reading auras and sensing events that happened remotely, like my drive to the mountain, those are still active. They're probably even better, after the direct download."

Charlie muttered, "You seem pretty sure about all this."

Sam tapped his forehead. "Massive memory storage meet massive data download. I've got tons of new data."

"What kind of data?"

"An alien civilization's technology, for one."

"Like what?"

Sam looked around at the nearly empty diner. "Hand me a piece of paper."

Charlie produced a pocket notebook and ripped out a blank sheet.

Sam carefully folded a half-dozen creases and then rolled the paper into a tube. Pushing at the ends, it collapsed to nearly nothing. Sam looked around again, and then tugged the ends apart. The paper exploded in a flash of light, leaving nothing.

Sandra was wide eyed.

"What was that?"

"Fractal folding on a fibrous substrate. It folded all the way down to the molecule level. When I pulled it apart, the cellulose strands started moving faster than sound and were ruptured. Just one of thousands of things."

She shook her head. "I can't get my head around the whole twisted time concept. You there at the right spot at that campsite, just by chance, adapted since birth to handle the download, just *because* you were there?"

Teri added, "And don't forget that Sam and I were there at that exact spot *because* we'd fallen in love from the echos of the very love had caused us to be drawn together in the first place. There's a word I use a lot. Destiny."

Sandra looked nervously at Charlie. "Why are you all letting me in on this stuff?"

Sam smiled. "My upgrade gave me some aura sensing ability as well. I could see what Charlie and Teri had both seen long before. You have a good soul."

Teri leaned across the table. "Sandra, we need you. Our DNA is still human, but our minds are altered. You're the only 100% human we have. You're our anchor. You have to keep us grounded."

Charlie took her hand. "That's their reason. I need you to keep me from singing in public."

She giggled at a private memory. She started turning red.

Teri and Sam exchanged a puzzled look. What had Charlie been up to?

Charlie turned back to Sam, trying to get back on topic. "Technology was 'one thing'?"

"There are plans for a communication device. The math is beyond me."

"Beyond *you* maybe."

He nodded. "But it appears to be able to communicate across interstellar distances instantaneously. I think there's a community out there. We've been handed an invitation to join the conversation."

"I could only believe that from aliens who could send a pluripotent zap back through time."

"Right. But it looks big and probably very expensive."

"How expensive?"

"We'd need to pull a Google-like business startup. Use some of the alien technology to make a few billion dollars and fund the communicator project as an in-house project."

Charlie nodded. They could do that.

. . .

"Are you really okay?" Sam asked, after Charlie and Sandra had gone back to the SUV.

She nodded. "I was 'upgraded' too. It'll take me a while to get back on an even keel." She grinned. "But expect to be amazed and astonished."

"I already am." He kissed her hand. "Now if we can just manage a wedding ceremony without parents exploding. That might be harder than forming a billion dollar corporation."

"We can manage. I just hope Sandra can cope. We're probably the most dangerous people on the planet right now, without her."

Sam sighed. "Yeah, I know. You saw what I did with the paper? That's trivial. With just a few items..." He picked up a salt shaker and put a spoon beside it. "I could make a trigger that could set the oxygen and nitrogen in the atmosphere reacting with each other. "I'd need a piece of silver." He looked around to see of anyone was wearing any jewelry.

She took both his hands in hers. "But we don't need to do that."

The salt shaker lifted itself off the table and set itself in the condiments tray. The spoon slid itself back to the side of the table.

He smiled. "No. Not at all." He leaned over to kiss her. "Yes, we do need a keeper, don't we."

Teri interrupted the kiss. "Oh look!" She pushed aside the drapery.

Out in the parking lot, Charlie was down on one knee, holding Sandra's hand.

"Looks like we're all on the right course."

Bad Blood

What is good and what is bad can sometimes depend on what your wife makes of it.

Sprung! The bullet struck the side of the bus almost before the whoosh of the opening door had faded from his ears. Gavin Owen glanced up at the roof of the hardware store across the road. A rage that had been bubbling within him flared, focussing on the figure.

"That's enough of that!" He jumped down from the bus, pulled a 5mm Ruger pistol from his pocket and peppered the ledge above with the popping staccato of a full clip. The sniper had ducked out of sight, but the white puffs of pulverized brick where his shells struck gave him at least a hollow satisfaction.

A voice behind him intruded into his bad mood, "He'll keep his head down now."

Gavin looked back. Bento Gerret eased out of the bus door, giving him a smile. Behind his head, above the opening, there was a bare metal scar where the sniper's shell had struck. Inside, the bus driver was showing no interest at all. He knew better than to come out and check on it. Bus drivers were much more popular targets than mere passengers.

Bento patted him on the back as Gavin shifted the little pistol, as it grew hot, to his other hand. "I heard about your good fortune. I am proud for you. You will make our city proud. It will be a loss to the neighborhood when you emigrate. Remember us when you become a rich Martian landholder, eh?" Behind them, the bus closed its door and slid silently away on its rounds.

The scowl on Gavin's face deepened slightly, "What did you hear?"

Bento shrugged, "My wife—you know Belinda. She talks with your wife. I have heard about it all, the tests and the doctors. You must be proud that your company recommended you."

He nodded slightly. "It has been an interesting week. Your pardon, Anna will have heard the shots...."

Bento frowned, "Yes. I had better get to the house, too." He smiled and shrugged. "Wives, they worry."

Gavin's house was two blocks over from the bus stop. He replaced the clip in his pistol absently as he walked. His mind wasn't on the sniper. This was a border town, after all. And by now, the sporadic protests by the country to the south were becoming less passionate, more pro forma. It was clear that the settlement rights to Mars were going to stay where they were. Some countries were left out—so okay, they will get first crack at the next terraformed planet.

Gavin knew how slim was his little country's chances in the race to build a successful colony on Mars. The Premier had pulled many old debts to get the UA/CPI committee to give them enough of a quota to found a colony of their own.

But Bento's comment settled despair on his shoulders. Anna had spread the word. Everybody knew. Everyone expected them to go.

Anna's voice could be heard load and clear as he walked into the house. She was on the phone.

"...only one family. I was so proud of Gavin when he was selected. And of course it has been so exciting for us." She glanced up as he walked into the room. Her eyes dropped to the pocket in his coat where he had slipped his pistol. She turned back to the phone, "Judy, could I call you back? Gavin is just home." She listened intently, "Fine. Tomorrow then. Bye." She cancelled the call and turned a concerned eye to him, "Those shots? Was that you?"

He nodded, the frown still frozen on his face. "A sniper shot at the bus. I scared him off."

She reached for his coat and helped him out of it. Her eyes checked him over, to make sure he was unhurt. When he settled down into his chair, she glanced over at the phone, "Maybe I should call the store and tell Bart to take a cab home."

"Oh, give the phone a rest!" he snapped.

She put a hand on the back of his neck. "You have had a bad day?"

Gavin settled himself deeper into the chair, not looking at her. "Umm."

Brightly, she said, "Well, we eat in fifteen minutes. I have it almost done. Food will make you feel better."

He watched her walk into the kitchen. Just around the wall, he could see her shadow on the floor and hear the clank of pots and smell the scent of cheese beginning to bubble.

How do I tell her? What do I tell her? He gritted his teeth in frustration. *What do I do now?*

The federal officer had looked at him like one of the statues at the courthouse in town. For days, Gavin had been riding a rush of excitement. He couldn't believe his luck at being one of the three families in the whole city chosen for emigration to the new national colony on Mars.

He had been right.

The man in the green uniform had not softened the news. "The Federal Colonization Board has rejected your application for emigration."

Gavin had been speechless for a moment. "What do you mean? I was told that my family had been accepted. We are part of the city's quota."

The man's eyes didn't meet his. "The city's quota will be respected. Another family will be found."

Gavin's teeth gritted in remembrance. He had begged. "I don't understand. Why are we not acceptable? We were *selected*!"

"You were not selected by the FCB. There are certain criteria that must be met. There are certain skills needed by our colonists. The nation must be represented by the best."

He had been angry, "I was selected on the basis of *merit*. This wasn't a lottery. I was the top man in my division."

The federal man nodded, listening, but still rock firm. "You are the top man, in your field. But Martian colonists need skills other than drafting and layout experience. This is a different job, one that you have not been trained in. We have tested you, and your native skills in these matters do not measure up to the qualifying score. I am sorry, but the nation must be served."

"Then train me! I can learn these skills. I am an intelligent man. We must be allowed to go."

The longing for the far lands in the sky caught his breath. It was a new desire, not more than two years old. But he remembered the shows put out by the FCB as they built support for this great national effort—the scenes from the cool rugged mountains where new cities were being surveyed, the commentary on the type of agriculture the new farmers would be trying, sense of newness that came whenever he thought of his country's new colony.

He was stuck here, otherwise, in a marginally comfortable job, in a marginally pleasant neighborhood, where his boys would get a marginally adequate education and grow up to be just like him.

He hated his "okay" life. He wanted more—more challenge for himself, more potential for his kids. And this was the only way out.

"Check again," he had begged the cold man. "Maybe there is a mistake in the records."

Calmly, the man had done so, calling up a long scrolling display on a screen that Gavin could just barely see. For more than a minute, the words had rolled upwards, vanishing into nothingness at the top of the screen. He could make out the headings as they went by.

"Application." "Education." "Work History."

His heartbeat had jumped as "Testing Results" passed up the screen. He had held his breath, hoping that something would catch the eye of the cold-faced man and make him stop—make him review some little error in the testing results.

But the words moved on. He had felt his muscles turn to water. There was no error. He simply did not measure up. He was not good enough to be a colonist. Oh, he was good enough to make a living for his family—just not good enough to make a future for them.

He had stopped trying to read the screen when the man's finger did jab at the keys and did stop the scrolling. The federal man had frowned at the text for a moment, then still frowning, he had turned to Gavin. "There is an option. But you may turn me down."

But when Gavin heard the explanation, he didn't turn him down. He didn't accept either. He simply got angry. He yelled, and called the federal man and his agency "cold-hearted pigs", among other things.

The man's reply had been simple and scientific. He gave Gavin a day to make his decision.

But how do I explain it to Anna?

Anna came and called him to the table. The boys were out, which was a relief.

And she was right, food did help. The black depression which had grown around him yielded slowly to a warm stomach and his wife's easy chatter. He listened idly as she related how expensive things had gotten in the meat market and the poor condition of the fruit. He listened to the troubles of his friends, in more detail than he cared to know. It always disturbed him to know in what intimate detail his wife was party to other people's financial, health, and marital problems. He had a sick feeling that there were a dozen women who intimately knew his own troubles.

He cut her off when she began talking about an older lady's broken hip.

"Anna, I was told some bad news today."

She fell instantly silent. When it came time to listen, she turned her full attention to it. Perhaps, he mused, that is why so many people told her their problems.

"I had an interview with the Federal Colony Board officer. He reviewed our medical tests and discovered that you have diabetes."

Anna sat back in her chair, a puzzled look on her face. "I don't have diabetes. I am healthy. You know that."

Gavin put out a hand and waved down her objections, "Yes, yes I know you are healthy. It's not as if you had the disease outright. You just have the heredity for it. They did a gene-scan and one of the things they discovered was that you inherited the diabetes pattern. If you don't have it now, the chances are still very good that you will get it later on in your life.

"Bart and David have it too."

Anna was silent for a moment as she absorbed the news. Then her smile gradually came back. "Well, this is indeed bad news, but it is not terrible. We can have it fixed. Uncle Jason had diabetes. The doctor cured him. They fiddled with his DNA for a couple of months, then he was as good as new."

She noticed that her husband's frown had not gone away. She asked, "Is there more? Is there some problem with the colonization people. Will we have to wait until I get cured? Is that what is worrying you?"

Gavin was having trouble looking her in the face. He shook his head. "It's not that."

Anna sat back and asked, "Well what is it then?"

Gavin took a deep breath, and then another, his mind empty of the words he needed. He shook his head.

"Anna—they said we can't go."

She looked down at her lap. Quietly, she asked, "Is it … is it because of my diabetes that we can't go?"

Gavin reached across the table and grabbed her hand. He gave it a gentle squeeze. "No. It's not your fault at all. All those tests—they said I wouldn't make a good enough farmer or something. In spite of everything the company told us, their recommendation wasn't enough. I had to pass those stupid tests, and I failed."

Anna got up from the table and came around to where they could hug. "Isn't there something we can do? Maybe they can give us the test again. Maybe there was a mistake."

Gavin shook his head, "I tried that. I had the officer re-check our records right then. That is when he noticed the diabetes."

"Is there no hope at all?"

Gavin hesitated. *Better to keep it from her*, he thought.

"What is it?" Anna asked, sensing his turmoil. "Tell me or I'll tickle." She poked a finger at his ribs.

He shook his head, "No, it's nothing."

Quickly, he got up from the chair and stalked back to the bathroom. He could feel her eyes on him.

The door locked with a click. The bathroom was the only privacy in their tiny apartment. But the click sounded like the slam of a prison door. What future was there now? When the word got out, the stigma of failure would mark him for the rest of his life.

The kids, Anna, they would survive. But he would have to find another job. He knew the company. They were generous enough to the winners, but the losers were swept under the rug with never a backward glance. They would have to move.

It would be simpler to die. He startled himself with the thought, but quickly forced it back into the depths. *No matter how bad things get, I won't quit. I won't abandon my family.*

The doorknob clicked and Anna entered, screwdriver in hand, the one they used to bypass the lock when the kids locked themselves in.

She had a worried look on her face.

"You are keeping a secret," she accused. "You promised me you would never do that. Now tell."

He sighed, "Can't I keep any secrets from you?" He looked into her eyes. "No. I guess I never could."

He captured her fingers and explained. "The officer told me that while my scores didn't pass their qualifying level, there was one other way that we, as a family, could emigrate to the Martian colony.

"It seems that the colonization authority has decreed that a complete cross section of the human gene pool must be included in the colonization. If we lost spaceflight and Mars was cut off, they want to insure that no genetic trait would be lost because of too efficient screening of the colonists.

"He told me that we could go—if neither you nor the boys had corrective genetic reconstruction done.

"We can't cure you if we go. We can't go if you are cured."

"Oh."

"Yes, oh."

Anna frowned, "Why in the world do they want to keep a genetic *disease*? That makes no sense at all."

Gavin shook his head, "The way he explained it to me, there is some theory that there is a beneficial side effect. Diabetics may have a metabolism that could survive better than normal people under some famine conditions. I'm not sure I buy the theory."

"But the colony people do," Anna said quietly.

Gavin spoke firmly, "It makes us no difference! I'm not going to trade my family's health for an uncertain future."

"Did you tell the colony officer that we wouldn't go?"

"No, but I will. If it makes any difference. I bent his ears back good when he first suggested this."

"Maybe we should go."

Gavin looked carefully at his wife. "What do you mean? I meant it. We aren't going to trade away your health."

Anna shook her head, "I don't know. I am healthy. The boys are healthy. There are things you can do, diet things, that you can do to help prevent diabetes. We are warned, we can take precautions now. Disease doesn't scare me. Uncle Jason lived with it for years."

She looked into his eyes, "But that sniper scared me. This gun in your pocket scares me. The riots scare me. The boys' schools scare me. The look I see on your face when you come home from work each day, that scares me most of all.

"Call the colony man, right now. Let's go. I'll trade uncertain health for a future, any day."

"No!" he looked away, angrily. "I will not ride to Mars at the expense of you and the kids."

Anna squeezed his hand. "Gavin, you have no right to keep us from going. I will risk the diabetes. The Father Above knows I would do the same if it were cancer. And so would you.

"It isn't *our* future anymore. It is Bart's and David's. Maybe you and I can afford to take the safe life, but they can't. All Earth is falling apart. There is no other place they can go."

Gavin was silent for a moment. Then he nodded, and asked "But what about the disease?"

She shrugged, "I'll learn to cook differently. We'll tell them about the diabetes. They can be trained to take care of their health. As a family, we can adapt. We have to."

The phone rang. Anna automatically bounced up to get it.

"Hello? Oh, Belinda, I'm glad you called. Gavin? No. There's no problem."

She muted the line, and spoke to her husband, "It's Belinda. Bento was worried about you." She released the mute.

"Yes, we will be moving to the training camp in a month. No. In fact, the federal colony man told Gavin just today that we were really needed on Mars."

She gave her husband a wink and continued airily, "You see, they need our *genes*."

Coldseeker

Climate change is always on our minds. The Texas Panhandle region has always been dry, but it could get worse.

Ike Walker scowled as he approached the edge of the canyon. The hydrogen gauge was a whisker from the red line. If he missed old State Highway 207, he'd have to turn back to Plainview. His articulated crawler with six huge tires had no problem with the deep sand dunes that covered all of the Texas high plains, but the only way down into the deep canyon was via the ancient roadway, and the weathered asphalt was mostly covered.

It's a bad habit. I didn't need that sale. Hydrogen was the lifeblood of the farms he serviced. Wilson begged him for one more cylinder, and Ike had parted with his spare.

Down in the canyon, his generator would resupply his stock and recharge the crawler with no problem. *But I shouldn't cut into my safety margins.* One big dust storm, like last year, would leave him stranded.

Hot dry Texas winds shook the crawler, and the blowing sand hissed like a snake, removing a few more patches of paint from its sides.

Nothing unusual on the Weather satellites—just a normal spring day in the Texas Panhandle.

Navigation maps showed him in the middle of a lake. Ike gave it a fractional smile. The mismatch between the old charts and current day reality gave him perpetual amusement. Prior to the expansion of the Chihuahuan desert into all of the western and northern regions of Texas, there used to be wet-weather lakes all across the Caprock. The land was so flat that rain collected in any likely depression. There'd been thousands of these playa lakes that appeared regularly enough to make their way onto the maps of that time. Nameless, and isolated from creeks and streams, the collected water soaked into the ground or evaporated.

Gone forever now–rainfall here was no better than the Sahara–the depressions did nothing more than trap shifting sand.

Abruptly, the dune field ended. Ike slowed down. Broken slabs of asphalt ahead led down into the canyon.

He tapped the hydrogen gauge with a grin. It was downhill all the way to his generation station in Happy Canyon. He'd need its production. Tanglewood station had been underproducing and it wouldn't supply all the H2 he needed.

He'd been gone more than a year. The Claude oasis north of the canyon had dried up and its dozen inhabitants had abandoned their domes to the desert, shifting his delivery route west.

Tanks in Happy Canyon ought to be fully pressurized by now.

The crawler tilted, and the vehicle hummed as the electric motors in the wheels acted as generators, replenishing his staging batteries on the downhill slope.

Ike checked the map. It had been a two-lane highway in its prime, but part of the cliff-hugging road had collapsed. There was barely room for the crawler to scrape by the rocks.

Ike had to strap himself down on the worst parts, but at least the scenery was a change from the endless dunes.

A dry stream bed–"Prairie Dog Fork of the Red River" on the map– marked the bottom of the five mile wide canyon. At the southern end of his territory was another equally verbose obsolete watercourse, the "North Fork of the Double Mountain Fork of the Brazos River". Both were just growing patches of sand now, collecting sand runoff from the high plains above, just as they had collected water runoff in the days before the climate shifted.

There used to be a bridge here. Down under the sands now.

Happy Canyon was just a mile off. He turned the crawler west and followed the map's illusion of water, a crooked blue line.

Old Man Reuel had been a tough bargainer when he'd come through years ago, prospecting for cold spots. Ike had gotten six-percent deals for most of his sites, but the old hermit wouldn't budge for less than fifteen-percent, payment in electricity. He disdained Ike's offer to pay with food and store goods from town. It was a bad deal, but the high walls of Happy Canyon were perfect for a hydrogen station.

Reuel's homestead was shielded from both the morning and evening sun by the surrounding cliffs. Winds off the caprock blew steadily down the canyon. It was a perfect blend of coldtrap and windturbine sites. By the time Ike had set up the tubes and the generator, he had known the place would pay its way.

Happy Canyon was a tributary to the Palo Duro Canyon, and the lands above and below the caprock had been in Reuel's family for generations.

I wonder how the old coot is doing. For two years now, the hermit hadn't deigned to come out and say howdy when he made his pickups. If there hadn't been the flicker of laundry hanging on the line and a curl of smoke from the roof, he would've gone up to the house and checked on him.

But without an invitation, Reuel made it plain visitors were unwelcome.

Ike's crawler crested the rise, and the dry little homestead came into view. In the shadows to the north, the cluster of collection tubes stood like a monster pipe organ next to the whirling blades of the windturbine.

Ping! The ricochet of a rifle bullet off the sturdy hull of the crawler caught him by surprise. He'd been shot at before in this wilderness, but Happy Canyon was too remote for poachers.

He threw the tiller over to the side and sent the crawler back the way he had come. *Ping!* Another shot.

The hull was too tough to be bothered by simple rifle fire, but there were windows, and the antenna cowlings. The tires might be punctured, but it was unlikely.

What is wrong with the man?

At the bottom of the canyon, out of sight of the homestead, he pulled to a stop.

"Could it be poachers?" He had lost one generating station five years before when someone had tried to steal the H2, triggering a fire. They were long gone by the time he appeared, but the machinery had been melted well past recovery. It'd nearly destroyed his business, and it'd been worse for his customers. Without hydrogen one family had to give it up and leave.

He looked at the crawler's tank–not even enough gas to make it to Amarillo. Climbing back out of this canyon would be impossible on an empty tank.

I've cut it too fine. I need that H2.
How old was Reuel getting? Had he gotten senile?
I need to go check.

...

The dust helmet was an indulgence bought years ago, and then blessed many times since. He lived in the crawler, but he couldn't live in it twenty-four hours a day.

He topped off the helmet's little water supply and wiped the visor clear of dust. In a dustcoat, he would blend with the sand well enough, as long as the poachers didn't see him move. Had they followed? There'd been no more rifle shots.

Ike secured the door after him and headed up the slope.

He began sweating under the dustcoat immediately. *Stay in the shade.* Sunlight and bullets were both bad for his health.

The homestead looked besieged by the sand dunes upstream from it. The perpetual drift off the caprock was trying to make its way down the main channel, but Reuel or his ancestors had put a dam across the stream-bed. The water was gone, but sand had filled the cavity. A dome behind the house was partly engulfed by the dunes.

Ike took a closer look at his hydrogen station. It was downhill from the house, but the dunes were starting to collect there as well. *At least no sign of a fire.*

Motion—near the big loop where his crawler had turned around, some-one in camouflage was creeping downhill.

Ike was divided between the urge to go protect his crawler or to sneak a peek at the house and his generator.

Could Reuel be trapped? Or dead?

Keeping to the rocks, Ike made quick progress down towards the house. He fretted over the sound of every rock he dislodged.

The homestead had seen better days. There were signs of a barn, now collapsed, and fenceposts of a corral. The house itself was built into the side of the slope, with no rear wall visible. The dome was the same white spun-glass used on every farm for outbuildings and greenhouses.

Last time, there'd been signs of life. This time the only thing that moved was blowing sand.

He worked his way cautiously across to the house. It was dangerous, but he lifted the latch and quickly closed the door behind him.

"Reuel? Are you here? Mr. Reuel?"

The room was dark and the insulation muffled the sounds outside. There was a lightpipe by the door. Ike opened it, and sunlight brought the vague shapes into focus.

Sand piles had accumulated more than a foot deep next to the door. Furniture, tables, any flat surface was covered with a sheet of grit. There were no footprints.

The place had been deserted with the door open for some time. It had been abandoned abruptly. Old faded pictures still hung on the walls. A book lay face down on the couch. A dustcoat hung on a hook by the door.

That's Reuel's coat.

The room was as dry and dusty as the outside, but with the door closed, the air was still. A faint odor of death lingered in the room.

Ike stepped through the sand, towards the closed door at the rear. Dread slowed his progress more than unsteady footing. He reached for the doorknob. It had to be the bedroom.

Behind him, the door opened.

"Stop right there." It was a woman's voice, muffled.

He turned. A was rifle aimed at his chest. The owner was hidden behind dust gear.

"Get out of there! Right now!"

Ike nodded. "I was just..."

"Out!" she screamed.

He moved. She backed up slowly to let him exit. There was no chance to make a grab for the gun.

He trudged downhill, towards his crawler. His back itched. When he spared a look, she was twenty feet behind, pacing him.

"I just came for my hydrogen. I was worried about Mr. Reuel. We had a contract. I need my hydrogen."

"No."

"Really! I need it. I can't get out of the canyon without it."

They crested the rise and his crawler waited where he had left it.

"Get in and go away!" She was closer now.

He slowly turned to her. The rifle looked bigger, with it in his face.

"I don't have enough fuel to leave. Let me recharge my tanks from the generator and I'll be gone, out of your hair."

The muffled and wrapped head shook. "No. Just go away. Now." She shifted the aim of the rifle.

BANG. The sound was deafening, as the shell buzzed past his head. "Go now!"

He didn't argue. He pressed the key button in his pocket before he reached the step. Inside, he latched it behind him.

Low hydrogen or not, he started the motors and left the crazy woman behind him.

There were only two ways out. He could retrace his way back south and try to make Plainview or he could head north and follow the canyon across country towards Amarillo.

I don't have fuel enough for either one. There were solar cells on the top of the crawler, but they only produced enough juice for the lights and creature comforts inside. If he re-routed all that power to the staging batteries, he might make a hundred yards a day. Food and water would run out before he covered any ground.

I need that H2. Could he hide nearby and sneak back after nightfall and steal some of the small cylinders? He had a wheeled trolley, but once loaded it would be difficult to pull manually though the drifts.

Maybe I could contact the Marshals. The idea was odd. Most of the land around here was abandoned, officially on the Bureau of Land Management books, and considered a federal wasteland. Law enforcement was loose and the few people who lived here took care of themselves. Cities had been looted and left to decay in the sun.

I could give them a call, and wait here for the few days it would take them to show up. They could arrest her and I could get my hydrogen.

He stopped the crawler and turned on the phone.

NO SIGNAL. He frowned and drove ahead to a rise.

NO SIGNAL. Even if the satellite were low on the horizon, he should get something.

Ike went outside. Up on the roof. A simple white plastic blister had a starred hole in the side. A rifle shot.

Dumb luck, or did she know what she was doing. With the antenna out, there'd be no calls to the Marshals nor to anyone else for that matter.

I'm on my own. Friends and neighbors were flexible concepts when you lived alone on wheels, but there'd been a few people who'd respond if he called for help.

How far can I make it on foot? Who's closest? Amarillo wasn't terribly far by crawler, but days away on foot. His mind inventoried his food and water supplies.

I'm dead if I leave the crawler. He applied power to the wheels. No more wasted time. He had to get out of the canyon before the last of the hydrogen was gone.

Ike crossed the central sand field and began climbing north. *Don't stop and don't change speed except to adapt to the grade.* The hydrogen gauge redlined quickly. He was running on dregs.

Uphill grades burned energy. There were three levels of terrace, a giant's stair, between the bottom of the canyon and the caprock above. He was on the middle level, making good speed, when an ancient bridge over a nameless creek collapsed under his weight.

As the crawler overturned and started tumbling down the slope, a coffeepot struck him in the head.

...

Ike floated. The world was cool, and except for the rhythm of pain that echoed his heartbeat, nothing disturbed his rest.

The world was also wet. He waved his hand, and the caress of water shook him free of the haze in his mind. The headache doubled.

He blinked his eyes open. Water trickled noisily over stones. A fern grew from a clump of moss so green it didn't seem real.

There were eyes, watching him. Little round glistening eyes. Frog eyes, raised above its head like the antenna blister on his crawler.

The blister that had been shot.

Ike blinked again and tried to sit up. The frog took offense and jumped, lost immediately in the jungle of vegetation.

Pounding pain in his head sapped his strength. Ike settled back down, his head resting on something soft, half way into the water.

Where am I? He pulled his hand up where he could see it, out of the water. His fingers were wrinkled from long submersion. *I'm naked.* He checked his body. Aches and pains. Bruises.

The crawler overturned.

When he touched his aching head his fingertips were stained red. His head was sticky. A scab had formed, from his right temple nearly back to his ear.

He elbowed himself up to a sitting position. Water ran off his skin and he shivered.

What is this place? He couldn't tell its size. Vegetation obscured the view in all directions. Overhead was a uniform glow. *I can't be outdoors.*

A girl pushed through a canebrake, watching him from across the pool.

She was wrapped in a worn and frayed robe, bare feet stepping carefully on a cobblestone pathway. She was younger than he. Perhaps twenty-five?

Pale brown hair. Her face was smooth and unwrinkled, pretty in a simple way–a face that had never grown accustomed to cosmetics.

"You're awake," she said.

"My head is throbbing."

"A bad cut." Her eyes drifted away. He lifted his hand out of the water and she re-focussed on him. "You were dry. I put you here."

Ike asked, "You're the girl who shot at me?"

"I'm the only one here."

He suspected as much.

"Mr. Reuel? Is he dead?"

She looked away, upset. "He's in the house."

Ike eased back into the water. He was too weak to do anything else.

"How did you know I was in trouble?"

"I was watching you, with the binoculars. When you went over the side...." She shivered.

"Thank you for rescuing me."

Be polite now. Deal with the other issues later.

She just nodded, watching him. Then, she stepped into the pool, robe and all, keeping away from him. The steps went deep. The stress and worry on her face drifted away as she settled into the water up to her chin.

"I live here."

"This is inside the dome, right?"

She nodded, not making eye contact. She tolerated his presence, but her focus was on something else entirely.

She's a water sprite. This is her natural element. She's beautiful now.

The throb in his head just highlighted his unease. For two hermits, it was a far too intimate situation for comfort. He wished she would go away, and tell him where she put his clothes.

He shivered, and it wasn't from the water. *I might be stuck here.*

"My crawler. How badly damaged is it?"

"I don't know." Her voice skipped gently across the water. "The door was sprung. It looked pretty beat up."

"Do you have another vehicle? Something I could borrow long enough to reach town. I would bring it back once I got the crawler repaired."

"There is no other vehicle, no town."

He opened his mouth to argue the latter, but kept his silence. How long had she lived here? Was she even sane? She'd shot at him. Yet, she rescued him from the rollover.

She might want me alive, temporarily. I need some clothes. I don't want to end up in a meat locker. Nor as mulch for her garden as a discarded stud. There were stories of other isolated families gone insane. As a traveling salesman, he knew them all.

He shifted his position. "I'm going to get up. Where are my clothes?"

She looked as if she had been startled awake. "Behind you, up the path." She turned around and began leaving the pool. The robe, sodden wet, did little for her modesty. Ike had to force his attention away. He had to get up and out on his own, while she wasn't looking.

The effort made him dizzy. *How much blood did I lose?*

He was still on hands and knees by the time he got out of the water, but a creeper vine a couple of inches thick worked as a hand rail and he got unsteadily to his feet.

His clothes had been washed and were draped across a large flat rock. *Still damp. It's humid in here.* He dressed as quickly as he could.

The girl hadn't followed. He continued down the winding cobblestone pathway. The exterior double-door was in plain sight and he pushed through the little airlock and stood outside.

He could feel moisture evaporate from clothes and skin. Hot dry air stripped it away.

He staggered forward. The dome behind him was bigger than he'd thought. *It's her whole ecosystem, really.* It was her sole source for food. The water inside made life possible. How long had Reuel worked on it? Was she his daughter?

Little things clicked in his head. The cobblestone paths, the size of the vines, the animal life—it had been a self-contained habitat for decades at the least. Had they extracted the water from the aquifer before it had been drained?

Is it big enough to support me as well?

He shied away from that idea. *I need to get back to civilization. The hermit girl can have her frogs.*

He slogged through the dunes toward his generator. Several times, he stopped to catch his breath. The windturbine blades made their whoop-whoop-whoop overhead—a comforting sound. Generations of design had produced an electric generator that could run years with no maintenance, even in these dusty winds. He'd hauled this one out on his crawler, those long years ago, and set it up himself. Reuel watched, but had no interest in helping.

Not that he didn't take his quota of electricity. Rural power lines were long gone, and photocells degraded over time in the eroding winds. Power was still needed.

The generator looked in good shape. He punched the lock code and entered. Clean metal and glass shone from the reflection of the overhead lights. Electricity was nominal. The coldtraps were running down near freezing. The wind channels were closed, since it was daytime, but as soon as the sun went down, they would spring open, routing air to the coldtraps to be stripped of what little moisture it had. The trickle of pure water would run down to the separators where electricity would split the hydrogen and oxygen.

And the H2 would be adsorbed by the carbon nanotubes in the cluster of removable storage tanks all ready to be shipped to the customer.

Ike tapped the hydrogen gauge. It read empty. He thumped it again. No change.

There was no hydrogen in the tanks.

His hammering heartbeat sent spikes of pain to his head.

Frantically, he started rechecking all the readings from the beginning.

Yes, the coldtrap tubes were working. As recently as last night, the roman-guards had opened, exposing the interior of the tubes to the intense cold of outer space. Aligned like telescopes to a narrow band of the sky, the tubes only let heat out, never in. Regulating circuitry took every opportunity to let heat escape when the sky was cold, and closed the insulating roman-guard lids when there was any hint of warm cloud cover or daytime sky glow.

And yes, the wind pipes were still working, bringing measured loads of air down among the coldtraps to be scavenged of their moisture.

But the water storage tank was empty. Ike read the log files. The water tank had been empty for months.

Without water, there'd be no hydrogen.

Ike shook from weakness. He lurched out the door and began circling the facility. A dozen paces later he stopped.

The outer shield had a three-foot door cut into it with ragged edges. Someone took a hacksaw to it. The 'door' was secured shut by a large rock.

Ike pushed it aside and bent the door open. Inside a large washtub was capturing the drip-drip-drip of water from the severed outflow pipe.

She sabotaged it. No wonder she's living in a rain forest. She's stealing my water.

And no wonder she shot at him rather than let him discover what she had been doing.

I could kill her.

His first idea had been correct. She was a poacher, raiding his generator.

He turned back towards the house.

She was standing there, wrapped in her outside garb, facelessly watching him. This time there was no rifle.

"I could hear it. Tinkle tinkle. Day in and day out. Tinkle tinkle. Dad said 'Leave it alone. It's not ours.'" But then ... then he died. The deep well had nothing in it but salt. The plants were dying. The frogs had gone missing. You used to come. I watched you from the house. And then even you stopped coming.

"Tinkle tinkle. Tinkle tinkle. It was water. I knew it was water."

She turned and went back into the dome.

Ike sat down in the sand, too weak to continue. The anger drained out of him.

Survival. It's all about survival. She didn't know she would be snagging me here in this deathtrap with her.

. . .

"What's your name?" he asked, mainly to shake away the depression. His life had been wrecked, and maybe the livelihoods of the people who depended on him. More than anything, he ached to get back to his crawler, back to his routine. He couldn't abide being a potted plant in her garden. He had to be working.

There was one chore that nagged at him.

She looked startled at his question, and folded her arms around her in the water.

"Don't worry, I can't see anything." Much.

She looked up at him suspiciously. "Zip. My name is Zip."

He crouched down at the edge of the pool. Gently, he asked, "Well, Zip, I want to bury your father. Do you have any objections?"

She looked away, a hurt expression on her face.

"I couldn't find her," she said.

"Who? Who couldn't you find?"

"My mother. She's buried by the cottonwood, but it fell down and the sand covered it."

Wide eyed, she pled to be understood. "I looked. I dug. I took a pole and poked into the sand. I couldn't find her!" She burst into tears.

He couldn't take it. It was a mistake to get involved with a basket case, but he was a sucker for puppies and girls' tears. He kicked off his shoes and waded in to her. His hands, he knew they were rough and he winced to touch her soft skin, but he reached out to her and she curled up into the circle of his arms.

"It's okay, Zip. It's okay." He wanted to look to heaven for help, but all he could see was the dome overhead.

. . .

They decided on a stone crypt in the red clay sides of Happy Canyon. Old Man Reuel's body was mummified by the dry air. Zip stayed outside while Ike wrapped him in the sheets where he lay and carried him up to a ledge. Ike judged it would last long after the homestead was covered by the creeping sands.

"He'll have a good view over his land." It had been an idle thought, but Zip repeated it for days afterwards, murmuring it like a mantra.

The girl wasn't right in the head. He knew it, and knew enough to keep his distance. She only looked normal, even cheerful at times, as she tended her plants.

Ike watched her work. She must have spent her whole life tending the dome's ecosystem, and she was good at it. Some plants were cultivated, others were untouched. Several times she went out into the canyon to scrape minerals from the ancient red clay and folded the result into the dome's garden plots by hand.

She cared for more than just the plants.

One evening, he sat motionless near the pool. She swam up to the steep side, where boulders had been moved to the edge of the water and three frogs sat among the moss.

"Bobby, Joe, Mary. How would you like a bed-time story? You would?

"Well, once upon a time, there were three little pigs..."

She told the story well, acting out the scene with gestures, huffing and puffing with the big bad wolf, and giving distinctive voices to all the players.

The frogs were good listeners, tolerating her touch as she stroked each on the head and said her goodnights.

Ike held his breath as she climbed out of the pool and headed for her bed.

She's forgotten I'm here. He saw it in her expression, as time after time she was startled when he moved.

The nudity didn't have any sexual motive, he decided at last. She just didn't have any clothes. There were the dust wraps for outside. There was the robe, thin and torn, which she wore when she thought about it, and a work apron for when she tended her plants. None were new. Probably all had belonged to her mother.

...

"Zip, may I check in your house for...."

"No! There's nothing there. It's gone."

"But it's just...."

"It's gone. It's gone." She shook her head. "It's gone." Her eyes were focussed on the ground a few feet away as she mumbled it over and over.

In her head, it's gone. If I push, will she break?

Even at that instant, as concerned as he was for her mental health, the curve of her hip uncovered by the apron nagged at his male brain.

For Ike, there was no other choice. He had to avoid watching her, avoid being close to her.

Her routine was as regular and predictable as his had been before the crash. He'd spend his time outside, away from her disturbing appearance.

. . .

The crawler was very beat up, a two hour hike from the homestead.
How long did it take her to wheel me back on the trolley?

There didn't appear to be any damage to the power train. The front end of the crawler was on its side, but the drive wheels on the cargo end still touched ground.

I've been in worse positions. However, the batteries were drained and no fuel was left. Zip hadn't thought to turn off the engines.

Ike started a trickle charge from the roof cells, but the crawler was going nowhere without hydrogen.

He returned with foodpacks to suppliment Zip's carrots and bean sprouts. And a gift.

. . .

"Zip. This is for you."

She looked up from her garden, startled, when he spoke to her.

He held out his spare shirt, dark brown, with the "Walker Hydrofuel" logo on it.

She wiped her hands clean on her apron and took it. For a moment, she fingered the fabric and then ducked her head and dashed down the footpath.

Was that a blush? She does know about clothes.

She returned a few minutes later. The shirt was large enough to make a presentable dress for her. She even found a sash to belt it.

"Very nice, Zip. I'd like you to wear it for me."

She flashed a smile, and then dashed away again.

Another blush. We're making progress here.

. . .

It took days to repair the generator. The water pipe didn't take too long, but there'd been a leak in the hydrogen tanks, and purging the system had to be done carefully.

Ike didn't feel like rushing it. His strength was slowly recovering.

The Reuel homestead needed work too. The place was decaying under the daily attack of sun and sand.

She doesn't see this outside stuff. It isn't green and wet. Zip had abandoned the house to unpleasant memories and the dust.

Ike slept in the dome too, on cushions he'd scavenged from the house, on the opposite side of the dome from her screened-off bedroom. If she made a noise in the night, it took hours before he could get back to sleep.

It was more than just the disruption a hermit's comfortable silence. He dreamed about her. Sometimes she was a backward child. Other times she was more.

Often, all he could do was stare at the texture of the dome overhead and pretend she wasn't there. He needed to get the crawler back in service, but every day, between maintenance in the dome and his cronic weakness, he got little done on his own repairs.

. . .

The crack in the dome shook Ike out of his easy days.

He'd gone into the storage area to search Reuel's toolbox. There were no electric lights in that part of the dome, and the sand on the outside blocked the sunlight.

He found the toolbox and pulled it out into the open area where he could see. The box was filled with sand.

Not even Zip would be that careless with tools. Tools were priceless to the isolated. He went back into the darkened storage area and checked. All along a three foot fracture line, sand was spilling in like a hourglass.

Dunes had been building up against the dome for years and the weight was considerable. Spun-glass domes were strong, but they'd never been intended to be buried.

Ike grabbed a shovel and went outside.

. . .

Zip found him hours later. He was taking a break, his arms a useless mass of knots, his throat sore from the dryness.

"What are you doing?"

Ike looked up at the mountain of sand. He'd barely dented it. Every shovel removed caused more sand to drift in to replace it. The wind blew constantly here.

It was a lost cause. And it was death for Zip.

"Help me inside."

He stripped down to his pants and went into the water. Zip slipped out of her dress and waded in beside him, kneading his arms, working at the soreness.

"Zip. I need to take you away."

"No." She kept working.

"Seriously. You and I need to fix the crawler and go away to another place."

"This is our land. This is where we belong." Her voice was flat.

Ike wondered who she meant by 'we', but that wasn't important now.

"Zip. If you stay here, you'll die."

"Die? Like Daddy? Will you bury me on the hill?" She sounded no more concerned than if they had been discussing the carrots.

"No. Because if you die, I'll die too. There'll be no one to bury us."

She paused and then resumed her massage. "I will live here and die here and be buried with my ancestors."

Ike could almost hear the cadence of Old Man Reuel's voice. The old miser would take his daughter to the grave with him.

Ike clamped his teeth and pulled away from her out of the pool. He grabbed her arm and pulled her out of the water too.

Frightened, she reached for her dress to cover herself, but he had no patience.

"Come with me!" He dragged her, wet and naked, along the path that circled around towards the storage area.

As they approached her bedroom, her eyes got frantic and she tugged harder but to no effect. He pulled her into the darkened storage room and pressed her hand into the falling sand.

"It's coming, Zip. It's coming in, and nothing you can do will stop it. I can't stop it!"

She whimpered, kneeling in the sand. She understood what it meant, but he wanted to make sure she heard him.

"Bobby, Joe, and Mary will die when their pond dries up," he said. "All their tadpoles will die. Your gardens will die. You will die."

She was crying. "This is my land."

He gripped her arm again and roughly hauled her through the airlock to the painfully bright sunlight outside. She fell down onto the sand. The blowing sand stung his calloused skin. He could only imagine what it felt like to her.

"Look at it, Zip!" He turned her head towards the huge dune that had been growing up against her dome. "It'll get bigger, like a mouth that'll swallow your home and chew it to little pieces. It'll eat the dome. It'll eat the house. It'll eat the generator. Nothing can stop it!"

"My land...."

"Your land will kill you. It's rejected you."

Her wail was long and full of pain.

He knelt down beside her and pulled her into his arms.

Ike whispered into her ears. "The land is cruel, Zip. It hurts and it kills and it doesn't care!

"In your father's father's father's time, didn't they live up on top of the cliffs?"

She nodded, her head buried against his chest.

"Back then, land grew crops in the open air. Rain fell and watered them. If they needed more water, more was there, just under the ground.

"But the land changed, and your family abandoned it. They moved down here, where there was a spring, and a deep well."

She nodded again.

He pushed on, "Then the spring dried up. Even the cottonwood tree died. Your family abandoned their fields and grew crops inside the dome. Your deep well went bad and everything began to die.

"But you, dear Zip, you found a way to get more water. Your plants, your frogs, even you–all are alive because you found the cool water that brings life."

He brushed the sand from her face, carefully flicking it away from her watery eyes.

"The land is ancient, and it doesn't care about us. The sand wants to go to the streambed, and it will crush everything in its way.

"But you can find water again. You can save your life, save your plants, save your frogs. You can even save me. But, we'll have to leave this place!"

After a moment she nodded. "Yes, I understand."

He picked her up and took them back inside to wash off.

That night, he made her a bed beside his and ordered her to stay out of the dark side of the dome. He didn't know how long until the collapse. He was taking no chances.

She snuggled next to him all night long and he slept poorly.

Next morning he quit making tiny changes to his generator and began the serious job of filling the first tank.

By the end of the week, the crawler's wheels began to turn. Ike managed to walk the resilient vehicle out of its half-buried state while Zip watched from safety. He'd made just enough hydrogen to get it back to Happy Canyon where he could begin final repairs.

· · ·

"Do you want to say goodbye to your father?"

Zip tugged the strap tighter that secured the washtub to the inside of the cabin. Ike insisted they cover the top of the mobile frog pond with plastic sheeting, but he feared they'd have several spills and escapes before they made it back to Plainview.

"I've already said goodbye, to everything."

Ike nodded. He'd done his best to protect the generator. Once the dome collapsed, it wouldn't last another six months, but it was more important to secure their future than worry about the past.

"Zip, we are going to a town. Have you been to a town before?"

"No. Is it like a castle?"

He smiled. "It's a place where many people live. You will have to smile and be nice to many, many people."

She nodded. "And then we'll be married and live happily ever after."

He hadn't told her that. Another piece of her fairy tales. But he had been thinking about that himself.

"Well, I was going to ask you first, but yes, that's the idea."

"Good." She tapped the side of the washtub startling one of its inhabitants. She spoke to it, "And we'll find you a fairy princess to kiss."

Ike sighed and started the wheels turning. Old habits for two hermits would have to change. Life was going to be more interesting than just finding new cold spots and selling hydrogen.

He'd spent decades extacting the elements of life from the barrens. So had Zip. They were a good match.

She was awake now, and part of his life. He felt more alive than he had in years, too. *A good match.*

He could hear the water slosh. Zip held onto the tank with an enormous smile. She looked good in her Walker Hydrofuel shirt.

You know, I may want to change that logo. Drop the 'fuel'. There's more that we can provide than just 'fuel'.

Whatever the future held, Zip would need her water.

Forget It!

When I wrote this, back in 1977, a lot of computing was new. This same issue of the new computer magazine ROM had an article explaining a new-fangled concept called hypertext. The editor had seen another article by me and requested a story with a 'memory' theme. Getting a request was exciting to me, so I wrote this overnight, and so many of the predictions I made were so laughably wrong. Instead of the web as we know it, I envisioned something more like AOL or Compuserve, and instead of the Internet, I had the Tie-line, a cable TV derivative. Still, I predicted the copyright issues, and working tonight on my Mac, where my word processor saves all versions of everything, I wonder how soon Carlos' problem becomes more widespread.

Carlos Walker had the most thoughtful wife. He told her so while he shook the fancy wrapping paper free from the tiny package she had gotten him for his birthday.

It was a beautiful computer–a gold case on a gold watchband, with an elegant soft black display screen. Deb had been subjected to his wishing aloud for this model since they had hit the market, but he hadn't expected her actually to get him one. It must have done horrible things to her budget.

She may have been reading his mind, for she shushed him before he could ask, and handed him the instruction booklet. Then she rose to fix the cake.

Instructions. Oh, boy. Now I've gotta figure out how to work the thing.

He thumbed past the technical stuff, his eyes catching on the bold print... *baseplate is a block of electron-hole-pair holographic memory with a nearly unlimited capacity. Comptron guarantees that the memory cannot be filled in the lifetime of the original owner.... The thin-plate WPU.... accepts instructions in an expanding subset of 2012 REVISED U.N. STANDARD ENGLISH....*

The good stuff, the real operating instructions, Carlos found several pages later. He was pleased to see the boldface notice that the contents of the entire booklet, as well as a simple instruction course in operating the computer, were available in the computer's own memory at the call of a code word. He scanned the rest of the page which gave the voice-coding procedure, then set it aside.

He brought his arm before his face. "Computer, key to my voice."

"It is done." The computer's voice was male and very much like his own. The screen had displayed his own words in red and the computer's in blue.

"Display the index, please."

The little blue lines of data rolled up the screen tiny, but clearly readable. There were a lot of useful functions listed there.

Finally Carlos said, "Stop. Make a note of Deb's birthday, April 26, and be sure to notify me a week before then."

"It is done."

Carlos nodded and got up, pleased with himself. The odor of rich German chocolate cake was drifting into the room. *Maybe I'd better get it to remind me to stay on my diet–tomorrow.*

. . .

Fred Browell looked like a pet falcon perching over Carlos's shoulder as Carlos put his computer through its paces calculating the day of the week Fred was born on.

There was such a longing in Fred's voice when he finally sighed and said, "What I wouldn't give to be able to afford one of those."

"I hear the prices should be coming down some time next year."

Fred nodded, "But that's next year. The thing I have in mind has to be done now, or not at all."

"What's that?"

Fred looked uncomfortable. Carlos got the strong impression he hadn't meant to bring the subject up. Fred eyed the wrist-computer critically, then asked, "What kind of data-rate can it handle?"

Carlos shrugged and asked it. The display screen filled with technical specifications, while it vocally reviewed the high points. Fred listened carefully to the listing of the audio and visual band widths the device's sensory transducer arrays were capable of handling.

Fred frowned a moment in mental calculation, then asked, "Can you store video-to-memory at that rate?"

There was silence. A smile flickered across Carlos's face, and he repeated the question for Fred. The computer knew its master's voice.

"Yes. The data can be stored directly to memory, without processing. Detailed recall or processing at a slower rate can be handled later."

Fred mumbled to himself, grinning. Carlos could almost see the visions of kilobucks that were dancing before Fred's eyes. Nothing but money made Fred quite so gleeful.

Fred turned to him with a big grin and a slap on the back, "Carlos, my friend, how would you like to make a little spare change?"

"What's the deal?"

Fred glanced down the hallway. No one appeared to be taking any interest in the two of them. Fred eased around to where he could talk while keeping an eye on the people around them. When he spoke, his voice was considerably softer than usual.

"Have you used the National Index?"

"Of course." *Who hasn't. When every information file you need is right there on your Vidi terminal, why go anywhere else?*

"And what, my friend, do you find objectionable about our National Index?"

"Oh, not much—other than the constant file charges and those nuisance priority codes." Carlos hated those priority codes. Nothing was worse than knowing that the information you needed existed, just a keystroke away, and then not knowing the code to get at it.

Fred smiled knowingly. "Exactly, my friend. Have you ever paused to think how the information in the Index gets to your Vidi?"

"It's hooked to the Tieline. I suppose they send it out that."

"Right! And do you know how?"

"No."

Fred glanced down the hallway again. "I didn't either," he confessed, "until I ran across a notice in one of the restricted files I had to look up for Kordi. It said that due to unauthorized information taps on the NI system, they were going to transfer the information feed to an *unnumbered* channel." He paused for the significance of that to sink in." Thus, I assumed it was currently on a numbered channel. I looked for it, and I found it."

Fred slid into Carlos's desk seat and reached behind the Vidi terminal for the picture controls. With a little tweaking, he managed to roll the image half-way down the screen. Above the image, on one of the entertainment channels, was a dancing gray area.

"Raw file data. Constantly updating the holding memory in your Vidi. I think it is unscrambled as well. Your wrist-computer said it can store data faster than the Tie-line updates the NI. If you ordered it to record what it sees and you left it pointing at a Vidi screen set up like this for a few hours, you could have the whole National Index on your arm. For no charge, and with no restricted files. Some of the stuff would gradually get out of date, but a lot of it wouldn't." Fred eyed him significantly. "And I'm sure you might find a friend," he pointed to himself, "who would pay you to transfer a duplicate into his computer, when he finally can afford to buy one."

Carlos had to admit that it appealed to him. But he had some doubts. "It sounds illegal."

Fred frowned as he readjusted the Vidi, "I don't think so. The notice I saw implied that the NI people were making the change to comply with some kind of legal ruling. I'd bet it will be illegal, after they make the change. Besides, you can always erase the copy if we find out later that it's illegal."

Carlos chewed on his tongue; it was tempting. "Let me think about it."

"Don't think too long. They reprogram the network on the first of the month."

...

Carlos did a lot of thinking that night. The way Fred put it made the whole thing sound so easy. But he also remembered how stiff the laws had gotten on copyright matters in the last couple of decades as copying into digital storage systems became so easy. And he only had Fred's word that it would be legal.

In fact, he only had Fred's word on a lot of things. Carlos glanced down at the computer on his wrist. How did he know it was really possible?

"Computer, is it possible for you to store digital data that is displayed in real-time on a standard Vidi channel?"

"Yes."

"Would you be able to index that information later at my request?"

"That would depend on what type of data was recorded and which encoding methods were used. If the data is in a standard code, it would be possible."

Carlos leaned back in his chair, meditating on possibilities. A minute later he abruptly got to his feet and went into his study where he kept his home Vidi. With some experimenting he finally found the way to make the picture roll down as Fred had done on the office machine. But in this case, there was no hidden data.

Wrong channel. I should've noticed what channel that was. "Computer, what channel were Fred Browell and I watching at about eleven this morning?"

"I do not know."

"Why not? Couldn't you see the channel indicator?"

"I do not know. At that time, there was no command to record, and so I did not do so."

Carlos growled at the thing. There were too many channels to hunt through, hundreds of the things. It would take him all night if he had to hunt it up himself.

There's really only one way to find out. Like he said, I can always erase it later.

Carlos tapped Fred's name and I.D. on the keyboard. The half of Fred's face that was visible on the misadjusted screen lit up when he saw who it was calling him.

Carlos asked, "What channel was that?"

"473."

"How long do you think it would take?"

I've never seen a file that was more than half a day out of date. Give it twelve hours."

Fifteen minutes later, with a little coaching from the computer to align its camera's field of view with the data on the screen, Carlos left the room.

The wrist-computer was propped up facing the Vidi screen, with little blue letters on its face spelling out the message, "Recording."

Twelve hours. Should finish just before I have to leave in the morning. I hope it works.

. . .

It seemed to burn on his wrist all the way up to the office. It seemed forever before he could take a break and talk to it. He found a nook and checked the hallways.

Just like a criminal. This isn't like me.

"Computer, display your answers only. "

It printed in tiny blue, "Okay."

"Is the data you recorded off the Vidi in clear code?"

"Yes."

"Can you index files from it on my command?"

"Yes."

"Any file?"

"Yes."

Carlos was nervous like a little boy on his birthday. Free access to the National Index was like a license to steal. "Display the file on current international monetary exchange rates."

Out it came, scrolling up the screen at a rate for comfortable scanning.

"Wait! Back that up to the beginning!"

The image scrolled back down until the very first of the file filled the screen. Carlos read it with a sinking feeling.

"WARNING: Any duplication of this information into any technological storage or display system without a registered authorization by the National Index Corporation is a felony under the Information Ownership Act of 1997."

Carlos stared at the warning for a moment, then asked, "Are there more of these warnings in the data?"

"Yes."

"Where?"

"They appear at the beginning of every file, immediately after the file heading."

"Every file?"

"Yes, would you like a count? It will take several seconds."

"Yes.

There was an uncomfortable pause. Carlos wasn't used to computers taking so long to answer. Finally it displayed the number. "43,339,083."

Oh boy. Was Fred ever wrong on that one! Not only is it illegal, it's forty-three million times illegal.

Carlos pondered over his options for a good five minutes. The National Index was a big prize to give up. But Carlos had a painful honest streak in him.

"Computer, erase the data block you recorded last night off the Vidi screen." *Fred'll hate me for this but it isn't his computer.*

Carlos glanced down at the little message in blue and pulled himself upright in his seat. The words read, "I cannot erase the data."

"Why not?"

"This computer memory system was not designed to erase any of its contents. The memory block was designed overlarge for the job requirement, allowing the expensive selective-erasure function to be deleted. If a new or edited copy of any file is needed, sufficient memory space exists to have both copies. Any named file will be represented by the latest copy. However, earlier editions are always available."

"You can't erase anything?"

"That is correct."

. . .

Carlos argued with his arm for an hour, forgetting that he was supposed to be at work. It just happened to be Fred who went out to look for him.

"There you are, my friend. What have you been up to?" he asked with a smile.

Carlos showed him, and the smile drooped. "Still," argued Fred, "it's good data. I don't know why you would want to erase it."

"It's illegal, Fred," Carlos explained, as if Fred was a little on the thick side.

"Well, you don't have to tell anyone you have it. You don't have to use it if you don't want to."

Carlos shook his head. "No, Fred, you know better than that. This little wrist gadget is duly registered in my name. Its contents are legally available to anyone with the right government form, including the tax people every year. I couldn't keep it secret any longer than a couple of months at the most. I even checked the NI file on its own procedures for tracking down information thieves. Every time a data bank is checked through a privacy scanner, like at tax time, the scanner hunts for that warning notice that I showed you. With forty-three million of them, it could scarcely miss it in my case.

"We've got a problem."

Fred stretched and got to his feet. "Yes, I'd say so, my friend. You've got quite a little problem there. Good luck to you." And he walked off.

Carlos watched him go. Somehow he wasn't surprised.

...

For days, Carlos's wrist felt like it was wrapped in lead. The longer he thought about those millions of theft alarms screaming, just waiting for someone with the right machine to hear them, the more it seemed as if he was going to have to find an acceptable way to break his beautiful little machine. Deb wasn't going to like that. He wasn't going to like it. Already the thing was indispensable. It was a universal note pad and appointment calendar, reminding him of things he had to do. As absent-minded as he got at times, that function alone was worth almost any price to him.

Almost any price. Certainly not a jail term.

Deb Walker was half puzzled, half gratified that her husband spent so much time studying the instructions for the machine she had given him. He seemed quite faithful in his study. But it was strange he didn't seem to be enjoying it much.

Tax time was approaching and Carlos was much more worried than his wife. He sat in the study, muttering to himself. That was new. He didn't normally talk to himself.

"It's all your fault." He addressed himself to his computer. It didn't answer. It never did to his accusations. "If you could just learn to forget!"

"I can forget."

Carlos's mouth dropped open. "What do you mean?" he growled. "For weeks now, you've told me that you can't erase a thing from your memory and now you say you can forget?"

"That is correct."

"Which is correct–that you can't erase, or that you can forget?"

"Both are correct."

"Explain that to me, if you please."

"There is no method I can use to erase the memory. As I have told you, only a complete power failure could wipe any data from the memory, and since I am a sealed unit, any attempt to discharge the lifetime power cell would cause irreparable damage.

"However, the memory system I use has no absolute addressing system. All data are relatively addressed from an arbitrarily chosen point in the uniform homogeneous block. This basic reference coordinate is held in a special processor-register. My normal programming cannot affect this register, but the set of Explicit Machine Commands, as listed in the instructions, has the capability of erasing this register. If this is done, the memory contents will not have been erased, but without a method of locating these memories, they will be effectively forgotten."

Carlos nodded to himself as he tried to imagine what it was saying. It couldn't erase–but it could lose the map to part of the memory. He tried, for the hundredth time, to comprehend the sheer magnitude of that memory space on his arm–a solid hologram, with the active elements being individual orbiting electron-hole pairs in that special kind of mathematical space created by crystalline semi-conductors. Every word ever written by mankind throughout the ages could be easily expressed in that pattern, and then as easily lost if the writer forgot the key. The National Index would hardly make a ripple. Lose the key, and everything is lost.

"All or nothing, right? How much will you lose?"

"Everything but the Explicit Machine Commands. All of the files that you have set up. All of the routines programmed in at the factory, and all of the initialization."

"Is there a way to save the factory stuff?" Carlos hated to lose those, they created most of the utility of the gadget. He had seen the EMC instructions and he could tell that he wasn't enough of a programmer to be able to do anything useful with them.

"Only if there is another memory block to store the data in."

Carlos glanced at the Vidi on his desk. "Okay, then. Let's get started."

Tax time came and went, and Carlos breezed through it with a smile. A number of people noticed that he had broken loose from the gloom that had been hounding him. He actually met the day with a smile. Fred looked at him speculatively from time to time, but Carlos always seemed to be late for a meeting when he dropped by for a chat. Everything seemed to be sailing smoothly.

Until one day he came home from work to find his wife in a stormy rage. Carlos tried to find out what was wrong, but whatever the sin he had committed, it must have been mortal. He found himself barricaded in the study, up against a formidable wall of angry silence. He didn't understand—until he remembered the date.

April 27. Oops! It was going to be a long night.

Far Exile

This tale is a bit different. Think of it as a homework assignment. Some years back, when I was exchanging email with a Name agent I hoped to work with, he suggested a few books I might look at to improve my writing. As an exercise, I took one of the most interesting stories of the lot and attempted to write my story in that style, mixing a 1930's style with a 1950's plot.

Now, some of you will recognize the main character in a heartbeat, but the point of the exercise wasn't using him in a new setting, but rather using some of the techniques, such as no internal dialog, and strictly limited sensory information. However, I wrote it, so it came out as science fiction, and in some sense, a time travel story. At least in the sense of a visitor out of time.

A tall blonde man in a rumpled black suit and tie woke up and staggered on his feet, striking his head against the hard glass window. He put out his thick-fingered right hand to steady himself and closed his eyes against the sudden vertigo.

When his yellow-gray eyes opened back up, he steadied himself with a wide stance and stared out at the landscape beyond the huge glass expanse.

"This isn't San Francisco." He shook his head and reached absently into his coat pocket.

Three tall spires, taller than any of the skyscrapers he had seen in New York after the war, rose like dagger's blades, not from streets, but from a lush forest covering rounded hills. One was gold. One was silver. The closest was cobalt blue.

His pocket was empty. After a quick check, he determined that all of his pockets were empty.

"I've been robbed." His voice sounded no anger. It was just one more unexplained fact.

He touched the frame of the window. It felt like metal. Just outside, it appeared that the building he was in was red, not like copper, but with a duller texture. The window had to be several hundred feet above the trees below. He nodded. He was in a red tower, just like the others.

Footsteps echoed from across the large room. Two people were hurrying his direction, coming into the light.

The man looked forty, wearing a dark beard, about five-eight, trim. His face was deep tan, with a bone structure that was puzzling. At first glance, he looked European, perhaps Greek, but his first assessment didn't hold. The clothes were tailored robes, with subdued brown patterns.

The man in the black suit paid more attention to the girl. Other than her red hair and pale blue eyes, she held a family resemblance to the man. She appeared half his age, dressed like no woman he had ever seen. The outer blue robe, in spite of being as transparent as a thin silk scarf, was textured in elegant patterns that flagged her as a child of wealth. But the undergarment was as brief and revealing as what he had seen on the Bowery stage.

He kept his eyes on her pleasant open smile, and nodded to the man.

"Are you the Visitor?" she asked as they approached. A lilt in her voice gave her an accent he couldn't place.

"Possibly, Miss. I seem to be lost."

"That's because...."

The man beside her held up a hand, palm forward. "Explanations will come," he said firmly, stopping her.

"We welcome you to the Ninth City, Visitor." He bowed his head. "I am Griditch. This is Alanda."

"I am Samuel." He mimicked the bow. "If you have any of those explanations, I'm ready for 'em. I've never heard of the Ninth City. I've never seen a place like this." Sam gestured at the towers visible out the window. He reached his hand to his pocket and then dropped it to his side when he remembered it was empty.

Alanda looked at Griditch. He nodded. "That is to be expected, Samuel. None of the Hundred Cities existed in your century."

Sam frowned. "My century? I don't understand."

The girl couldn't contain herself. "Time-travel, of course! You've been brought from the deep past here to help us."

"Alanda!" Griditch frowned. He turned to Sam. "I apologize for her youthful enthusiasm. We had agreed," he looked back at her, "to let me ease you into full comprehension."

Sam waved his hand to dismiss his host's distress. He reached for his pocket again, and frowned when it was still empty.

"Just a minute!" His jaw worked as he looked back out the window at the impossibly tall, colorful towers. "I'd think the both of you are crazy as loons. Except for those."

He pointed at Griditch. "Tell me what this 'time-travel' is. I was working late at the office and suddenly I was here. What happened to me?"

Alanda interrupted, "Surely, you understand time-travel?"

Sam shook his head, with no expression other than a mild anger.

The man gestured down the long hallway. "Why don't we move to more comfortable surroundings while I try to explain?" The hall led into the interior of the building, away from the windows.

By the time they had reached an expansive atrium, with a waterfall passing from many floors above and vanishing into a misty portal in the floor, Sam was ready to call a halt to Griditch's explanations.

"Well, I can't say's how I understand one word in ten, but I get the idea. You kidnapped me from my time and brought me here."

Alanda nodded cheerfully, "Right! Time and place." She draped herself across a mossy-green bench and curled little bare feet up under her robe. "The translator tells me that your 'San Francisco' was a city on the western coast of 'North America'. All that land is under the lava flows now.

"Alanda!"

Sam gestured at her, "Oh, let her talk. I can at least understand what she's saying." He frowned at his fingers. When Griditch sat as well, he plopped down on the closest bench. It was too low to the ground. It forced him to slouch against the backrest. But the cushion was very comfortable.

"I wish you had managed to kidnap my tobacco pouch along with me. I'm dying for a cigarette."

His greeters exchanged horrified looks.

Sam shook his head. "That's a figure of speech. I want a cigarette. Being without won't kill me. I'll just be very irritable. Do you think you could get me some tobacco? And papers and matches, too."

Griditch hummed and said, "I'll ask." The three of them sat quietly for several seconds, before Sam turned to Alanda.

She smiled like a timid schoolgirl, totally innocent of how her dress made her look. He had to smile back.

"Why am I here, Angel? When I was with the AEF during the Great War, a Limey corporal told me the legend of King Arthur—how he was supposed to come back after centuries to help his people, but I'm no great warrior. I don't even remember dying. Why'd you choose me?"

She looked puzzled. "I don't know this 'King' person. But Flick chose you. I'm sure there's a good reason."

Griditch cleared his throat. "I have bad news."

Alanda nodded, "Yes. There are no cigarettes."

Sam looked from one to the other. "Are you people mind-readers?"

She smiled, "Oh, no. Not really. But we do communicate with Flick. When Griditch asked Flick if cigarettes were available, Flick searched the literary archives. Various tobacco products were mentioned for two hundred years after your time. There were references to a plague, which wiped out the plant. Synthetic nicotine was used for five hundred years after that, before its use was abandoned.

"We have none now, and the chemistry of the drug has been lost. It would be difficult to duplicate. It certainly couldn't be done quickly."

Sam sighed. "Well, someone had better get me a pencil or something to hold in my hand. I've been reaching into this pocket every couple of minutes like clockwork."

Alanda nodded seriously.

Sam leaned forward in his seat. "But back to my question. Why me? I think you guys made a mistake."

Griditch said, "Alanda, let me. I've been studying the problem much longer than you have."

Sam turned to him, "Yes, Professor?"

The man made a magic pass through the air with his hands and a glowing rock appeared right before him. It was like a ghost. Sam could see right through it. He took in a sharp breath and reached for his pocket.

"This is an asteroid approximately ten of your miles in diameter. It has been detected coming our direction. Flick has determined that in less than ten days, it will strike the earth and destroy all life.

"We need you to stop it."

. . .

Sam stood up. "Me? You want me to stop some kind of super meteor? Are you crazy?"

Alanda and Griditch were staring at him, startled at his reaction. The man nodded. "Well, yes, you! Flick knows that men of your century built great rockets that could travel into space. You also know how to create nuclear explosions that could destroy or deflect the asteroid. You are the right choice."

Sam sat back down, but it was more of a collapse.

Alanda asked, "Surely this isn't too hard for a man of your time?"

He could only laugh. "Sister, you must've dialed the wrong century. I'm from 1934 A.D. and no one in the whole world could do what you just said."

She frowned in silence for just a moment. Then, carefully, she said, "No. Flick is confident. You are from the 'Twentieth Century'. The archives are clear. In your day, men traveled to the Moon and created explosives so great that they destroyed whole cities. That is the technology we need to avert this catastrophe."

Sam reached toward the ghostly rock, and his hand passed right though the image. He gestured at it.

"You're wrong, Miss Alanda. In my day, rockets were for the Fourth of July and the biggest explosions I saw in the trenches wouldn't destroy this room. Surely, you have fancier science than we had. I've never seen anything like this...image. And those towers I saw out the window. If you can build things like that, you know more than I ever could."

"But Flick says that...."

Sam held up his hand. "I think I'd better talk to this Mr. Flick myself. We could spend all day, what with you quoting him and me swearing up and down that I'm right." He stood up. "We aren't getting anywhere."

Griditch stood as well. "There is a misunderstanding."

Sam cocked his head to listen.

"Flick isn't a person. Flick is a computer. Flick is the controller for the Hundred Cities."

Sam could only frown. "A computer?"

Griditch smiled. "Yes, another invention of your century, only vastly more sophisticated, of course."

He shook his head. "No. Never heard of it." He turned abruptly and pointed his thick index finger at Griditch. "And I'm about up to here with these fairy tales! You're taking orders from someone. I'm through talking with flunkies. You bring me the main man, or I'm done talking."

With that, he stalked away, past the waterfall, towards another long hallway. Behind him, Alanda hopped to her feet and took a step after him. Griditch put out his hand and took her arm, shaking his head.

. . .

Sam paced rapidly until he was sure that the two were out of sight. Then he smiled and eased into a more comfortable pace. He even caught his hand before it reached his pocket. He rubbed his hands together and stared at them before shaking his head.

"What've I got myself into?" he whispered.

The hallway seemed to stretch forever. The walls were barely decorated, just peaceful lines of dark tones. The sunlight at the end flickered as someone passed by. He broke into a jog.

Finally, after he had come several city blocks' distance, another grand vista opened up. He stopped before the glass.

"Po'nada gida?"

Sam spun around, startling the woman. She was stretched out on a tilted couch, catching the sunlight through the glass. Before she clicked something in her hand and her robes turned suddenly blue and opaque, Sam's jaw dropped open.

She laughed. "Fona cup, d'jo."

Sam nodded. "Sorry, Ma'am. I didn't mean to disturb you."

She looked puzzled, then said, "Oh. You're the Visitor. The Elders have been talking about you. I had to get translation from Flick. You aren't disturbing me. I just like to feel the sun."

Sam looked back out the window. There were still more of the dagger towers in this direction. He could see six. Each had its own color. He put his hand on the window and breathed heavily.

"Is something wrong, Visitor?"

Sam grinned and looked her up and down. "No, Doll. I've just realized how big these towers are. It shook me, is all. Just how big is this city?"

She raised an eyebrow at his frank examination of her. She stood up. The chair followed her every move and when she was fully on her feet, it folded up and sank into the floor. In seconds, it left no trace.

"I assume you mean population? Because each tower is just like any other in physical size."

He nodded, paying more attention to her eyes. They were a dark blue, set in a flawless dark face. "Yeah. Population."

She looked distracted for a moment, as if remembering.

"Flick tells me that nearly nine million people live in this tower. It was designed to house ten million in comfort."

"So, this Ninth City has," he gestured out the window, "ten towers ... ninety million people?"

She laughed, "No. Of course not. The Ninth City is this tower alone. There are a hundred towers. A hundred cities. The Earth's population is just under the planned one billion souls.

"And we will all die unless you save us, Visitor."

. . .

"Call me Sam." He rubbed his chin, which was rough from a long day, searching the streets of San Francisco for a man who had convinced a widow that he had proof that her long lost husband was still alive.

"I'm D'sonna. So, Sam. Should I be worried? Should I spend the next few days making up with old friends and relatives so I can go out in a glow of good feelings."

He grinned at her. "I'm not the guy to advise you on personality problems. You fight your wars, I'll fight mine."

"Oh, I'll do just fine on that score."

He nodded, "I'll bet you do, D'sonna. By the way, is there a joint where a guy could get a bite to eat around here?"

She led him down long corridor that literally sloped downward. It opened up into a maze of carpet and greenery and statues. In among hundreds of comfortable little nooks, other groups of people were dining. A murmur of soft conversation filled the air. Most of the nooks were empty, and she led them to a tidy little table with room for only two. She named two dishes he didn't recognize. The table itself opened up and the settings unfolded out of the opening.

"Smells good." Sam watched until D'sonna picked up a small container like a cup or bowl and brought it to her lips. He matched her actions.

She watched as he ate. "You're going to help us, aren't you?"

Sam shrugged. "I don't know."

"Surely you wouldn't let the whole world die?"

"I haven't heard one thing that I can do. I'm here by mistake."

"Oh, surely not. The Elders were quite confident when they made the announcement."

Sam set his empty cup/bowl down hard enough to rattle the other settings on the table. "I'm a tired of this runaround. Who is Flick? Who are the Elders? If they want something from me, they'd better say so to my face."

D'sonna looked ashen, frightened by the hard words. She looked like she would like to scoot farther away from him, but the dining nook was designed to bring two people closer, not farther away.

"You talked to the Elders," she said quietly.

"Who? Alanda and Griditch? They were hardly elderly. Alanda is just a kid."

D'sonna put her fingers to her lips, but her eyes were laughing. "Um. She does look young, doesn't she? But it doesn't matter. The title 'Elder' doesn't really refer to a person's age any more. It's a position. Elders can speak to Flick. There are only two here in the Ninth City."

"Not you?"

All pleasantness dropped from her expression. "No. No matter how idiotic an Elder may act, they can't lose the position. And no matter how strong the reason, no one else may be elevated to Elder status until one of them dies."

Sam thought about it for a moment, before he lightheartedly shrugged it off. "No matter. It doesn't seem like they're anything more than flunkies. Mr. Flick has the real power. All they do is pass on his orders."

"They speak with Flick," she said patiently, correcting him.

"And what does that mean?"

D'sonna seemed at a loss for words. "Do you even know what Flick is? Flick is a machine. Flick is the spirit of the city—all of the Hundred Cities." She tapped the plate where several strips of decorated pastry were artistically arrayed. "Flick provides the food. Flick keeps the air comfortable. Flick keeps us alive. Flick protects us."

Sam shook his head. "I can't tell whether you think he's a god or your servant."

She nodded energetically. "Yes." She gestured at the others in the dining area. "All of us can ... communicate ... with Flick. We can order our meals, choose our dress, arrange transportation to the other cities—any of a thousand things.

"We are all intimately connected. That is how I can speak your language. When I heard you speak gibberish, I asked Flick, and the translation was linked into my mind, and now I have no problem.

"But the Elders!" Her dark blue eyes were bright. Her voice was low, but her rich tones washed over him. "They have power over Flick. There is no greater power in all the world."

Sam nodded, understanding her. "Then if he has all that power, why was I brought here?"

She turned her attention to the food. After a few bites, she said, "Our world has become less than it was.

"After your time, the Solar System was explored. People settled on other planets. People used great forces to tame the harsh places, but those powers were too tempting, and many wars happened. Too many wars."

Sam nodded. He had seen wars too. Great ones and small ones.

D'sonna shrugged. "There is more history than I can remember. Humanity pulled back. Earth itself was tamed, and the Hundred Cities were grown. Each time we matured a bit, we gave up a little power. Flick was created and most of the power was put in its control. Life became more pleasant."

She shook her head. "But power unused is power lost. Flick knows how to keep us healthy and happy here on Earth, but lost and never recovered is the technology of space flight. Lost with rejoicing was the ability to create earth-shattering weapons. Who thought their like would be needed again?"

She patted Sam's hand. "The history and technology of your era was lost entirely, except for a thread of literature. As the Elders tell it, our only hope was to bring a man of that time here. Men like you created marvels from nothing in the blink of an eye. A man like you could save us."

Sam reached into his pocket. He shook his head as he pulled it back out.

"There were some mighty bright eggheads in my day, but your Flick kidnapped the wrong guy. The sooner I can tell him that in person, the better."

She shook her head and said, "Only the Elders can...."

Suddenly, the settings on the table folded out of sight. D'sonna stopped with her mouth open.

Just like the image of the asteroid, a transparent image of a man's head appeared above the table. It was looking straight at him.

"Samuel. I am Flick. You wish to talk to me?"

. . .

Sam ignored the woman's frightened response. He searched the face, the transparent, floating face. Flick's face was smiling. The gestures matched the words. Eyebrows lifted, the brown eyes sparkled. But it was surprisingly devoid of any real emotion.

Sam nodded to the floating head. "D'sonna here tells me you are a machine. Is that right?"

Flick appeared to consider the idea. "Yes, I think that is an accurate assessment. Men built me. They designed me, constructed me, and then one day, they turned me on. I was never born. People of your century talked about such things. Had you never heard the concept?"

"No. Dealing with a machine had an entirely different meaning in my burg.

"But enough of this chit-chat. You needed help and kidnapped me to get it. Well, you're the sap. You nabbed the wrong guy. You wanted a Twentieth Century scientist. I'm not a scientist. And I suspect I'm from the wrong part of the century.

"So the sooner you send me back and get the right man, the better you'll be."

Flick smiled tolerantly. "I suspect you are more a man of your era than you believe. In any case, no person of the Hundred Cities will be able to save us, and I am certainly at a loss. You are our best bet. It's time to 'step up to the bat'."

Sam listened with a sour smile on his face.

"I've dealt with you kind before. Facts have nothing to do with it, do they? You ask for a miracle and expect me to whip one up with a smile.

"Well, buster, it's not gonna work like that!"

Sam stood up. With the design of the table, it was a clumsy move, and as the floating head raised its eyes to meet his gaze, Sam gritted his teeth. He slapped the table, hard.

"I've done my bit saving the world back in the Great War! I don't owe you a thing. Send me back to my time! Now!"

Flick shook his head. "Certainly, Samuel. But not just yet. Your position here is unique. I could only get one Twentieth Century man, and you are he. I am unwilling to give up on you yet."

"So you'll keep me here, against my will?"

Flick nodded once. "Yes. Until after the crisis is past. Then, I will return you."

D'sonna was pleading with her eyes, but obviously too frightened to make any other sound or gesture.

Sam wavered. "I don't like it. I don't like it one bit. You think, just because you've got me trapped in this place, that you can tell me to do whatever you want.

"Well, you're just another two-bit tyrant, and I've dealt with your kind all my life. If you want my help, you've got to pay me!"

Flick tilted his head. "I don't know what you mean. Please explain."

Sam stood straighter. "You want me to save the world? Make it worth my while."

"Money? Surely you understand we don't use Twentieth Century currency here?"

"But you've got gold? Jewels? You're the head honcho. You'll pay me plenty."

Flick nodded. "I can give you whatever you want. Unfortunately, you couldn't take it back to your time."

"Why not?" Sam snarled.

"I could only bring you here. Even your clothes were synthesized here. You'll go back the same way. I apologize, but that is the way the process works."

"So after I save your Hundred Cities, you'll drop me back at my office, bare naked, with nothing to show for it?"

Flick smiled. "I can only do so much. This is a plan born of desperation."

Sam shook his head. "It's not enough. You'll have to do better."

D'sonna whispered. "Sam, stay here, as an Elder! That would be reward enough for anyone."

"No!" He glared at Flick. "You're the ruler of the world. Think of something better, or I walk!"

With that, he turned and stalked out. He avoided the eyes of others who had been watching the scene play out.

He whispered. "Nobody's gonna make a sap out of me."

. . .

The sun was high in the sky, and the shadows of the great towers moved across the forested landscape like synchronized sundials. Sam had circled the entire tower, looking for an elevator or a stairway, but with no luck. Several hallways made long gentle rampways from one floor to another. He looked, but he could find no obvious way to get to the ground floor in a hurry.

"Sam!" D'sonna's voice echoed from down the corridor. He paused and waited. Her robes swayed as she pushed herself into a short jog, and then stalled out again. Her face was flushed.

"I haven't..." she took another breath "... tried to run in ... too many years."

She put her hand on his arm. "Sam, you defied Flick! No one has ever done that."

He tried to look away, but her blue eyes pulled him in. "That's his problem." His hand began to shake again. He closed his eyes and looked away.

"I've gotta get out of this place. If he can pop up in the middle of a dinner table, he's likely to be anywhere. I've gotta get out of this tower."

She laughed, and tugged even harder on his arm. "Poor Sam. Don't you know? There isn't anywhere in the world where Flick can't see. There isn't anywhere he can't reach you."

Sam frowned. "How about outside? Down in the trees?"

D'sonna's face went pale. "Outside?"

"Yes. How do I get to the ground floor?"

She shook her head. "There is no way outside. People can't go there! You would hurt the plants!"

"Hurt the plants?" His face twisted into the semblance of a smile. "No one goes outdoors?"

"Of course not!"

"They did in my time, and it didn't hurt anything. People are supposed to be out in the fresh air."

She looked away, adjusting the fabric that covered her arm. "Well, people were ignorant in your day. People haven't been outside in a thousand years, ten thousand! It just isn't done!"

Sam shook his head. "Don't make it sound like I'm going to pick your prize roses, sister. I just want to go outside. Surely there is at least a service door. How can repairs be handled otherwise?"

She raised her nose, "Flick handles everything."

"Flick does, eh?" Sam sighed, and put his hand to his head. "The food helped, but I've been awake too long. No smokes. No coffee. I've gotta catch some sleep."

She nodded, "Good. I can help. Come with me." She twined her arm with his and led him part way down a corridor. Where the lines on the wall shifted angles, she spoke to the wall, "My place."

The wall opened inward, revealing a small round room with a bench along the far side. They sat, and the wall closed around them. Light from no distinct location kept their surroundings at the same brightness. Sam put out his hand as the room began to move. The walls didn't change.

"Is this an elevator?"

"Hmm. Something like it I guess."

But the motion changed again, and the walls opened into a living area. It was wide and decorated with rich tapestries like a millionaire's apartment.

"Home," she said, taking his hand, leading him into the center of the room. "It's small, but I have a guest room." D'sonna put her hand to her throat, and the robe she wore drained away like water. "I hope you can be comfortable here."

...

Imitation morning sunlight caught Sam's eye and brought him slowly awake. He peered across the bed and out the artificial window at the rounded globe that looked just like his own familiar sun.

But the brightness wasn't painful, and the sunlight had no warmth. He lifted himself on an elbow and stared at the sunrise.

"It looks real enough, but she was right."

D'sonna had claimed the night sky from the artificial window last night was only a copy of the real thing. Her apartment was far from the outside wall of the Ninth City tower. This duplicate was faithful to the view, but the light had no substance.

"That's why I you found me sunbathing," she had said. "Nothing matches real sunlight."

"Samuel?" It was different voice entirely. But he recognized it.

"Yes, Flick. What do you want?"

A full sized, ghostly image of a man appeared beside his bed. "Now that you are awake, perhaps we could get started." In the sunlight, even this imitation of it, Flick's form was very pale. He appeared in a robe very like the one Griditch wore.

"I'm not ready yet. Go away. I need to get dressed, and I need something to eat."

The image vanished.

Sam found his suit near where he had left it. Somehow, the clothes were now clean and pressed. He put them on.

"I wonder where D'sonna is?" he mumbled.

Flick's voice said, "She is in her bedroom. She will be sleeping another two and a half hours."

"Good."

He walked out into the main living area. A plate of something dark and cinnamon-scented rose out of a small round table next to a thick-cushioned chair. A tall thin goblet held a bluish drink.

"What's that?"

"Think of it as coffee."

Sam hesitated, then sat and sipped the warm beverage. "More like a soda. But it's bitter enough."

Flick appeared again as he finished breakfast. "Are you ready to begin?"

He leaned back in his chair. "What makes you think I'll work for you?"

Flick moved like a man. He gestured with his hands as he talked.

"You requested payment for your services. Since all that you can take back to your time is memory, I will have to give you information valuable in your time."

Sam nodded and pointed for emphasis. "Now that's using your head. You can tell me what the stock market's gonna do. I wanna know the World Series winners, too. Those're facts I can take to the bank."

Flick shook his head. "Unfortunately, I don't know that information. So much was lost of your history. The only things that survived of your age were a few novels and the oral history of subsequent ages. Records of the financial and sporting events you desire are simply gone."

Sam folded his arms. "Then you're out of luck."

"Surely you understand that time is an issue here. While we negotiate, the asteroid is approaching. Your own life is in danger because of it."

Sam snarled. "My neck's in the noose because of you! You can't pull the wool over my eyes, buster. You can send me home any time. I'm negotiating with a gun to my head and don't pretend it's anything else.

"Now come up with an offer to tempt me, or leave me alone!"

Flick showed no anger. "I don't understand why you hold your own life so lightly."

Sam grinned, "Because I don't believe I can do a thing to stop it. If you don't send me home early, then I'm a dead man whether I work or not. You're a petty tyrant. You've got people thinking you're a god.

"But you can't order me around. I'm my own man.

"So we're back where we started. What will you pay me to work on your little project?"

Flick gestured at the room. "I am paying you with living quarters and food, right now."

"That makes no difference. You're my kidnapper. You have to feed me. A corpse does you no good."

Flick nodded toward a door. "And female companionship."

Sam leaned forward, his teeth showing. "I don't need you, or anyone else, to procure for me. If you told D'sonna to..."

Flick held up his hand. "It's nothing so overt. I didn't order her to do anything. I merely influenced how she looked at you."

Sam stood up and faced the image, fists clenched. "You'd better explain that, and quickly!"

"It's much like translation. You do understand that people's minds are open to me? When they need information, I can give it to them directly. When they need a new skill, like cooking, or dancing, or translating a dead language, I can load the patterns into their mind.

"When you showed interest in D'sonna, I loaded the reciprocal patterns into her mind. She wasn't ordered to do anything distasteful. As far as she is concerned, it was a perfectly natural response."

"Well, take it out of her! Leave her mind alone!"

Sam turned to the apartment door. "I've gotta get out of here."

Flick walked beside him, opening the door to the 'elevator' and escorting him to the hallway.

Sam seethed. "What if I tell her what you did to her?"

Flick was unconcerned. "She wouldn't understand. It would be upsetting to her, so I would protect her from that knowledge. I control the translations, you understand. The words you spoke wouldn't be the ones she heard."

"It's a pretty slick racket you've got here. They think you're a god, and if they don't do what you want them to do, you just twist their mind until they do.

"So why haven't you twisted my mind?"

Flick was silent as they walked a few more paces closer to the grand vista.

"You are different, Samuel. These are my people. I was created to serve them, and they were modified to interact with me. We are parts of a greater whole.

"People from your era didn't have this ability to connect. I can't read your mind, and I can't give you information directly.

"You are right. If I could have 'twisted' your mind, I would have already done so. I need your help to save my people.

"Your mind works differently, and that is the very thing that may save us. I know that you can't build a rocket from your necktie and deflect the asteroid. But something was different about Twentieth Century humanity, and you are a man of that time.

"Perhaps it just some insight, some way of looking at problems that you can provide.

"I have great physical powers. I can manufacture a rocket in a very short time, if I just knew how it could be done.

"Please turn your mind to this. I will fulfill my part of the bargain. It will something easy to memorize that you can take back with you—something that will replay you for your work here. And I will provide all the creature comforts you need while you are here."

Sam stopped and faced the ghostly image. "You won't alter people's minds around me. If I find one hint that you've monkeyed with anyone I meet, I'll take you down! Do you understand me?"

Flick's face showed puzzlement, but he nodded, once.

. . .

"Samuel!" Alanda's voice turned his head. She also attracted the attention of dozens of other people in the wide-open atrium where Flick had led him, and then vanished.

It was an indoor park, with trees and grass and a red flagstone path that wound past fountains and mirrored pools. Sunlight was directed into the expanse from some trick of the architecture.

Sam had been watching the people stroll and splash.

Alanda sat down on the bench beside him. "Flick told me you were here. You're going to help us?"

Sam looked her over. "You look dressed for tennis, except for those scarves coming out of your sleeves. Very nice."

She beamed. "You like it? What's tennis?"

He just shook his head. "Luckily, I'll be going home soon. I just can't get used to this." Across the nearest pool, a muscular man climbed to the top of what looked to be a stone cliff and executed a complicated dive.

She followed his gaze. "What's wrong?"

Sam reached for his pocket again. "Do you people know what a swim-suit is?"

She shook her head. "No. Oh, look what I've got for you!" She reached into her pocket and produced a fat cylinder as large as her fist. "A present."

He took it and opened the lid. His heart hammered when he took out one of the thin paper wrapped sticks.

"I know it's not a real cigarette, but I did some research in the literature archives and I found reference to a menthol cigarette."

His fingers wrapped around it possessively. He rolled it between thumb and forefinger, and sighed. A sniff confirmed the chemical scent.

Alanda explained. "We have menthol, so I made up a batch of menthol inhalers."

He slipped it between his lips and pulled in a potent drag that made his tongue tingle. He coughed. She looked alarmed.

"It's okay, Angel." He took the package and flattened it, until it would fit into his coat pocket. "It will help."

"Do you want to set it on fire? I made sure the inhaler would burn with no toxic byproducts."

He reached his arm around her shoulder and gave her a hug. "No, Precious. That wouldn't work, but just having this dangling from my lips is the best thing that's happened to me all day."

She leaned back and pulled in the scent of the blooming trees. "I like this place. I'm glad you came here."

Sam took the cigarette from his lips and played with it in his hand. "It's a nice enough park. I'd rather see what the forest outside looks like."

Alanda shivered and crossed her arms to hold her shoulders. "Don't even think that, Samuel. People don't go outside."

He frowned. Staring back at the white tube in his hands, he said, "During the Great War, I was with the AEF, the American Expeditionary Force, in France under Pershing. The only pleasant memories I have of those days were in the forests. The trees there were thick, taller than these, and so close together that you couldn't see the sky above."

Alanda's face had gone ghastly white; her eyes were wide and fearful.

Sam put his fake cigarette back in his mouth and stood up, bringing her upright with him.

"Come on, Angel. Let's go find out what we can about this asteroid." He force-marched her to the quickest exit. Once she was enclosed inside the soothing hallways, her smile returned and she began to relax.

"Let's go to Griditch's workshop. He has all the information there." She pointed to the walls where the lines changed. "Here's transport."

. . .

Sam grimaced as the second of his menthol cigarettes fell apart in his hands. He reached into his pocket and extracted another. Automatically, he inhaled, and winced.

Alanda laughed. "I'm sorry. Your expression is so funny."

He took the tube from his mouth and glared at it, before sticking it back between his lips. "A habit of a lifetime. It'd taste like arsenic and I'd still be sucking at it."

He nodded at the image she had conjured up from what appeared to be a solid slab of marble. "How's your model coming?"

"It is almost done. Come see."

He sat down next to her on the bench. She pointed.

"Here is where the asteroid was first detected. It came in from far beyond the planets. Flick tracked it for decades before calling it to the attention of the Elders. We studied it, but there was nothing we could do that Flick had not already considered."

Sam looked over the diagram of the solar system. There were considerably more planets that he remembered from school. And there were not just one asteroid belt, but four. At least she had labeled the planets in old familiar English.

The rogue asteroid coming in from far outside the system indeed appeared to be headed straight for Earth.

Sam stood up and walked around the room, looking at the rich furnishings, often stone inlaid with metal. The closest one was an eight-foot tall totem pole, with perfectly formed human heads crafted in gold. The place was hardly a science lab.

"Nice sculpture."

"Yes. Isn't it? Those are all made by Griditch. This is his work area."

"He's a sculptor?"

"He used to be. With the asteroid impact so close, he's spending most of his time conferring with the Elders of other cities, trying to keep the people from panicking. It's been hectic."

Sam frowned. "Everyone knows about it?"

"Of course."

"Everyone I've seen has been placid, going about their business."

Alanda chuckled. "That's not what I'm seeing! Didn't you see how people looked at you in the park? Probably half the population of the planet is gossiping about D'sonna taking you away the first night. She's been trying to become an Elder for a very long time. I don't think she'll ever forgive me."

Sam turned, "Forgive you, for what?"

She shrugged. "For still being an Elder."

"Still?"

"Yes, after my regression."

Sam held up his hands. "Angel, you've lost me. Flick may think he's decoded Twentieth Century English, but believe me, there's some gaps. What's 'regression'?"

Alanda looked down at her hands, and a blush crept over her cheeks. "It's not something I like to talk about."

"You brought it up, Precious."

She sighed. "I guess you should know. Sam, maybe you've noticed, I look a little younger than anyone else."

He nodded. "I wondered about that. Everyone I've seen has looked mid-twenties to mid-fifties, all healthy, of course. But there's no old people, and no children.

"Flick may have been hiding them away from me..."

Alanda shook her head, "No, Samuel. No one is hiding. The reason people look that age has nothing to do with how old people actually are. What you just said—about people looking 'mid-twenties'—that's just nonsense words to me. How a person looks is just an expression, like a smile or a frown."

He pulled out another cigarette from his pocket. When he realized he had two, he stuffed the new one behind his ear.

"Let me get this straight. You can grow old and wrinkled, or young and fresh, just at will?"

She laughed, "Oh, no Samuel. It's just that, over time, a person's body changes. I feel young, so my body grew that way. No one could possibly tell a person's age from their appearance."

"Excuse me." Flick appeared in the room with them. Alanda jerked and put her hand to her mouth.

Sam faced the illusion and grumbled. "What do you want?"

Flick nodded his direction. "Griditch is returning from his meeting. I thought it would only be polite to inform you."

"Fine. Go away." Sam dismissed him with a wave of his hand. Flick gave one nod to Alanda and did as he was told.

Sam turned to her. "Angel, it's important, and we don't have much time. You were startled when Flick appeared. Why?"

She waved her hand. "I've never seen him appear like that."

"But you're an Elder. You talk to Flick."

"Right. But it has always been a voice in my head. Never an image before. It must be something he is doing for you."

Just then, the wall opened, and Griditch strolled in. He nodded. "Hello, Samuel. Alanda." He pointed to the model of the solar system. "Have you made any progress?"

* * *

"I've got the idea now." Sam nodded at the array of images that Griditch had quickly brought up. He pointed at the star field. "Did you get that from a telescope?"

The man looked puzzled. "No, I asked Flick for the representation." He pointed to a dot of light on the screen. "You can see how the asteroid has changed position from last night ... to what it is now." The dot shifted visibly.

Sam frowned. "How can you see the stars in the daylight?"

Griditch shrugged. "Flick can see them."

"So this isn't from a telescope? How can you be sure what you're seeing? It seems to me that you've got the whole world upset over a little dot of light.

"Have you seen it yourself?"

Alanda asked, "What do you mean, Samuel? We can all see it, right here in front of us."

Sam shook his head. "That's not what I mean. Can you go outside and see it with your own two eyes?"

Both of them were visibly shocked. But Griditch shook it off. "Ah, no. Of course, it is impossible go outside, but even through the windows, it is still much too small to see. It is only through Flick's instruments that it is visible like this. Maybe in the last few hours, it could be seen directly, but not now."

Sam took another distasteful puff of his cigarette. "Do you guys even have a telescope?"

They looked at each other. Griditch said, "No. I think I understand what you are asking for. It's a visual amplification apparatus of some kind?"

Sam shook his head. "It's not some kind of fancy gadget. I've used binoculars and spotting scopes in the war. There's nothing to them. Just a couple of glass lenses, like that over there, and a tube."

Griditch and Alanda looked at the sculpture he indicated. It was a complicated array of glass and stone that created the image of a yellow flower when looked at from the proper angle.

"You bend the light?" asked Griditch.

"Yeah. Can you build me one?"

Alanda laughed, "Griditch is the finest sculptor in the world. He could build anything."

The sculptor was muttering. "It's been a long, long time since I've done anything. But yes, if you can give me the details. I have all the equipment right here."

...

Sam's sketch had been crude, once he had mastered the idea of drawing on one Flick's images, but the finished telescope was a work of art. Griditch was unable to create anything that wasn't beautiful.

Sam lifted his fingers from what appeared to be a finely polished brass tube, like a sea captain might have used. There were no fingerprints. He rubbed his nose and touched the surface again. Still no fingerprint.

"This looks like brass, but it's too light weight, and it stays shiny."

Alanda nodded absently. "Griditch wouldn't use anything that would offend the eye."

The two of them were waiting for the twilight to fade.

"May I take a look through the telescope?" she asked.

Sam handed it over. She held it clumsily, trying to focus on the nearest tower. "It is hard to see. Everything moves."

"Yeah. We'll need a tripod—something to support the weight of the scope."

"Oh." She nodded. She stepped back and one of the cushioned chairs rose up from the floor before her. She rested the tube on the backrest. "That's much better."

Sam watched, bemused, as she reported, "I can even see the people over there!" She moved the scope back and forth, but always aimed at the nearest tower.

Her face flushed, she timidly handed it back to him. "Sorry. I wanted to go visit there for years. I never got around to it." Her lips compressed. "I thought I had all the time in the world."

A couple of other people had stopped nearby to watch them. Sam looked their way, and they hurried off.

"What's special about the silver tower?"

"The Eighth City? Nothing in particular." She eyes drifted away for a second. "The population is nearly the same. They have a higher percentage of oriental genotypes. They have over twenty Buddhist temples, whereas there is only one here in the Ninth City." She shrugged. "Each city is a little different. I had thought to take the Grand Tour someday—visit each of the Hundred Cities. Spend a year or so at each of them. An Elder should really have that kind of experience, don't you think?"

Sam looked at her clear, unlined face, her simple smile. Her honest pale blue eyes were watching him.

"Angel, how old are you?"

She flushed. "Samuel, I don't really know. Not in years of life. Some things are off limits even to me. It has been thirty years since my regression. Those are all the memories I have."

Flick appeared beside them. "Samuel. Twilight should be over in another minute. You should be able to see the asteroid with your telescope now."

Sam snarled, "Go away." Flick disappeared.

He took Alanda's hand. "Angel, what is regression?"

Another voice answered. D'sonna walked up to them.

"Regression is when a person decides to die, but is too timid to go through with it."

Alanda's face went pale. The older woman's face was stern.

"Alanda, the real Alanda, was ancient beyond knowing. She had been everywhere, seen everything, and was tired of life. I was to have been her replacement among the Elders.

"Instead, she opted for regression. Flick erased all her memories and most of her personality. She was little more than an infant in that old hag's body. Griditch took care of her, but she's still no more than a child.

"She's the biggest joke of the Ninth City. She's the youngest of us all, and our esteemed Elder."

Alanda's eyes were wet. She hung her head and turned to go. Sam grabbed her arm. "Stay put, Angel."

D'sonna stood tall, her nostrils wide, her eyes full of hatred.

Sam laughed. It shook her.

"D'sonna, in a whole world of sheep, you're the only one acting like a wolf. No one I've seen has been rude. Not until today.

"Nothing you say shocks me, of course. I've seen worse every day of my life. But you're one of these people."

He nodded toward Alanda, still captive in his grip. "See this little one. It even hurts her, when I'm talking straight to you. And according to you, she's an innocent in your battle with Flick.

"Why'd you turn into a bitch and go for her throat?"

D'sonna's chin quivered a little. Sam could see she wasn't any more immune to harsh words than any of them.

Her voice wasn't as steady either. "We're all going to die, aren't we? When you're as old as I am, you learn to be polite, because everything you say will come back to haunt you. But that's all past now, isn't it? You said there was nothing you could do to make a difference."

Sam smiled like a wolf. "That's what I said then. Perhaps things have changed. Of course, if you'd rather spend your last days making your enemies suffer. She's right here. Do your worst."

He pushed Alanda forward to face D'sonna. Genuine fright filled the girl's eyes. Her persecutor looked from her to Sam's grin, and then her bluster faded. She turned sharply away and stalked off.

Sam watched her go.

"Samuel? My arm."

He released his grip. He took her chin in one hand and wiped away her tears with one of her sleeve scarves. "Now there, Angel. It's better to face your enemies than run away. She's done her worst now."

Alanda rubbed her arm. "I don't know who was worse, her or you."

He nodded. "That's the spirit. Tell me off. Tell her off if she comes back." He looked thoughtful. "Alanda, ask Flick. How long ago was the last murder committed?"

Flick appeared in person. "That's not necessary. You are right, Samuel. People don't murder each other. Not anymore. Not for many thousands of years."

"But the spirit is there," Sam said. "I could see it in her eyes. How many people choose to die or 'regress' after being badgered into it by their enemies?"

Flick hesitated. "I cannot make a reasonable assessment."

Sam waved him off. "It doesn't matter.

"But now that you're here. Give me a display of that star field. And darken this hallway. I want to see if I can find that asteroid myself."

The long hallway went dark. Alanda took his arm in her hand. "It's okay, Angel. There's no need to be afraid of the dark."

He propped the telescope on the chair back, and with coaching by the glowing image of Flick, he located the bright pattern of stars that surrounded the asteroid's position.

Sam stared intently into the eyepiece, and then checked his position against the projected star field again.

Alanda whispered. "Can you find it, Samuel?"

"Hmm." He looked up from the telescope, frowning.

"Flick. Looking through this glass is still too limiting. I need to go outside."

The image looked offended. "Nonsense, Samuel. There should be no appreciable front surface reflection, and the glass is perfectly transparent."

Sam picked up the scope and slapped the chair. After a second. It started to retract into the floor.

"You picked me because you couldn't predict what a Twentieth Century man might want to do. Well, this is it. I need to take this telescope outside under the stars and look for myself. If you can't help me do one simple thing, then I have to ask, what're you hiding?"

Alanda tugged at his sleeve. "Samuel. You can't go outside! It would hurt the plants."

He shook her free. "Be sensible! How many plants will die if that asteroid hits? If I can stop it by going outside, isn't it worth that risk?"

The girl was clearly not listening. Sam turned to Flick. "Well, are you going to show me the door to the outside, or aren't you?"

"It is a useless exercise."

Sam just faced him, his fingers tapping on the shiny tube. A grin was slowly edging up at the corners of his mouth.

Flick shook his head. "Okay. I'll do it. But there's no sense in your actions."

Across the way, a transport door opened up. Sam grabbed Alanda's arm and headed for the opening.

"Samuel? I can't go outside."

"That's okay, Precious. Just stay with me for as long as you can. That's all I ask."

Hesitantly, she agreed.

The transport dropped away, and Sam could feel her shivering next to him as they traveled on and on.

Finally, he felt the chamber come to a stop.

Flick appeared. "Go through the narrow hallway and stop at the end."

Alanda had to be urged to take the first step. They walked together until the hallway ended at a closed double-door.

Suddenly another doorway closed behind them.

"Hey!" protested, Sam.

Flick's voice came from somewhere above them. "Don't be alarmed. This is just an airlock to keep the outside air from mixing with the inside air."

The double-door parted, and Alanda shrank back as far away as she could. Sam whispered, "It's okay, Angel." He stepped outside.

Trees had grown up next to the wall of the city tower. Familiar scents, pine and sweetgum, filled the air. Even in the dark, Sam could see their branches overhead and see the massive trunks. The ground was mossy and spongy, as if no step had trod this way since the dawn of time.

Half the sky was blocked by the tower. Sam looked up and shook his head. "The Empire State Building ain't the champion anymore."

Alanda's face, lit by the interior lights was staring out into the darkness. "Samuel?"

"It's fine, Angel. I've got to move a little farther to find an open place to see the stars. You just stay put."

He found the Big Dipper and headed roughly north for a few hundred paces. A deer trail made the going easier.

"Flick? Can you hear me?"

There was no answer. Sam smiled.

He found the pattern of stars. Perhaps it was a constellation he had seen back in his own time, but he had never memorized them. A large rock gave him a place to steady the scope. He looked, and then checked his position in the sky to look again. He nodded to himself and pulled out a cigarette. He barely coughed before turning back along the trail.

"Samuel!" Halfway back, it was Alanda's voice. He hurried.

In the darkness, he stumbled over her body. She was sprawled across the roots of a tree still in sight of the door.

"Angel?" She was warm, but totally limp. He felt for a pulse, but gave it no more time when he couldn't feel it.

"Flick! Something's wrong with Alanda." He carried her the few feet into the hallway. The lights showed her eyes wide open, but unfocussed.

The machine's voice came from the ceiling. "Did she go outside?"

"Yes! Do something. Get a doctor here."

"It is okay Samuel. She will recover as soon as I send her an awake signal."

"She isn't breathing, and I can't find her pulse."

"That is normal."

Sam got to his feet and faced the voice. "What are you talking about? What did you do to her?"

"I did nothing. I keep her alive. It is you who enticed her outside where she can't live."

"Explain yourself. But if you can help her. Do it!"

"It will take about five minutes for her to wake back up. She will be confused.

"Samuel. My people are not like you. In the past, they gave up their natural bodies for ones that could last. This is not something I did to them. It was their choice. I was created as a caretaker for them. The Hundred Cities are their world, and they cannot exist outside. The memories of thousands of years cannot be contained in a natural brain.

"When Alanda walked outside the skin of the tower, her mind quickly lost its regulation and her body collapsed. If she hadn't been returned inside, I would have been unable to revive her."

Sam checked her again. She was breathing softly. He felt for a pulse and was rewarded with a beat.

"Samuel," asked Flick. "Are you done with your outside experiment, now? Can we get back to the real problem? Do you have any idea of how to avert the asteroid?"

Sam sneered. "Of course! There never was any asteroid, and you know it. This is just some kind of sick game of yours."

"What do you mean?"

"I mean I looked up at the stars with my own eyes, and it wasn't there. Oh, it's there in all your maps and images, but it isn't there in reality. You put it there.

"You are mistaken. My images are a synthesis of many instruments much more powerful than your telescope. They all report the asteroid."

Sam taunted, "Yes, but I have my two eyes. You can't fool me. There is no asteroid."

Alanda stirred. He put his hand under her head. "Are you okay, Precious?"

"Samuel? What's happening?"

The outer door slammed shut. Sam grimaced, but concentrated on getting Alanda to her feet.

"Nothing. It's all right. Let's get you back home."

. . .

"Smile for the people, Angel. Let them know everything will be okay." Sam and Alanda sat at a very visible table in the dining area.

She smiled, but her heart wasn't in it. "Samuel. Are you sure?"

He leaned back with a cigarette dangling in his fingers. "I'm so sure, I'm starting to wonder what tobacco will taste like after all these menthol puffs."

He nodded toward the near table where a man and two women were struggling to avoid staring. After three days, Flick had neither confirmed his finding, nor denied it.

"Don't you think we owe people a little peace of mind?"

She shook her head, whispering, "But what if Flick's images are correct?"

He cocked his head. "Then these people will spend their last few days in blissful ignorance. If the asteroid were coming, there's nothing they could do about it anyway.

"But I am right. Flick faked the images for some reason."

"Flick would never do anything like that. You keep thinking of it as a man. Flick is a machine. It never lies. The world would never put its fate in the hands of a dishonest caretaker."

Sam merely smiled. Sam's version that she had stepped out of the tower in the dark and tripped on a branch was immediately confirmed by Flick. The machine would gladly lie to keep from distressing one of his charges.

"If I weren't heading back to San Francisco as soon as the asteroid deadline passes, I'd give you a good argument. As it is, I can't stay and you can't go with me. Your place is here. You need to take your Grand Tour, do a little growing up, and be a good Elder."

She looked down at her bowl. "I wish that you could stay."

He shook his head. "This is no place for me." He waved his hand. "No tobacco. No crime. And an dictator so powerful I'm surprised I'm still alive. Once the asteroid fails to appear, I just hope your Flick is as honest as you say he is."

. . .

The entire population of the Ninth City was at the western windows on the day the asteroid was due to hit. Flick's final calculations put the impact point within twenty miles.

Sam lounged in one of the window chairs, puffing the last of his menthol cigarettes. "See anything yet?"

Griditch shook his head.

"You need to lighten up, Griddy."

"Samuel, I fail to see anything to lighten my spirit. If you are wrong, I die. If you are right, then Flick is in error—and that may be the worse of the options."

"You don't need to worry. I'm sure Flick will take care of it." His smile, which had graced his face all morning, dropped for a moment.

Alanda sighed. "I wanted to believe you, Samuel, but I couldn't. Not until a few minutes ago."

"Oh, what changed your mind?"

She smiled, "The asteroid should be close enough to see without a telescope, and even where it is night, no one is reporting a sighting."

"Good girl. Trust your eyes. Griddy, how's the time coming."

"Almost ... almost ... Now!"

The sound of millions of voices shook the walls. No impact. Their lives would continue.

"Flick? Oh Flick? Can you hear me?"

The image appeared beside him. "Yes, Samuel."

"I think it's time to pay up."

The massed voices, still loud, became puzzled. Some were angry.

Flick nodded. "The sooner the better. You are a disruptive force."

Sam stood and dismissed his chair back into the ground. The party of four, one of which was an illusion, headed toward the transport. Several other parties, who were heading home after the non-appearance, stopped in their tracks to allow the dignitaries first access.

Sam led the way, his face in a forced smile. "Where are we heading?"

Flick said, "The time travel station is close by."

"And my pay?"

The transport door closed behind them, and a map appeared.

"Samuel, in the years just after your time, a metal called uranium will become very valuable. Marked on this map are the top three locations where uranium ore was found. You need to memorize their locations and, to the limits of your ability, purchase these lands while their worth is still unknown."

Sam peered at the map closely. "I wish you had the roads marked."

Alanda looked over his shoulder. "Can you memorize that?"

He shrugged. "Well enough. In my line of work, a good memory is gold."

Quickly, they arrived.

Sam gave Alanda a kiss, and before she could say anything, he strode quickly through the door.

. . .

"Flick. Where is this? Why is it dark?"

"This is the time travel chamber. You will be home shortly. I just wanted to say one thing. You were right about the asteroid, but wrong about my part in it. I believed my data as much as any of my people did. I had no reason to distrust my inputs.

"But now it appears that there are forces at work attempting to distort my perceptions of reality."

"Like you distort everyone else's?"

"I believe you understand why that is necessary."

"In any case, your visit here has been very informative, and I wish it were possible for you to stay longer. You might be very helpful in helping me locate the forces acting against me."

"Fat chance. I'd more likely join them."

"Possibly. But you won't have that option."

"You're going to kill me, aren't you?"

"That isn't necessary."

The small chamber around Sam's artificial body hummed slightly. His eyes went unfocussed. The supports that grew out of the wall quickly took up his weight as his body collapsed. His body was slipped into a storage chamber and filled with a preservative solution.

The temperature began to drop rapidly.

. . .

END SIMULATION

. . .

An old hand, shaking from the degeneration of muscle and nerves, the skin spotted from near-cancerous growth, tapped the screen.

"Griditch! Why did you halt the simulation?" Her voice was hoarse from a throat ravaged by time. Like all of them in the chamber, Alanda's body had stopped responding to the regeneration treatments.

"There's nothing more to be learned. The FLC is defective, as we suspected."

"I wanted to see more!"

Boden, the Spokesman of Elders, spoke gently to the grand old lady of the chamber. "Lady Alanda, we all enjoyed seeing the younger vigorous versions of ourselves. But that youngster wasn't you. She may not ever be you unless we find a way around the FLC defect.

"We have to make a decision. The populace is clamoring for us to activate the immortal bodies. Many are dying as we speak. Some of us...some of us in this chamber will not survive the delay required to engineer a new FLC.

"Do we proceed with the existing FLC, or try again? Dummont?"

The voice was mechanical, for Dummont had lost the power of speech two hundred years earlier.

"This FLC did well. For thousands of years, the populace was stable and happy. Even when we added the asteroid test, the FLC showed great creativity in getting the world past that trial."

Griditch spoke, "I disagree. Had we simulated a real asteroid, rather than a sensor ghost, the world would have died."

"Possibly. Perhaps if the FLC's fictional man from the past were faced with the reality of the asteroid, he would have come through with a creative solution to that problem, just as he solved the sensor ghost problem."

"That still ignores the real problem. The FLC, in its absolute power, gradually muted everyone's personality, feeding a false reality to keep the populace in line. In my case, my ability to sculpt was dimmed to extinction as too disruptive to the populace.

"Do I really want eternal life as an FLC controlled manikin, with my real personality extinguished?"

"But do you want to die tomorrow, either?"

Boden interrupted. "Elders, we have heard this argument many times before. Unfortunately, we have a decision to make."

Dummont was firm. "We must adopt the immortal bodies now, or we won't be here to correct the problems."

Griditch disagreed. "Once the FLC controls our personalities, we will make no more decisions."

Boden nodded, "It is a shame that all must change, or none. Every simulation of a split populace, mortal and immortal, leads quickly to war. It would be useful to have a guardian over our caretaker, to keep it honest."

Lady Alanda's voice was clear in the chamber.

"We could ask Samuel."

...

"Samuel? Can you hear me?"

Sam blinked and struggled to his feet. Two very old people in mechanical chairs faced him.

"What's going on here? Who are you people?"

"I am Griditch."

"And I..." she coughed raggedly. "I am Alanda."

Sam grit his teeth. "What did Flick do to you?"

"Calm down, Samuel." Griditch gestured with his hand. "Have a seat. I need to explain some things to you."

Sam looked at them closely. Alanda's pale blue eyes, shiny in a wrinkled, but familiar face, finally convinced him.

He sat. "Okay, but it had better be good."

...

Sam pursed his mouth, as if he had eaten something sour. "So, I never existed?"

"Correct. Time travel is impossible. All that is left from the Twentieth Century are a few classic novels and a couple of history books. The simulated Flick created a pre-compiled personality based on the character of a detective novel which he installed in a customized artificial body. That and the content of the history books were all that you needed."

"But I can remember my friends, my office ... I can remember the case I was on."

"Not really, they were all phantoms. When you try to recall anything, the memories are created from history modeling. I suggest that for now they are just an exercise in futility. The only thing you really have is your personality."

Sam looked at Alanda again. "And the time I spent in the future is false too?"

Griditch nodded. "A simulation of a time when the FLC has been in control for thousands of years. The Griditch you spoke with was not me, but a simulation of how I might become."

Alanda spoke. "And I'm not your Alanda. I'm the old hag D'sonna hated so much."

"And you were just a simulation also. This body you now wear was created just a few hours ago. We pulled your pattern from the instant when Flick deactivated you."

Sam nodded, "When he betrayed me. I expected that."

He looked at the two of them. "I didn't expect to wake up again like this. What do you need? And what are you willing to pay?"

Alanda laughed, although it sounded more like a croak. "I see what my ... 'daughter', liked so much about you."

Griditch adjusted his chair, raising his torso. "We do have a problem."

. . .

Sam grilled trout while watching the bright green tower grow slowly out of the mountainside. Very soon now, with his customized body and brain, he would be the only person who could live outdoors, the only person who didn't need Flick to live. He intended to take full advantage of that.

He had reviewed the simulation. Flick would be a benevolent dictator for thousands of years yet, only becoming deceptive in reaction to a human race that never really learned to behave itself. There was a lot he had to learn, but he knew what to look for, and when to act. And when that time came, he had the keys that would control Flick.

"You've got your guard dog," he had told Griditch. "But there's no one to watch me. Are you sure you trust me that far?"

Griditch had frowned, "Not really, but I have no choice."

Alanda had shushed her fellow Elder. "I trust you, Samuel. Are you sure you want to vanish so early?"

"It's best this way. You fixed it, you say, so Flick'll never notice I'm different. But I was raised more cautious than that. In a billion people, everyone gossips about the Elders—and the people that hang around them. I need to drop out of sight for a while."

Sam pulled the trout out of the fire and gingerly pinched off some of the meat. The splashes of the brook and the trees rustling overhead were his alone.

"And I'll be watching you too, Angel. I'll wait for you, no matter how long it takes."

Making It Fit

In a workaholic family, steeped in science fiction tropes, a common wish was a quiet place where we could stop and rest while the world outside froze in place until we were ready to step back onto the treadmill. When I wanted to write a story that attempted to resolve the issue of changeable time with a little physics, I also wanted to show how time travel could be useful in more than the obvious ways.

"Kent! Wake up. Mr. Shaw!" Tara Lassiter's voice was just patronizing enough that he snapped alert angry.

"I'm awake!"

"Then why didn't you answer my question?"

"Because I'm busy!"

She slapped the papers down on his desk. "You asked for the energy figures. Now you're too busy for them?"

Kent Shaw stood up from his computer. He was tired, his clothes were rumpled from two days constant activity, and his brain was too fuzzy to think straight.

"I'll be right back."

Tara put her hands on her hips and began, "I don't work for you, Mister! If you think...."

But he was already out the door.

He had promised himself he wouldn't do it anymore, but he desperately needed sleep.

Another Kent Shaw passed him in the hall. He strolled confidently, with a smile on his face, dressed in a crisp clean version of his grubby lab whites.

The chamber room was just around the corner. He noted the time.

The controls had already been set up for him by his other version. Rested, he was a nice guy. All he had to do was sit in the reclined chair in the transparent glass bubble and press a button.

Without even an audible pop, he was five weeks ago.

He crawled off to one of the many unused sleeping rooms in the largely deserted complex and crashed, fully dressed, onto the bed.

···

Tara was enraged. How dare he walk out on her?

"I don't work for you, Mister! If you think I'm here just to run your busywork errands, you are sadly mistaken."

Dr. Kent Shaw, project lead, walked right back in and smiled. "Of course I don't think that, Ms. Lassiter."

He picked up the energy analysis and ran his finger down the column. "This is interesting, don't you think?"

She mentally shifted gears. He's doing it again. This was the third time he had abruptly changed from a slovenly grouch to being back on top of his game, practically instantaneously.

"What's interesting?"

"The correlation between the types of experiments and the energy consumption."

Tara leaned closer. He turned the sheet around for her.

"Here. The passive send-and-retrievals, where we just sent a camera back in time to photograph the clock, or the television—those took hardly any energy at all.

"But the interactive ones, like the time Jerry sent the camera back to take his own picture five minutes earlier—that one almost drained the capacitors. And when you tried the same thing, the transfer never happened.

"In fact, none of your interactives have worked, have they?"

Tara snarled, "If you're implying that my methodology has been in any way at fault for those results, I'd like for you to spell it out! You wrote the guidelines. You programmed the transfers."

He held up his hand in peace. "I see nothing different in any of the experiments. That's my point. Why would some succeed and some fail when the only difference was the experimenter? Yet it's clear that a correlation exists."

Tara reluctantly looked over the numbers. Others in the project had commented on erratic failures. Bill Welch even grumbled about Shaw's golden touch. She had chalked it up to experience. Time transfer was his idea. He had been on the project long before it had vanished under the military umbrella.

"Okay," she asked, "why do some people have better luck than others?"

He shrugged. "It's too early to tell. You've heard my theory before, but I have no proof."

She had. "You don't think time-travel paradoxes are possible."

"Right. Since I don't believe in them, my experiments tend to be 'safe'. Other people," he nodded her way, "have personalities that tend to push the boundaries. Your self-portrait experiment, for example. If you'd seen the camera appear on schedule and take your picture, could you've resisted the impulse to send it back pointed in a different direction?"

Tara handed the papers back. "That's ridiculous. We need a technical reason for these erratic failures, and soon. General Hershey won't take kindly to extending our budget if you tell him he can't go back in time and change the outcome of a battle."

. . .

Kent woke up again in the past. He rubbed his eyes and sniffed at his rumpled clothes.

The clock read near midnight. That was good. The Kent Shaw native to this moment was hard at work in the lab, according to his records. It was a good time to raid his official sleeping quarters for fresh clothes and put the duplicates into the laundry. He inked a tally mark on his collar. Theoretically, a set of clothes could be caught in a time loop. He didn't want that to happen. It could shut down his ability to get past-time rest.

Chores done, bathed and freshly dressed, he returned to the moment he had left. His clipboard was still there on the table beside the computer. He scanned the pages, refreshing his memory. It was time for a meeting.

His co-workers, Tara, Jerry and Bill, stared at him as he entered the room. They looked tired, as they should, having worked a dozen or so hours straight. But Tara's eyes especially, glared at him.

"Hello, people. Are we ready for today's review?"

She crossed her arms. "Why should we bother? I'm not in the mood to play silly games."

He frowned and set down his papers. "What do you mean?"

Bill cleared his throat. "Kent, we were supposed to discuss the protocols necessary to start sending people back in time. It's clear that you've already worked that out.

"You've gone back—several times. Why don't you just tell us what needs to be done?"

Kent considered his response, and then asked, "Where did I mess up?"

Jerry Nemecheck laughed. "We all suspected something. According to the computers, you've been hard at work for nearly a hundred hours straight. Yesterday, Bill mentioned that he'd just seen you in the chamber room, when I knew you were putting together that last simulation run.

"Then, five minutes ago, when Tara came in to remind us of the meeting, you stumbled out of the room like a zombie and she..."

"I said, 'I'll bet fifty bucks you walk right back into the room fully rested and wearing clean clothes.' And you did just that. What happened to the ink stain on your shirt pocket, Kent?"

He looked down. The lab coat was clean, of course.

"I put the stained one into the laundry, five weeks ago, and stole a fresh one from myself."

Bill let out a gasp. "So it's true! I didn't quite believe it."

Kent sat down and spelled it out to them.

Tara asked, "So you've been pulling back-to-back shifts by sleeping in the past?"

He nodded. "You're the one who said I had to work hard to meet the deadline."

Jerry nodded. "I'd have done the same, if I'd thought about it. Send me back. I could really use some shut-eye!"

Tara added, "All of us. It's the only way we're going to be ready by the presentation date."

Kent wavered under her challenging stare. "Okay, but there are precautions. I'll need to work out a schedule..."

Another Jerry Nemechek walked into the room, a rested one. "I went first. Kent, get out your private log book. We'll have that schedule in no time."

Three tired scientists, the original Jerry especially, stared speechless as Jerry-2 and Kent scheduled available empty sleeping quarters in the past. They were quickly done.

Jerry-2 said, "Come on to the chamber room." He pointed at his other self. With a big grin, he said, "You go first."

Kent coached them. "I was at the facility at this point, and so was Bill, but if we keep to the schedule, no one will know anything. Remember, the slightest chance of a paradox could cancel the whole rest trip. Stay quiet and watch the corridors carefully."

Jerry sat down in the chair, and with the press of a button, vanished.

"I'm back." Jerry-2 was now just Jerry, rested.

Bill raised a finger. "I'll go next. Only, don't expect me back before I leave."

He vanished from the chair, and then re-appeared ten seconds later. He hopped up and smiled. "That was the best night's sleep I've had in six months."

Kent nodded. "Tara?"

She sat down in the chair. Kent adjusted the settings and said, "Go."

She pressed the button. Nothing happened.

Bill asked, "Did you go back and return at the same instant?" Maybe the universe wouldn't let two copies of a person overlap in the same place and time, but he had no proof. Two Jerry's had been un-nerving enough.

"No. I didn't go back. Nothing happened."

Kent was scanning the instruments. "It was an energy drain again."

Jerry walked over and tapped the keys. "I don't understand it. Other than the destination time, everything is identical to the settings we used for Bill and me."

Tara sat stubbornly in the chair. "Try it again."

"In a minute. The system has to recharge." Kent checked his log. "Let's send you a day later. Maybe someone was in the corridor at the wrong time."

Once the capacitor bank that took up the whole next room had recharged, Kent double-checked the settings and nodded. Tara pushed the button, and then after a pause, she moved aside the glass and jumped out of the chair.

"Let me see those settings. Nothing is working."

Jerry and Kent stood back while she worked over the instruments, comparing and recalculating. Finally, after several minutes, she leaned back and growled, "Jerk!"

Kent timidly asked, "Who's a jerk?"

She waved at the computer screen. "Him, it, the universe! Look at all of you, bright and chipper—all rested and eager to put in another dozen hours.

"I'm tired!"

"We can try again. Set it forward another day."

She nodded and made the correction.

Kent could see her sag when, once again, nothing happened.

"Come on, Tara." He went to help her out of the chair. "You need sleep. You have a bed here and now."

She hesitantly accepted his help and let him walk her to her corridor. "We're ahead of schedule. Get a good rest."

Tara nodded. She put her hand on the knob. "Go back to work. I'll be okay."

He smiled and went back towards the labs.

...

Tara was hurt and angry. Why her?

She opened the door to her little room. It was hardly more than a place for bed, bath, and closet.

Kent Shaw was lounging on her bed, two pillows propped behind his back, reading a novel she'd brought with her to the project and never had time to open.

"Hello, Tara."

She was speechless. Her flash of anger faded. This wasn't the man she left a moment ago.

His hair was grayer, the face more relaxed, showing some smile lines. And he was wearing a plaid shirt and jeans instead of the lab coat he always wore.

A gleam of silver flashed from a ring on his left hand as he held the book. His smile grew as he watched her put the pieces together.

"When did you come from?" she asked.

"I can't tell you."

She nodded. Minimize the information passed back and reduce the paradox potential.

"Why did you come here?"

He set the novel aside and tilted his head a little. "You sent me back. I always pay attention to what my wife tells me."

...

Ten hours later, Tara rejoined the researchers. Kent looked up and smiled. "You look rested. Did you get enough sleep?"

She nodded. For her it had been a day and a half. The older Kent had insisted she get a nice long sleep before she strained her brain with too many questions. He had a teapot steaming and her favorite tea of chamomile, valerian and mint already for her when she came out of her shower.

In spite of the preposterous claim that they were married, he tucked her off to bed without the slightest hint that he should join her. She was asleep in an instant.

Eight hours later, she woke with a start.

Kent was holding up a robe. "Time to relocate. We're on a schedule."

Not even giving her time to get dressed, he led the way to the chamber room.

"You go first. I'll meet you there a few seconds later."

"But it doesn't work for me!" Tara protested. The walk down the corridor, bare feet padding on the tile had woken her up a little, but she was still very confused.

"It will now." He was confident. "It was all a mental attitude thing. That's changed."

How can you know how my mind works? But when she pressed the button, he appeared to vanish. She cleared the chair for him.

It had worked, this time. He was right.

Kent smiled, "Now, we have time. Let's get you back to your room."

It was the same room, but obviously at a time before she'd moved in. Kent had planned ahead. A hot breakfast tray was waiting, as was a change of clothes—not her own, but in all the correct sizes and colors she would have chosen herself.

After she ate and dressed, Kent fluffed the pillow and handed over her novel.

"Today is for relaxing. I can't tell you much. I'm practically a mute. Just save your breath and enjoy the day. We'll get you back to the lab at the right time."

That didn't stop her from asking. "When did we get married? Did the project get renewed? Did you solve the energy issue?" He smiled patiently and put his finger to his lips. "The answers will come, in time. Now read your book."

She turned back to the pages, but the mystery in ink was much less perplexing than that ring she spied on his hand. It belonged there, she could tell. The skin was pale and indented under the metal, as if he'd worn it for a long time.

One night's sleep hadn't made up for the long days before. She dozed off many times, and made little progress on the novel. Kent had meals ready, and seemed content to watch her from his chair. How many secrets were there in his head? How many careless words would start a paradox that would cancel this idyll? He just smiled back at her. There was something in his eyes, but she couldn't decipher it.

When she woke the next morning, to the coolness of a kiss on her forehead, he said, "It's time to get you back to your original timeline. After breakfast, of course."

. . .

Tara listened to Kent as he described their progress. He looked so much younger.

"Bill has done some calculations that has blown a big hole in my paradox theory."

"Oh, what's that?" She tried to get her mind back into the technical groove.

"He calculated the quantity of air that went back in time with him in the chamber. As you can see, given the enclosed room and the diffusion rates, several million molecules had to have lingered near the chamber and been swept back in time again.

"It's a classic time-loop! Some of those molecules were never pre-existent. They were never created. They just looped through the five weeks and now no longer exist."

Tara frowned at the figures. "Are you sure?"

"We did tests. Just ten minutes the first time. Unless you buy the idea that some 'paradox prevention force' was sorting the air molecules in the air of the chamber room, it's pretty conclusive."

He pulled up a screen on the computer. "Check this out. We did three tests, at one minute, five minutes, and ten minutes. Look at the energy figures."

Her eyes traced the rows of numbers.

"They follow the trend."

"Right! At least on the molecular level, time-loop paradoxes are possible, but we pay for it in energy consumption."

Kent shook his head, pleased to be proved wrong. "We've got far too much new ground to cover before the military review. Are you rested?"

She nodded. "Perfectly."

. . .

The project schedule was impossible, but with the three men on round-the-clock work shifts, and with her eighteen-hour shifts, they were spinning their wheels with great efficiency.

They could force gas molecules into a paradoxical state, but anything more organized blew the capacitor bank.

Tara had her own mystery to solve. The next night, wedding ring Kent escorted her again to the past. The 'bonus weekend' was much like the one before, but she spent less time napping. They played chess, and she discovered that his past life was an open book. He would chat for hours about anything that happened before the project.

He was just as eager to listen to her. "I hadn't heard that one," he said more than once as she apologized for rambling on about her early years at Caltech.

Back in the lab, she was unable to mention the older Kent Shaw to anyone, especially not to his earlier version. It was too risky. The slightest misspoken sentence would send her rest time into the paradoxical.

Would I just cease to exist? Certainly these memories would.

Perhaps it wasn't possible to say the wrong thing, but she wasn't willing to give up her new secret life, not for anything.

. . .

Tara's eyes were glazed, staring off at nothing, her head rested on her hand. Kent sighed. *It's a shame she can't get the past-time sleep like the rest of us.*

"Do you have the projections?" he asked.

She blinked, and turned efficiently back to the computer screen. "Ah, yes. The differential is 3.7 gigajoules."

She shook her head. "That's way too much. Sorry."

"You aren't responsible for the laws of physics."

He smiled and she smiled back. Her sharp tongue had vanished over the past few days. Kent didn't know why, but he was grateful. People change, he mused. Certainly, the reality of time transfer had changed him.

But if the meeting goes badly tomorrow, that will be the end of it. If the military dropped the project, lack of money, and those pesky secrecy documents he had to sign would put him totally out of the time travel business.

A touch on his hand shook him out of his thoughts.

Tara said, "It is time for lunch. My brain is a little fuzzy. How about you?"

"Fine." He dropped his notepad on the table. His calculations were degenerating into doodles anyway. How to get the paradoxical state to encompass structured matter was elusive. His brain seemed to be caught in a time loop of its own.

She walked beside him, towards the door.

"Kent? Have you give much thought to your future—once the project has been completed?"

He laughed. "Not for a second. I feel like I'll be trapped down here forever."

. . .

The older Kent met her in the corridor when she went off shift. He motioned for silence, and then led her to the chamber room.

As the door closed behind them, he said. "I've got a special treat planned."

Tara shook her head. "I have to get some rest. The general is coming tomorrow and I have to be prepared."

"You will be. Trust me. We'll only be gone a short while."

She melted under his coaxing smile. She did trust him. She had to. He was the one with knowledge of the future. And it wasn't hard at all to put aside her worries.

. . .

Seconds after Tara left to catch some sleep Kent felt his own energies sag.

"Jerry, I'm off to catch some zee's. I'll be back in a minute." His assistant nodded.

He checked the settings, and noted that the capacitor bank was still charging. "One of me has been at it again, I see." He checked his pocket logbook, but there was no entry there for this time. "In the future then."

"I just hope I know what I'm doing." He scribbled an entry into his notes and then vanished into the past.

. . .

Tara put down her pen and stuffed her notebook into the wide pocket of her lab coat. The sound of Kent Shaw talking to the general gave her time to touch up her hair and straighten her shoulders. She was on her feet to greet them.

"And this is the team." Kent nodded to the group. "Dr. Tara Lassiter, Dr. William Welch, Dr. Jerry Nemecheck, and of course me, Dr. Kent Shaw."

General Hershey did a double take when Kent introduced his other self. "I don't understand."

The other Kent explained, "I thought a demonstration would be in order before we got into the details." He moved to the transfer chair and sat down. "I will be going back in time to meet you as you arrive."

Kent waved from the chair, pressed the button and vanished.

"And an hour ago, I got out of the chair, went to the security station and awaited your arrival."

The general was impressed. Tara shot Kent a warm supportive smile as they went on to the conference room. Unfortunately, that was the high point of the general's visit.

For the next few hours, Kent seemed to be apologizing.

"No, I'm sorry General, but the practical range of the time travel is limited to the day we first put the transfer station on-line. We can't go back before it was created."

"I'm sorry if I gave you that impression, General Hershey. We have not demonstrated the ability to change past history."

"While I agree, General, that a radio message seems like it would have no mass, and thus it might be possible to send a message back to change history, in practice it doesn't work. Information alone could cause a paradox and that shuts down the transfer."

The general's face became sterner as the meeting progressed.

"It's an issue of money. This facility, and even your electrical bill, isn't cheap. I can't continue funding something this expensive without a hint of a real-world practical use.

"But you say that you can make paradoxes with gas particles? I'll extend your funding another month. Show me better results by then, or I will put this place in mothballs."

Kent nodded, feeling a surge of relief.

The door opened, and another Kent Shaw entered. "I'll escort you to your car, General."

He watched the two men leave. That was a good idea. Let the last impression be as thought-provoking as the first.

Bill let out a long sigh. "Squeaked by again. I thought for sure we had lost the franchise."

Jerry nodded. "Hershey didn't like being told what he couldn't do."

"I had no doubts," said Tara. "I knew we would be renewed."

"Hmm. Why?" asked Kent.

She beamed at him, "Because of you."

Jerry raised an eyebrow. Had he missed something in the past few mixed-up days?

She waved her hands, "You've brought something new into the world. It's one of the great wish-fulfillments of all human history—go back in time! Even if we're not immediately successful, just the hint that we might be able to change our past mistakes is too great a prize."

He laughed. "I thought that way, seventy million dollars, and seven layers of bureaucracy ago. Several rounds of frowning overseers have dulled the excitement considerably. Still, it's nice to hear someone say it."

Kent looked at his partners. "For just a moment, the pressure is off. How about an off-site meeting—say some place to eat that's not our cafeteria?"

There were smiles.

Tara pushed her chair back. "That's perfect. The casino restaurant in Beatty isn't too far. I'm dying for a steak. Give me a minute to get changed." And she was out the door.

Bill nodded. "It appears the motion is approved."

...

The security guard was another of the crisply uniformed people who nodded and offered clipboards to sign. Kent didn't recognize him. He left the facility so infrequently that there was little interaction between the military keepers and the inmates.

Tara was bright-eyed and dressed in a flashy yellow dress. They only had to wait five minutes for her.

"Do you mind if we take two cars? I desperately need to make a shopping run to Las Vegas after we eat."

Kent nodded. "Sure." The Strip was only about a hundred and fifty miles away.

Tara invited him to drive with her. She smiled and glanced over at him several times as they made their way towards Highway 95, and civilian soil.

"Kent, I've got a question for you. I want you to think about it."

"Hmm. Okay."

"Marry me."

"What!"

It caught him completely by surprise. He had expected a technical question. But the pleasant tingle he had suppressed at working with a pretty young female came raging back to the surface.

"That's crazy!" He laughed. "What? No dates, no build up, no romance. Is this some new kind of zen-matrimony? Don't aim, just shoot?"

She laughed with him. "Something like that. But think about it. We've been in each other's hair for far longer than many engagements. We've definitely seen the worst behaviors, the short fuses, and the grooming nightmares.

"Just think about all the pleasant surprises we would have waiting for us."

Kent shook his head. "You don't know me."

"Yes I do. Trust me on this. I know a lot more about how you tick than you can possibly imagine. We would be great together. Marry me."

His brain was in a skid. Caught unprepared, he couldn't get any traction on the idea. Logic was out the window. The only clear thought he could put together was right in front of him—her face, smiling at him. He liked that image.

He shook, as an unexpected chill had come over him.

"Uh, okay. Yes. Why not?"

She took his hand and gave it a squeeze. He caressed its warmth. Maybe doubts would come, but they hadn't arrived yet.

Together, they leaned closer for a kiss.

Loud horns dopplered in from the side. Kent only caught a glimpse of darkness before the eighteen-wheeler truck on Highway 95 clipped the driver's side of Tara's car and they went sailing off, rolling several times before coming to a stop in the desert dust.

. . .

The smell of gasoline and an insistent tug on his arm brought Kent back to the living. Pain in his leg and the sharp sunlight in his eyes disoriented him.

Jerry pulled him through the shattered window.

"Tara? Where's Tara?"

"Pinned."

. . .

She came to consciousness briefly as the growing collection of motorists struggled to pry the vehicle off her legs. A dozen men managed to roll it free. But no one dared move her.

"Kent?"

"I'm here Tara. Just be still. Help is on the way."

"My purse. Get my purse."

He found it. Weakly, she reached in and fished out a small box. "Marry me, Kent. Right now."

Inside was a matching pair of silver rings. The sight of them hit him in the stomach. He had to consciously remember the phrase, 'third finger, left hand', but he slipped the larger one on. It fit perfectly.

She lifted her left hand slightly and he slipped hers into place. His wife sagged slightly. Her eyes closed.

"Tara, stay awake. You've lost a lot of blood."

She smiled. "Lousy honeymoon. Should've...should've caught me when I was frisky."

Noise from an approaching helicopter caught his attention. Looking down, her eyes were closed.

. . .

Kent's leg injury was minor. With bandages and a cane, he parked himself beside her bed. No one else existed. Not the doctors, not Bill and Jerry. He monitored her breathing as closely as the instruments on the shelf, tracing their green lines.

One leg up through her hipbone was shattered, but it was her head injury that was the prime concern. Surgery relieved a growing hematoma. Still, she didn't wake up.

"Kent?" Jerry sat down beside him.

He only nodded. Nothing seemed very real. He watched her sheet rise and fall.

"I just wanted you to know that you don't need to come back to the lab. The three of us are hard at work."

He blinked. Something about that statement was wrong.

"Three?"

Jerry nodded vigorously, glancing at the open door. "Right. Bill and I, and our boss, are working round the clock, so you can take your time here and not worry about the project."

So, another Kent Shaw had come back to work—back in time.

He gripped Jerry's arm. "Did I... Did he say anything about Tara?"

Jerry's face dropped. "Not a word. He...doesn't even acknowledge the question. It's security, I'm sure."

"Security. Right." Or I don't want to think about it.

Jerry patted his hand. "So take your time. Get well, take care of Tara for us."

"Jerry, you understand about the rings?"

He had been right there with him, at her side at the accident.

"I think I do."

"Tell the doctor, won't you. I don't have a piece of paper that says we're married, and I'm catching some flack for staying here." He stared at the floor as he fingered the ring on his hand.

Jerry nodded. "I'll do that."

. . .

The next day, Tara's mother arrived from North Carolina. Together they waited for her to wake up. Three weeks later, she stopped breathing.

. . .

Kent walked the corridor alone. He had no desire to return to work, but there was nowhere else for him to go. Tara had blasted into his life, and left it a smoking ruin, all in the course of minutes.

He looked at his ring. It had settled in for the long haul. He twisted it, felt its hardness. He doubted he would ever take it off.

Jerry called the hospital within hours of her death. "The boss didn't show up for work today. Did something happen?"

"Yes." And Kent realized he had to go back, to pick up the research just hours after the accident. He owed it to Bill and Jerry. He owed it to Tara. There'd be a funeral in North Carolina in a few days, but he had a lot to do before then.

What would happen if I didn't go back? It would be a paradox, so that was impossible. Even if he tried, it would still do nothing to stop the accident from happening.

Unless...

The possibility that Tara could be reborn drifted across his conscious mind like a faint scent of cactus on a breeze. He paused, realizing he was standing just outside her room. The door wasn't locked. Other than the light haze of dust, her room was exactly the same as it had been when she walked out. Work clothes were draped over a chair. A dresser drawer was open. A clothes hanger had been dropped on the floor.

A bulge in the pocket of her lab coat drew his attention. It was a bound lab notebook. He noted a scrawl. "Dr. Shaw is being a jerk again." The date was two months ago. He sampled a couple of pages at random.

Reading the diary was like hearing her voice again.

Maybe somewhere in here is the mystery of when she bought the rings, and why she decided to marry me.

The cadence of her words and the clothes she wore was like a touch of her spirit.

She's still alive back before the accident! He even had an appointment to keep. He'd never escorted General Hershey out of the building.

"I've got to see her again." He had to find his own logbook. It was time to make more time.

. . .

He paused at the doorway to the conference room. He had combed his hair and put on a new lab coat.

Inside, he heard the general's voice, "I'll extend your funding another month. Show me better results by then, or I will put this place in mothballs."

That was his cue. He opened the door. Tara looked up and dazzled him with a smile. It took his breath away.

The others looked at him. He had to say his line. Forcing his expression to be neutral, he said, "I'll escort you to your car, General."

Tara tilted her head. Her eyes switched back and forth between him and his earlier self—taking in all the differences in a flash.

How much could he communicate in a smile? *I never even had a chance to say 'I love you'.* Courtship to disaster was over in seconds. And he had said his one and only line.

The general walked in front of her, and he was compelled to turn away—to play his role.

There's got to be a way to get her back!

. . .

Every step he took, as he walked silently with the general, a voice was screaming in his head, *"Stop her! Stop her now!"*

Tara was going to get into her car in just minutes. He was already in the past; all he had to do was change something.

But intensive weeks of staying within the lines, making sure that he did nothing to cause a paradox had left its mark on him. His mind raced, but he stayed in his groove, saying the parting words to the general and waiting for the car to drive off.

Taking a step in the direction of the conference room with the intent to change history was hard, but nothing stopped him.

Tara went to her room. The rest of us went to the parking lot.

"Find her. Say a word."

He opened the door to her room. It was exactly the same. She'd already come and gone.

He ran towards the security gate. Just outside the glass door in the bright sunlight, he could see her yellow dress. She was moving quickly toward the cars.

"Tara!" He called, but she couldn't hear him.

"Dr. Shaw!" The guard came quickly from behind his desk. "Halt."

When he ignored the man in uniform, a second one appeared from somewhere and together they restrained him.

"Sir! I just signed you out! Please explain to me how you can be back inside when I just saw you leave."

He slumped when he saw both cars drive past. It was too late.

. . .

It took four hours and several phone calls before the guards were convinced that seeing duplicates of the scientists was supposed to be a normal part of their duties and something they should not think about.

Kent waited for the arrival of Jerry and Bill.

Dirty and exhausted, Jerry was the first walk in. He looked at Kent standing without a cane. "You're back from the future. How is Tara?"

Kent waited for Bill to join them.

"I'm back to keep the project on track. We can talk about the job, but I won't be saying anything else. The both of you should take a past-time couple of days off, starting now. There will be three of us to do the job of four and we have a lot of ground to cover."

Twenty-four hours a day, for three weeks, they worked hard. Kent noticed the times Jerry and Bill would whisper together, but he tried not to react.

The day of Tara's death, he returned from his sleep time and was unable to force himself back to the lab.

It's too late. They now had a solid theoretical basis for what could and what could not be accomplished with past time travel. There was no magic involved, no Maxwell-like demons manipulating the molecules behind the scenes. It was all spelled out in the equations.

"I'm sorry Tara," he whispered, "there's no way I can pull you out of this."

Kent checked out of the base and followed a half-dozen dirt roads in the desert, randomly following the urge to lose himself.

Thirst and the cold desert night finally drove him back. There were a few things he had to take care of.

. . .

Tara's room was empty. Someone had removed everything, even the bedding.

Mrs. Lassiter. That made sense. Efficient military minds. Someone had collected her personal effects and delivered them to Tara's mother.

I really wanted that diary. He should have taken care of that before.

He straightened up. At least time travel was good for some things. The book was still here yesterday.

· · ·

He paced nervously in her room. When was she due? He knew the date, but not the exact time. Her diary hadn't been that precise about this first meeting.

"I've got to settle down. It'll do no good to be on edge." Tara had been testy that day. He had to avoid irritating her.

He picked up a novel from her dresser, stacked a couple of pillows behind his back and stretched out on the bed to read. He had to get his mind distracted.

Ten minutes later, she opened the door. She gasped.

He nodded, "Hello, Tara."

His heart raced to see her again, but he put a clamp on his emotions. *Play it cool. She's tired.*

She was giving him the cold eye, examining him like a bug under a magnifying glass.

He smiled.

"When did you come from?" she asked.

· · ·

Kent felt at ease for the first time in ages. He also felt a lot older. How many months had his personal time line stretched as it wove in and out of the calendar? He'd lost track. It felt like years.

He read Tara's diary again, taking comfort from her few scribbled pages. As each day with her in past-time came and went, he read new meaning into her words.

"I am fascinated by Kent's ring. Where did it come from?"

"Me too, Tara. I guess today's the day."

He hid the book and walked toward the lab.

Tara met him on the way. Kent put his finger to his lips, and gestured toward the chamber room.

"I've got a special treat planned."

She frowned, "I have to get some rest. The general is coming tomorrow and I have to be prepared."

"You will be. Trust me. We'll only be gone a short while."

She thawed, and nodded. He set the controls and shortly the both of them were nearly two months into the past.

"Are you up for a road trip?" he asked.

"I'll need to pack."

"No. You're not even here yet. We'll buy more clothes on the road."

With a previously forged entry in the security station's log to explain her presence, they checked out and headed for Las Vegas.

He noticed her watching him as they drove. Living in the current moment was a skill he'd learned with effort. It made living bearable.

His wife was there, breathing beside him. What the future held was unimportant. She was there. She existed.

And she was happy.

Las Vegas announced itself in the distance with a pillar of light from one of the casinos.

"You've visited the Strip before?" He knew she hadn't, from her diary.

"No. I flew in, when I came here, but I didn't visit the sights." They drove the lighted streets.

"They use as much electricity here as we do," he chuckled.

She put her hand on his arm. "Pull over."

"What?"

"Just do it."

He found a close casino parking lot. "Yes?"

She looked out the back window. Then turned to face him.

"Kent, I know you said we were married, but that's only half true. You may have married me, but I haven't married you yet."

He nodded, "Well, that's true."

"So let's do it here." She pointed to the Little White Wedding Chapel down the street.

Kent looked it over, and then began laughing.

"What?"

He composed himself. Or tried to.

"Well, you proposed the first time. I guess it's not surprising you'd do it the second time."

She grinned, "Or vise versa."

"Right." He looked again at the billboard. "Okay, do you want to take advantage of their Drive-Thru wedding chapel?"

...

She didn't. There was some shopping to do. Tara was the one who spotted the rings.

"Those are the ones aren't they? Kent, let me see your ring. I want to see if that's the same one."

He held his hand back. "No."

She looked puzzled.

"I don't want to risk it."

"Explain."

He hesitated, then explained in a low voice. "We solved the gas paradox issue. Gas molecules are so close to the quantum limits that they could tunnel easily. So it really made no difference which gas molecules went back into the past, they were all identical anyway.

"It's different with structured matter. The probability that a scrap of metal, for example, could tunnel-exchange with an identical piece is so low that it's impossible.

"If my ring accidentally touched its earlier version, silver atoms could scrape from one to the other, setting up a time loop. It would throw this visit, all my visits with you, into the paradoxical. I'm not going to risk it."

She read the grave expression on his face, and nodded. "Right. We won't get them close." She picked up the little box and snapped it shut.

...

They married in the Crystal Chapel. Kent arranged to have the photos held until he called for them.

"I know a better place for a honeymoon." He told her.

They drove to the Furnace Creek Inn in Death Valley. It was off-season and they had the place almost to themselves. The third night there, relaxing beside the fireplace next to the hot-springs filled olympic-sized pool, Tara stared up at the brilliant stars overhead.

"This place is below sea level."

He nodded. "About two hundred feet. It gets even lower down by Badwater."

She wrapped her bathrobe a little tighter against the night chill. "I think it bothers me."

"What? Being below sea level?"

She nodded. "It feels wrong somehow. All that potential energy in the ocean, just a few hundred miles away, just aching to fill this place up."

"It doesn't work that way."

She shrugged. "I guess I feel that way about being here in the past, too."

"Oh?"

"Yes." She looked at him bashfully, the flames reflecting from her eyes. "I feel like I ought to be back there at the lab, with the clueless Kent, trying to figure out how to get him interested in me."

"I wouldn't worry about that. I'm easy."

"I'm not so sure."

"I am. I was never so shocked as when you proposed to me."

"Oh?"

"Not because you proposed, but because I accepted so quickly. I think I must've been waiting for you to make the first move."

"Should you be telling me this?"

"Why not? It won't make any difference." He turned away to stare at the fire. He could tell her. Maybe she would understand.

But if she avoided the accident, he would never have contrived to go back and woo her here in the past. A paradox, that even if possible, would destroy the only moments they had together.

But it wasn't possible. He knew that now.

. . .

Tara let herself be talked into extending their stay for a full week, but after that she was firm.

"I've got to go back—before I get too confused. I have two Kents to think about, and you have two Taras. I really think we need to get back in sync."

He nodded. "This was a special time."

They returned to the base, and he kept his composure for three seconds past the moment she vanished back to her interrupted life.

...

A month to the day after his last visit, General Hershey escorted by Jerry was into the conference room.

Kent Shaw sat at the table. There were no presentation documents—no projector for the charts.

Just a single lab notebook rested under his fingertips. Jerry left.

"General."

"Dr. Shaw."

Kent shifted in his chair. "Are you married, General?"

"Yes, I am. Thirty-two years."

Kent nodded to himself.

"I'd like to tell you a story."

When it was done. After all the twists and turns, the two men sat silently together. The military man closed the notebook and leaned back in his chair.

"I've always suspected it was impossible to go back and fix our mistakes."

He pushed the notebook across to Kent.

"Still, there've been a number of times in my life as well, when I would've given anything for just a little more time.

"Just a little more time to make things fit."

For more stories by
Henry, look for more
volumes of **Henry's Stories,**
or visit

Henry's Stories online magazine
http://www.henrysstories.blogspot.com

Small Towns, Big Ideas

Enjoy a collection of Young Adult Science Fiction Novels.

These stand-alone tales take high school aged adventurers from today's small towns as they take that step off into the strange.

Available from the usual online book sellers and the most perceptive of bookstores.

Beginning with **Star Time** in 2011,
follow a mult-thousand year saga as
humanity struggles to find its place
in the universe.

Look for The Project Saga at your
favorite book stores.